Praise for The Old Orchard

It reads like a fast-paced and twisting thriller, but built around rich complex characters and dotted with beautiful, often moving, descriptions of feelings and place. I loved the short chapters and easy format. Very original.

What a cracking story! I loved the way it all unfolded at the end. Really clever and credible and I didn't see the twists coming - very well done!

As in his previous book, 'Best Eaten Cold', Tony Salter captures our attention and keeps it, as the story unfolds chapter by chapter. Full of lovely prose, characters that you feel you know and some surprise twists and turns, this is a truly sumptuous and satisfying read.

FLIPPIN' BRILLIANT!

The Old Orchard is a pacy, tense, domestic thriller which builds an original and satisfying plot around real characters we can believe in. The prose is light and evocative with vivid descriptions and many moments of real insight and human wisdom.

This is a different book from the author's debut, although the author's originality and individual style remains. The Old Orchard is not quite as dark and twisted – at least not on the surface – but it is an equally compelling read. Flipping between 1995 and 2017, the exciting plot develops and holds the reader's attention as we learn how easy it is for a family to break itself in two. We also learn to care what happens to the characters and there are plenty of moments of genuine human emotion to move us.

About the author

Tony writes pacy contemporary thrillers. Exploring different themes, but all sharing Tony's thought-provoking plots and richly-painted characters.

Highlights of his early career include (in no particular order) three years as an oilfield engineer in the Egyptian desert, twelve years managing record companies for EMI Music in Greece, India and across Eastern Europe, running a caravan site in the South of France and being chauffeur to the French Consul in Sydney.

Having survived the Dotcom boom, he went on to be a founder of the world's largest website for expatriates, a major music publisher and a successful hotel technology business.

In amongst this, Tony found the time to backpack around the world twice (once in his twenties and once in his fifties), learn six languages (including Norwegian and Greek) and to find a beautiful Norwegian wife.

He now lives in Oxfordshire and writes full-time. He is fifty-eight and married with three children and four grandchildren.

Also by Tony Salter

Tony's debut novel, Best Eaten Cold – a dark, psychological thriller – was released in March 2017 and continues to attract new readers from around the world.

Following the launch of The Old Orchard, Tony will publish his third novel, Sixty Minutes, in early 2018.

He is currently working on the sequel to Best Eaten Cold.

You can find out more about Tony at www.tonysalter.com

THE OLD ORCHARD

Tony Salter

www.tonysalter.com

ETS Limited

Dawber House, Long Wittenham, OX14 4QQ

First published in Great Britain in 2017 by ETS Limited

ISBN: 978-0-9957977-3-4

CONTENTS

To everyone who helped me along the way and especially to my mother who would have been my best critic.

She would have loved the journey.

Easter in the Orchard

Early April afternoon sun cut sharply through the apple trees: dark, crumbled charcoal branches a stark contrast to the delicate budlets of spring's early blossoms, smatterings of white just showing within the pink.

Deeper in, behind the mossy trunks, the sound of laughter was magnetic, a primitive attraction tugging onwards amongst the old trees, a steady lodestone drawing you ever in.

There were nine of them gathered around the long table in the orchard. Scattered plates, bottles and dirty cutlery told the story of a lunchtime well spent. A turkey carcass, a yellow chattering of fluffy chicks and the shattered remains of an enormous chocolate egg completed the scene.

It was a moment to cherish, to freeze in time, to preserve in fading sepia memories and to allow to slowly crumple and blister behind dusty glass. Do you remember the last Easter in the Orchard? Can you stand back, retire to the edge of the trees, and look on? Can you see how happy everyone is? What a perfect family celebration! Isn't this what we work for, and dream of? Isn't this what life is all about?

Sadly, no-one remembered to take a photograph, or to find a moment to burn the image into their memories, although it was indeed the last Easter in the Orchard. No-one realised that this time would be different from any other, that the tangled skein of family life was quietly being teased out while they sat, and ate, and drank, and laughed, in the comfortable lap of their innocence and ignorance.

The Fates were busy and had plans for them all, but they were in no hurry to reveal their work. Each of those present had their own thread, which would be spun for them alone, measured for them alone and, eventually, cut for them alone.

1995 - Jane

If only she had been able to see the three sisters of destiny at their close and cunning work, Jane might have questioned what these Greek Goddesses were doing at her Easter celebration in the first place. She would probably have seen it as quite presumptuous and inappropriate but, having been properly brought up, she would almost certainly have offered them a glass of wine or a cup of tea in any case.

Jane was the only member of the family who really gave a damn about Easter. The rest of them would struggle to disinter even the bare bones of the Easter Story without help. They'd all been taught about it when they were young, but the stories and messages didn't seem to matter any more. Jane had given up on them all years ago; they were a bunch of total heathens.

But family is still family and, to be completely honest, she had been wondering for some years now why she bothered with religion herself. It was important to have someone, or something, to thank for all of her good fortune but, as far as her Christian faith went, things didn't feel as clear and bright as they once had.

Easter was always early in the year to eat outside and they had all brought warm clothes; just as family is family, family traditions were family traditions, with Easter Sunday lunch outside in the orchard being the most traditional of them all. Rain or shine, this was the one day of the year where there was no room for excuses.

If it was actually raining, a small marquee might go up as a concession to the season and the elements but, often as not, they managed without. The tradition had started in the year Jane and Mike had bought the house, almost thirty years earlier, and Jane had

3

no intention of allowing things to change any more than was strictly necessary.

Some change will happen, of course. Either for the good, or the not so good. None of their parents' generation were around any more and Alastair and Jenny had been through a few more partners – many deeply unsuitable – over the years than was strictly necessary.

Maybe the biggest, brightest and somewhat surprising change had been that she and Mike had become grandparents. Quite why she'd been surprised about that remained a mystery; it was probably just the unexpected way that time and life's milestones had a habit of sneaking up without warning.

The weather this year had been exceptional. It had been warm enough all day to be in shirtsleeves and even now, at after five, no one had bothered to put on jackets or jumpers. Simon and Alastair were bare-legged, but that was typical. Simon had turned up in their back garden twenty-eight years earlier with skinny eleven-year-old legs poking out of his shorts and both boys had been allergic to long trousers ever since.

Jane sat back in her chair and looked around. It was a golden moment in so many ways. What would that be in Latin? 'Annus mirabilis' didn't quite do it; she would need to look it up.

So many things to be thankful for. All of them in good health, or as good as could be expected, both of the children apparently happily married, everyone with decent jobs, Alastair with a more-than-decent new job, two gorgeous grandkids who were almost civilised, and one more on the way. The list went on and on.

Maybe she should hang on to her faith for a little while longer. She laid her guilty fingers on the worn boards of the trestle table just in case. It never hurt to hedge your bets.

1995 - Alastair

I really shouldn't have had so much Malbec. A schoolboy error. This week has been absolute crap and I doubt I've slept more than a few hours in the past four or five days. Come to think of it, I don't remember when I last had a good night's sleep.

It was always going to go wrong. Mum sitting at the top of the table with that terrible self satisfied look she always gets at times like this, Dad just off somewhere in a world of his own, Jenny and Danno loved-up as always, and Fiona and Simon giggling away on the other side of the table like a pair of school kids at the back of the cinema. Whose fucking wife is she anyway?

I'm putting on my best party face of course. Have to keep up appearances. Christ, the only thing that can make this any worse is ...

... Oh yes, here she goes. Mum's standing up and banging a glass with her knife. I really can't bear it. I just can't.

'Dearly beloved!' A slight pause for the obligatory murmur of polite canned laughter. 'We are gathered here today...' Another pause, more giggles. '... for three reasons. The first should be obvious to you all and has to be worth a little toast. Happy Easter.'

'Happy Easter,' we all chorus in union, standing and clinking glasses, laughing, crossing hands and making sure everyone, without exception, clinks with everyone else and looks their fellow clinkers squarely in the eye. There are a bunch of unwritten rules in this family and this one is unwritten so deep into the stone that you really, really know not to break it.

As I look around, I'm struck by the terrible realisation that the rest of my family are genuinely having a good time and not only pretending. When did I turn into such a grumpy bastard? I used to love this event more than any other, but my mind has been in an ugly place for way too long.

Bloody Head Office. Conference calls every evening and most weekends on top of everything else, and I still have to play along as though everything is normal, at least for now. I think I've got a solid work ethic, but there are limits, or at least there should be.

Accountancy was supposed to have been a smart career choice. The early years were the tough ones; you signed your life away, did your time working for one of the big firms – stupid hours and huge pressure – and then you either made partner or got a job with an outside firm. Either way, things would then become more civilised, and you would be able to reap the rewards of those years of hard graft.

Well, they were certainly right about the tough beginning, but Fiona and I made it through despite everything and, for a couple of years, I foolishly allowed myself to believe that my period of slavery was over, and we were entering an age of blissful emancipation. I'm not quite sure what happened next. It's as though I turned around for a fraction of a second and, when I looked again, the shackles were back; they were solid gold now, but a shackle is a shackle.

The glass being bashed again drags me back into the moment and my mother, who is in full toastmaster mode, is now looking at me 'The second reason to celebrate is Alastair's new job. I still have no idea what he actually does, but am reasonably sure that three promotions in two years is a good thing. Well done, Alastair.'

This time the glass clinking and gaze holding is all focused in one direction and I give a massive power boost to my game face.

'Well done, Alastair.' Again, I feel a moment of surprise as I realise all of the smiling faces are honestly pleased for me. Why is that so shocking? This is my family: my parents, my sister, my wife, my kids and my best friend. If they can't be pleased for you, who can? The thing is that none of them – even Fiona – has any idea how little I wanted, or needed, another promotion just now. What I do need is more Malbec.

Mother Toastmaster kicks it off again for a third – and hopefully final – toast. 'I've saved the best for last,' she says, a huge grin spreading over her face. 'Next year, there'll be one more of us at this table.' For a split second, I'm afraid Fiona is pregnant again but quickly realise how ridiculous that is – for all sorts of reasons. Mum continues. 'Jenny is expecting a baby. He, or she, is due on the tenth of October.' The announcement gets the open-mouthed surprise it deserves and Mum's glass is raised sky high this time. 'To Jenny, to Daniel and, most of all ... to family.'

Lots of excitement, raising glasses and poorly synchronised group hugging. I don't think I can cope for much longer and am going through my escape options when Simon saunters over, bottle of armagnac and two glasses in one hand, cigars and matches in the other. 'Fancy a little smoke on the water?' he says, nodding his head in the direction of the river.

Timing is everything, as they say ...

Simon doesn't appear to be inclined to say much as we make our way through the long grass, and the odd strategically placed stinging nettle, down towards the river. I don't feel particularly chatty either, although I have a feeling a couple of stiff armagnacs and a Montecristo might change that. Simon works for a major wine importer and tends to get hold of the good stuff.

I am quite happy just walking along quietly, grateful to have escaped. Don't get me wrong, I love my mother dearly, and she is an amazing woman. It's just that, sometimes, the whole family thing is too cloying for me and, to add insult to injury, my personal life is really not in great shape.

I experience a brief moment of pure, relaxed pleasure, simply strolling along and enjoying the early evening sun. Not thinking about anything important. Not actually thinking about anything at all.

It's too early for the dragonflies but in a few weeks the whole place will come alive and, for a moment, I can feel all of that burgeoning life holding itself ready to burst out in a flurry of electric-blue, shimmering energy. Too much wine, too little sleep; I am clearly losing it.

The moment couldn't last forever and Simon bursts the bubble as we scramble down the bank to the small half-rotten jetty. 'Is she actually going to have a child with that little hippie moron?' He is laughing, but there's no humour in his voice.

He's had a crush on Jenny since she was about thirteen and they even went out for a few months, maybe five years ago. Everybody knew it was never going to work and, come to think about it, Simon's had a crush on almost everyone in our family at some point or other. Ever since he "adopted" us. Strange, really. In any case, the break-up with Jenny hit him unusually hard and he's still got a strong possessive streak where she's concerned. Danno – or Daniel as my mum still insists on calling him – is a long way from Simon's idea of a "suitable" partner for Jenny.

Simon takes a sharp breath and goes on. 'I mean, he's four years younger than her for Christ's sake. He's never had a job worth talking about, and he spends half his life playing guitar and smoking weed. She could have done so much better.'

'What, with someone like you?' I can't resist it, and there's plenty of humour in my voice. 'Isn't it about time you got over her? It's been years now and, you know what? Danno's not so bad. He's a decent enough bloke and I've never seen Jen looking so happy. They'll be OK.'

Simon clams up, a look of pure fury flashes across his face and then disappears as if never there. 'Whatever!' he says, balancing the bottle and glasses on the rusty cast-iron bench next to the jetty. 'Let's have a drink.'

As he pours the armagnac, we shift effortlessly back to that comfortable silence which only exists between old friends. The sound alone is magical, a soft schloop as the cork is pulled out and then the gentle gurgling of the pouring. Add in a spoonful of golden sunshine captured by the amber liquid in a snap of primeval time and my mouth is already watering. All that, before even smelling or tasting anything. I might like alcohol more than I should, but, when the booze is the right quality, drinking really is a stunningly sensual process.

We continue to sit in silence as we light the cigars, drinking in the moment, the peace, the gentle sounds of the river, and the armagnac of course. This is what I have been missing: simplicity, time to breathe and be at ease in the company of people I trust. I am filled with a deep and rejuvenating calm.

The moment continues for what seems like hours before Simon breaks the silent spell.

'Well, what the fuck is wrong with you, mate?'

1995 - Girl in Casino

We get all sorts in here. Mostly rich Arabs, though not as many as back in the eighties according to the head barman, Joe, who started working at the Beach when it re-opened in 1973. On top of the obscenely rich regulars, there are normally a few pissed blokes out on the town after some conference, meeting or whatever, trying to find something to do after the pub, rather than go back to their sad, lonely hotel rooms.

Two things they've all got in common. First, they've forgotten that the house always has the odds and second, they're all hoping – somewhere in the back of their minds, or maybe not so far back, and maybe not really in their minds – that they might get laid tonight.

Everyone in the business knows this and everything we do is geared to making a turn from it. It's all "above board" these days and the police and gambling authorities are all over us, but it hasn't changed so much when push comes to shove. They are weak and stupid little boys who shouldn't be let out without their mummies and certainly not with a pocket full of cash and credit cards.

Still, as the casino pays us shit and we live off the tips, I don't lose too much sleep over what their wives have to say when they come home with stonking hangovers and the holiday plans have changed from Barbados to Tenerife. Most of these guys don't have a clue how lucky they are anyway.

I've been here two years now. I got the job straight after I got back from Thailand and, even though I like to have a whinge, it's not too bad a life. I started out as a cocktail waitress which was fairly shitty, but mostly because we've got a lot of gropers around Mayfair.

I'm not talking about the stupid little boys here, they're harmless enough. It's the rich Saudis and Greeks and nowadays a whole new bunch from Russia and Eastern Europe.

I can't really be doing with the posh rich types but at least when they're being arrogant, condescending twats, they know it. The other lot who've had gazillions thrust into their grabbing paws overnight, can't seem to deal with it and are much more difficult to manage. I guess grabbing becomes a reflex action after a while.

To be fair to the Casino, after I'd done my time as a waitress and worked hard for a year, they offered to put me through a croupier training course where I learnt how to run all of the games we play here – roulette, blackjack, stud poker, baccarat and craps. It's not as easy as it looks. You need to be able to explain everything to the players, manage the tables, work out and pay out winnings quickly and keep everything moving.

Basically, if you don't keep right on top of things, you either make mistakes or, even worse, you stretch out the average time between bets, which means active punters make less bets and the casino makes less money. If you want to work in a casino, you'd better figure out pretty quickly that management don't give a damn about anything apart from making money.

I got my license with the Gaming Commission more than a year ago and, even if I say it myself, I'm getting pretty good at this. I figure I'll hang around here for another six months and then see if I can get a cruise ship gig. That's supposed to be a real laugh, at least for two or three years. You never know, I might meet a rich sugar daddy who can whisk me off into the sunset.

Seriously, I can't think of anything worse. I've always been crap at relationships; my judgement is as random as the Red Queen's court in Alice in Wonderland and I might as well be sentencing myself to decapitation every time I pick a new man.

I seem destined to always make crap decisions, but I do try my hardest to make good ones and for the right reasons. I choose blokes who I actually fall in love with, or at least think I might fall in love with, not people who could be useful to me. With my brilliant taste and judgement, the result is that I manage to miss one bird with two stones every time, and end up having to wriggle my way out of mess after mess while scrabbling to hold on to a few scraps of dignity and self-belief.

Still, I'm a born optimist. If, at first, you don't succeed ... and all that. I normally have a laugh on the way, and Mr Right is just "up around the bend" as Creedence would say. I'm not going to find him in the Palm Beach Casino though. My Mr Right isn't swimming in a pond full of lost, little conference boys, posh twats or fat-fingered, nouveau riche oafs. One of these days, I'll have to go fishing somewhere else.

2017 - Jane

Jane knew she wasn't going to like the new house from the moment she got out of the car. It wasn't anything to do with the place itself. It just wasn't home. During the four years she'd been on her own, Jane had strengthened her resolve to stay at The Old Orchard and to keep it as a haven for her and for her family. She also imagined a small candle was always burning in the window to guide Alastair home. Who knows, with his father out of the way, maybe he would come back. Maybe.

The new house glared at her accusingly. It really was a lovely little cottage. Exactly the right size, and only half a mile from Danno and Jenny.

Even the weather was conspiring against her. Clear blue skies and clean, fresh, velvet warmth in the air, the first touch of spring appearing as a rare and precious gift, a reminder of winter's flight. There was a small apple tree in the garden, blossoms just starting to show, which took her back to another spring day twenty-two years earlier. The blossoms had also been perfect back then, and everything in the world had appeared so fragile and sweet. Like a newborn child or an unsullied, dewdropped spider's web at dawn.

Looking back, it was then that things had changed, and changed forever. It was the last Easter in the Orchard, the last time everyone was properly together, the beginning of the end of so many things.

A bit melodramatic maybe. No one died, or at least not for a while, and an outside observer would no doubt say they were all still extremely lucky. It was a matter of perspective though, wasn't it? It was always a matter of perspective.

Jane didn't actually give a fig for what that outside observer might have said. She wasn't so interested in what other people might think at the best of times. For her, in her heart, that day had truly been the beginning of the end for many, many important things.

'Why can't I just stay at home?' she said petulantly, and not for the first time, knowing the whine in her voice was that of a small child rather than an eighty-two-year-old woman. Or maybe that wasn't true; maybe it was exactly what eighty-year-olds were supposed to sound like.

How did the seven ages of man thing go? Or did she mean the Riddle of the Sphinx? She had studied English literature at university and, although she sometimes mixed up the names of her grandchildren, she could still quote from poems and plays she had learnt sixty years earlier. That in itself made no sense but, then again, so little did.

The words came back effortlessly and her lips moved softly as she ran through the lines in her head:

'... The sixth age shifts
Into the lean and slippered pantaloon,
With spectacles on nose and pouch on side,
His youthful hose, well saved, a world too wide
For his shrunk shank, and his big manly voice,
Turning again toward childish treble, pipes
And whistles in his sound. Last scene of all,
That ends this strange eventful history,
Is second childishness and mere oblivion,
Sans teeth, sans eyes, sans taste, sans everything.'

Well, she'd never had a big manly voice but she thought she deserved a bit of poetic license and, in any case, she was talking about the seven ages of woman, which might well go more like:

'... Her rich womanly voice turning again towards a childish treble, pipes and
whinges in her sound ...'

As for the last lines of the speech, they summed up her feelings about this proposed move perfectly, being shovelled off to sit out the remaining few years left to her in *'... second childishness and mere oblivion ...'*. She'd been fighting so hard against the inevitable. Could she be bothered to fight any more?

The worst, and most frustrating, thing was that she didn't want to be a burden to Jenny and Danno, or anyone for that matter, but she knew how easily she could become one. They had their lives to live and, after years of struggling, everything was coming together for them. Even the words 'oh, I don't want to be a burden' were straight out of the cliché of the live-in grandparent and reminded her of every awful television sitcom she'd ever seen.

'Why do I need to move house at all?' she went on. 'I'm fine where I am.'

Jenny took her arm and helped her gently out of the car. Where she found her patience was a complete mystery to Jane. It wasn't something the Johnsons were famous for. 'Come on,' said Jenny. 'Let's not have that conversation again now. We can talk about it later. Right now, we're here to look at this lovely cottage. The estate agent is standing over there waiting to show us around. Let's not leave him hanging around. You know how you hate to be late for people. It's the worst kind of bad manners, isn't it?'

The thing when people get old is that – because they may be a little slower off the mark and appear frail – everybody assumes they are also a little stupid which, for some unknown reason, gives them a blanket license to be patronising. Jane was fully aware that, when Jenny quoted her and hijacked Jane's own rules about manners and punctuality, it was an obvious tactic to manipulate her into behaving better. She wasn't slow and not yet totally gaga.

What amused her most of all was that, despite being able to see through such simple subterfuges, Jane found herself increasingly tempted to play along and to fit into the role which was expected of her. Jenny meant well and, let's face it, the poor spotty chap from the local estate agent had done nothing at all to deserve exposure to either moaning or sarcasm from an old biddy like her.

'All right, all right,' she conceded. 'Let's go and have a look at the house. But it doesn't mean anything. I haven't agreed to anything. We're only having a look. No promises.'

Jenny laughed and looked at her mother. 'Have you got any idea how much you sound like me when I was a teenager? It's uncanny.'

Jane didn't think this justified any response, shrugged off Jenny's arm, and strode towards the young man in the cheap blue suit which didn't fit so well. He was presentable enough, she thought. Or at least presentable enough for this day and age. At least, he'd shaved properly, which was quite impressive considering the challenges of manoeuvring a razor around the minefield of acne which covered his chin.

'Good morning, young man,' said Jane, giving him her best, firm handshake. 'I'm Mrs Johnson, Jenny's mother, and I believe you would like to show me around this house.'

Jane half expected a clumsy stuttering response and was pleasantly surprised by the confidence and strength of his voice. 'Good morning, Mrs Johnson. I'm very pleased to meet you. I'm Jason, and I would be happy to show you around this lovely property.' He looked over to Jenny with an amused smile. 'Morning, Jenny. Nice to see you again.'

The house really was charming. It was almost a caricature of the perfect thatched cottage, oozing history from its stone-flagged floor to the brooding thatch hanging low over the lead-paned windows. The oldest part dated back to the sixteenth century and had originally been a single-room peasant's house built around a pair of elm cruck beams at either end. There had been numerous extensions and modernisations since then but all of them had been sympathetic and it felt like a friendly place to live. Jane still had no intention of moving though. It wasn't worth the kerfuffle.

'Well, Mrs Johnson, what do you think?' Jason stood at the gate and waved his arm dramatically towards the house. 'Beautiful isn't it? And such a nice homely feel?'

'Yes,' said Jane. 'It's very lovely and thank you so much for showing us around.' She turned to Jenny. 'Did you say something about lunch, darling?'

'I did, indeed. We're meeting Danno, and Natalie's coming. She's down for the weekend.'

'How wonderful. It seems like forever since I've seen her.'

1995 - Fiona

As Simon and Alastair disappeared into the trees, Fiona was left sitting alone at the table. The kids had wandered off to play tennis earlier, and Mike and Jane were still so occupied with interrogating Jenny that she had a few welcome moments of peace and quiet.

The first time she'd been at the Johnson's Easter party had been in 1982 – only a few weeks after meeting Alastair – and she'd not missed a year since. The Old Orchard was a beautiful, rambling family home which was the perfect setting for such a proper, old-fashioned family gathering. Events like these were new and different for Fiona; her parents had died when she was ten and she'd been brought up by her uncle and aunt who, although they were kind enough, didn't have much time for either parties or family.

1982 had been a great year. She'd passed her bar exams a couple of years earlier and, although she was still earning a pittance, it was the first time in her life when she could really afford to go out and let her hair down.

The night she'd met Alastair had been an absolute classic. She'd been out with a friend, Vicky, from her chambers and they'd planned a mini pub-crawl, starting at the Admiral Cod in Chelsea. It was early April and one of those rare spring heat waves, which burn themselves forever into our collective selective memory, was transforming London into a pavement city. In those days it was still rare to see any chairs or tables on the streets, but that was fine as there wasn't room anyway.

The mass of sweaty, sloaney bodies made an incredible racket, with their heads craned back and braying mouths wide open. David Attenborough could have filmed it for Life on Earth:

... spread for mile after mile, the Sloane Flamingo has come here to breed. Sometimes travelling for as much as twenty minutes, the females return to the same watering hole year after year in order to find a mate. The males are resplendent; pink chests puff out, necks arch backwards and they strut up and down, filling the narrow streets with their raucous squawking. From close up, the noise is deafening and the smell ... almost unbearable. The females gather in small groups and observe the males carefully; they are looking for the loudest and pinkest contender to ensure the strongest genes for future generations ...

Alastair had been with Simon and another friend who she couldn't remember and hadn't seen since. They'd moved in with a series of predictably lame chat-up lines, but big smiles and decent looks made up for that and the girls accepted the offered drinks. Fiona ended up talking mostly with Simon, who was interesting to talk to, and the most handsome of the three, but a bit too serious for her liking. Vicky had Alastair and his mate totally cornered from the start.

After an hour or so, Vicky announced that they were moving on to the Grenadier in Wilton Row and they might see the boys there. 'Treat 'em mean and keep 'em keen,' she muttered to Fiona as they left.

It wasn't until two more pubs, and a lot of Pimms later that she finally pried Alastair away from Vicky. She'd seen him glance at her a few times and was sure the attraction was mutual. Even though they were both too drunk to have any sort of coherent conversation, there was something between them, something different and exciting.

Closing time, ten minutes before the last tube home, and a potential future universe was suddenly spiralling out of sight like the last, gurgling memory of an empty bath. She could still remember the sharp pang of sadness and regret which slammed into her like a knife in the stomach. Fiona was a modest, well brought-up girl but, in a rush of assertive decisiveness, she took out a pen and wrote her number on the back of Alastair's hand. 'Call me,' she mouthed, before turning to follow Vicky.

But he hadn't. Her heart was in her mouth every time the phone rang, but it was never him. It had taken an eternity – actually three days – before Alastair eventually called. He mumbled and stuttered nervously, but managed to invite her out for a drink. That had been thirteen years ago.

She looked at the spot in the trees where the boys had disappeared, wondering whether Simon would be able to talk some sense into Alastair, or at least to find out what was going on. She wasn't holding her breath though. What had got into him? They'd been married for ten years and had hardly been apart since that first date. By most people's standards, they were happy and well-matched.

Of course, they'd been through plenty of ups and downs along the way – work, money, family, sex, drinking – basically all of the usual relationship complications and in pretty much every possible combination.

The worst time had been when their first child, Arabella, died; she was stillborn at thirty-four weeks. Arabella was a perfectly formed, beautiful baby, her heart just didn't work properly. They named her and then buried her. Each of them had mourned Arabella in different ways and at different times but they had somehow managed to be there for each other when it was needed. Surely whatever was eating Alastair now couldn't be worse than that?

She imagined listing all of the fights they'd ever had on coloured Post-It notes stuck on the walls like they sometimes do on training courses - pink if the woman started the fight and blue if it was the man. They would probably need a very big room, but even so she didn't feel their relationship was unusually fiery and, if she compared them with most of their friends, they were paragons of harmony.

One explanation for the relative harmony, Fiona felt, was that there had always been a fair balance in their arguments. If you looked at who was responsible for what on each occasion, the results would end up fairly even. Who started it, who escalated it, who ended it and who, most importantly, initiated the making up process. To her mind, the Post-it covered walls would be half pink and half blue.

She smiled to herself, thinking this was a better definition of a balanced relationship than you'd find in all those self help books put together. Well, at least, that's provided you're talking about normal relationships, which involve real people.

She didn't know what had changed, but she didn't like it and she was worried about him. He'd never refused to share problems with her before and his silence left her frustrated and impotent. This couldn't go on much longer. Something was going to snap.

If she was honest, she was also fairly worried about herself. Maintaining even a semblance of youth and beauty took more and more effort every year and the clock kept on ticking. With Alastair working so much and behaving so strangely, her life had become a dull, repetitive cycle of school runs, exercise classes and a few, lonely glasses of chardonnay alone in front of a rented film. If she wasn't careful, she'd end up doing exactly the same for the next twenty or thirty years. There had to be something more to life.

Fiona had a decent group of girlfriends in Sevenoaks and they'd meet up for lunch most weeks, but it wasn't enough. She missed romance, passion, someone who gave a damn about how she looked. What was the point of all of the swimming, yoga and aerobics sessions if there was no-one apart from herself to care. She'd be forty in a few years and, whatever anyone said, that had to be the beginning of the end.

She wasn't the only one of her friends who felt the same way. Their girlie lunches often degenerated into bitching sessions about absentee husbands. They all liked the money and the comfortable life, but most of them had expected something different for their generation. Becoming exactly like their mothers hadn't been the plan, but now their children didn't need full-time care, they'd started looking at each other and suspecting that it might be too late to change things. Too late to start again.

Her closest friend Elaine thought they were all idiots. 'Just enjoy the freedom,' she would say. 'I don't know what my husband gets up to when he's on his business trips, but I've got a pretty good idea, and there's no way I'm going to sit at home waiting around to give him his slippers and a whisky when, or if, he makes it home. There are plenty more fish in the sea and I have no intention of sitting back and watching life pass me by. You have to take the bull by the horns, as it were ...'

Elaine never went into specifics but it was well known that she'd been through a string of lovers over the years. Nothing too serious but, although she seemed to be careful not to dally with anyone they knew, most of her friends tended to keep a close eye on their husbands when she was around. They were all jealous of Elaine but, as they were too lily-livered to take the plunge themselves, gentle disapproval was all that was left to them.

Fiona wasn't sure she could make the leap, although there had been a couple of times recently at drinks parties when it had crossed her mind. Only a week earlier, one of the men had taken the usual flirting a bit far; he had drunk too much and was inappropriately tactile all evening. A touch on the arm, a hand lingering on the small of her back as he moved her out of the way of a waitress, nothing obvious but the suggestion was definitely there and she'd caught herself a couple of times thinking 'what if?'.

Would it be so wrong? What would Alastair do if he found out? Maybe it would kick him into shape, make him realise he couldn't just take her for granted. He'd certainly not been slightly aware of that guy's unsubtle fumblings at the cocktail party. What would it take to get his attention?

Fiona was finding it easier and easier to see herself in the role of injured party. She felt cheated. Yes, Alastair was home for three or four nights a week, but he might as well not have been. Why couldn't he put a bit of effort into being more charming and solicitous? Why couldn't he try to inject some romance back into their marriage?

Maybe his talk with Simon would help? Now, there was someone who always made the effort ...

She was shaken out of her thoughts by a gentle, but firm, pat on the shoulder. 'Come on, you're drying,' said Mike, with his familiar clipped voice of authority. 'Here you go.'

She took the offered tray and stood up, resisting a girlish urge to salute. 'Well, it's got to get done at some point,' she said, 'and it really doesn't look like anyone else is going to do it.'

Mike had been a Colonel in the Royal Marines until he'd taken early retirement a few years earlier, and Fiona had eventually learnt it was easier to just follow orders when he was in this sort of mood. Fiona was no pushover – she'd been on her way to becoming a half-decent barrister before having children interfered – and, in the early days, she would never stand back and allow Mike to treat her like one of his junior officers or enlisted men.

The problem was that, whatever she said or did, it made no difference whatsoever. Objections went straight over his head and he carried on regardless. After a while, she no longer bridled every time, but went along with it, normally finding the game quite charming. She liked Mike.

Liking him didn't stop her from feeling sorry for Alastair though. It must have been tough growing up with a dad like that. Such a clear, simple worldview. No need for compromise or grey areas. Fiona had no idea whether Mike had always been that way, or if he was a product of his work environment, but she was certain he'd invariably been a tough taskmaster where his son was concerned.

Alastair was quite different from his father and that must have set them at loggerheads all of the time. Despite being an accountant, Alastair was, or used to be, a "thinking" man, interested in all points of view and believing that individuals could make a difference, that things weren't written in stone. His personal life philosophy was simple, and centred around his belief that you made your own life, your own choices, good or bad, and there was no point complaining about future consequences because, after all, they resulted from your decisions.

The lunch table looked, as always, as though a bomb had hit it and it took them three journeys each back to the house to bring up all of the glasses, plates and cutlery. Simon and Alastair could deal with the bottles later.

The kitchen wasn't too messy – Jane was a tidy cook – and they soon had a military production line going. Everything had to be done by hand, because Mike and Jane always used the silver and the best wedding service for Easter lunch.

Fiona could tell that Mike wanted to say something, but he wasn't the chattiest of men and he seemed to be struggling with how to start. She was about to give him a nudge when he spoke.

'What's wrong, Fiona?' he blurted out. 'What's wrong with my boy?'

Fiona put the wet tea towel down on the marble worktop and turned to face Mike. 'I don't know.' She rested her hand on his wrist, half-covering his hand. 'He won't talk to me. There's something really not right, but I've got no idea what it is.'

Mike pulled away and continued with the washing up. 'That's a pity,' he said, and paused for a long moment. 'You probably think I'm old-fashioned, totally institutionalised and emotionally stunted ... ?'

'... Of course I don't ...'

'... Well, it might be true to an extent but, actually, I've spent my entire life as a manager. I'm trained to understand people and to look after them. My guys were soldiers and they had to obey orders, but they were people nonetheless. All of them, all of us, had times when we were under huge stress.'

'I do understand,' said Fiona. 'You must have seen some terrible things.'

Mike turned back to her and smiled. 'With the greatest of respect, my dear, I doubt you do. You're a great girl, but I don't think you actually can understand if you weren't there.' He took a deep breath and looked away before continuing. 'That doesn't really matter though. My point is that I've got a lot of people experience. I have eyes, I know my son, and I can see he is struggling with something. We both know he won't talk to me or his mother, so what can I do to help?'

Fiona had never seen this side of Mike before, he was always such a rock. His standard problem solving mode was to tell you to be a man, don't show vulnerability or weakness, crack on and get the job done. She shouldn't have been surprised that there was more to him than that, but she was. Totally.

'He won't talk to me at all,' she said. 'I'm not covering for him.

I've really tried. That's one of the reasons why Simon took him down to the river. I asked him to try to find out what's going on.'

Mike's brow wrinkled. 'I'm not so sure Simon would be the best person for Alastair to be talking to right now,' he said.

'Why not?'

'Well, he's always been a bit jealous of Alastair. He didn't have much of a family himself and he always wanted to be part of ours. It was worse after Alastair went away to boarding school and started making new friends.'

'I know what you mean,' said Fiona. 'He's definitely got a bit of a chip, but I'm not sure it matters. They've been friends for a long time and I'm certain that Simon really cares about Alastair.'

'You're right, of course.' Mike put the last of the plates on the draining board. 'It looks like he needs all the friends he can get right now and Simon is closer than anyone else. There's just something ...' He blinked a few times and went on, 'Is there nothing you can tell me?'

'Well, not from anything he's said but we don't talk properly any more. He's definitely acting strangely. He works all hours, he's distant with me and the kids, avoids social activities and, except for today, I could swear he hasn't had a drink for a couple of months. I would know. I can always tell.'

Mike laughed. 'Now, that is unusual. He was always quite the party boy, even in his teens. His mother used to despair of him. Hollow legs as well. Nothing else you can think of?'

Fiona had noticed Alastair was developing some strange routines and habits, no single thing, but they all added up; his suits and shirts now needed to be perfectly pressed and hung up in exactly the right order, and he would get very tetchy if anyone moved his razor or toothbrush by even a millimetre. Lots of other little things as well which, when combined, made her husband look like a complete stranger.

He had always been a bit OCD, it probably came with the territory being an accountant, but this was different and he had also become very, very secretive. Password locks on his phone and computer, documents either shredded immediately or in the safe.

The list went on.

For some reason, she felt these things were too personal to share with Alastair's father and wondered if she'd already said too much.

'I don't think so,' she said. 'Hopefully Simon has found out something. Look, here come Jane and the others ...'

1995 - Alastair

Simon's sudden outburst leaves me momentarily dazed. Even though we've known each other for ever, it's not like him to be so direct and, as I was deep in a drunken, almost-yogic trance, the raw honesty of his outburst was doubly shocking. I'm jolted back to harsh reality against my will; the soft, gurgling of the river has become louder and more strident, the armagnac is sharp on my tongue and the smooth tang of the cigar smoke is now touched by an acrid undertaste. I needed that moment of tranquillity and resent its departure.

'What?' I snap my head up, turning to face him. 'Where did that come from?'

'Oh, give it a break.' He's now looking me straight in the eye. 'Who do you think you're talking to? I may not always be the sharpest tool in the box, but I'm not thick, and I know you better than anybody. Something's rotten in the State of Denmark, so spill.' He reaches over and puts a hand on my shoulder. 'Is it Fiona?'

For a few moments, I sit there blankly staring at him. Should I laugh it off and tell him he's imagining it all? Is there any point in trying to explain things to him? Simon isn't unintelligent, but my problems are complicated, technical and frankly boring.

Can I explain the reasons why I'm afraid. No, not afraid, terrified. The reasons why I think I've been shafted and I'm going to be hung out to dry. The reasons why I don't think I have a way out of this situation. Where would I start?

The other worry is that I've got so many confidentiality clauses in my contract that I'll probably go to jail for even thinking about talking to anyone about this stuff. All well and good, but my real problem is that I need to. I desperately need to unload some of the shit I've been carrying around for months.

I can't discuss it with Fiona. That wouldn't be Plan A right now. Mum would take my side and be sympathetic, and Dad would probably hit me. Simon is really my only option and I don't think I can keep it all in for much longer without bursting.

'No, it's not Fiona. Well, maybe it is now, but that's not where it started.' I speak quietly, dispassionately, keeping my emotions tightly reined in. 'It's about work, and it's complicated.'

Simon pours me another glass, now resting his hand firmly on my shoulder as he pours. He looks me in the eye one more time and sits back down. 'That's what mates are for,' he says, raising his glass. 'We've got all night and the bottle's still almost full. Tell me.'

I feel like hugging him and my voice cracks as I begin. 'Well, you remember when my old firm got bought out a couple of years ago?'

'How could I forget?' Simon's deep-buried jealousy shows a little pink mole-nose above ground for just a moment, as it did from time to time. 'Your mother emailed everyone she knows with a copy of the FT article announcing your promotion. She didn't seem to care about the buyers' reputation as totally unethical shits.'

I am not sure Simon can wear these moral high ground stilettos without getting a blister or two, but I'm in no position to argue. This is the tricky bit and I need to take a few moments. I stand up and lean over the river, peering down into murky green, before going on. 'When they made me Finance Director, I automatically became chairman of all of the European pension funds.' I turn back and look at Simon. 'But I was too busy tidying up all of the takeover mess to look at everything in detail to begin with. I relied on other people to deal with most of the formal admin, even though it was my responsibility. Because of that, I missed something important.'

Simon is leaning forward, totally engaged, cigar abandoned uncared for, on the edge of the bench. 'OK, so you're a lazy git. Nothing new there. What did you miss?'

'Over the past six months, the US owners have stripped all of the assets out of a dozen of our European subsidiaries. They're now worthless shells.'

'So what's the problem then? If they're worthless, you close them down and you're done with it.'

'It's not quite so simple. They're worthless, but they have over a thousand employees between them who will be made redundant, as well as almost three thousand former employees. All of them are either taking, or will be taking, a company pension.'

Simon looks confused. '... And they get their pension from a pension fund. I still don't see the problem.'

I have almost got to the nub. 'Normally there wouldn't be a problem but, in this case, when I say they stripped all of the assets out, that included the pension funds. Our global finance head told me that the employee obligations would be transferred to the central group scheme, but he was lying and I should have checked more carefully.' I empty my glass. 'Do you remember Maxwell?'

'Of course. Massive pension scandal at The Mirror. Disappeared off the back of his boat a few years ago. Found drowned a few days later.'

I stand up again and turn to face the river. I have almost finished. 'Well, this is about the same and it appears I'm technically to blame. It's all my fault.'

Simon is looking at me as though I've just hoiked him out of the river on a hook and line. His mouth is opening and closing, but nothing is coming out.

'Fuck,' he says, before going back to his fish impression for a few seconds. 'Fuckity fuck. What are you going to do? Have you seen a lawyer? What did they say? What are you going to do?'

I cut him off before he does himself an injury. 'Of course I've been to a fucking lawyer. My guess is that my lawyer's bill is already sitting at around ten grand. Their initial advice was particularly helpful; basically, they told me my assessment was right, and it looked like I was stuffed. If I'd come to them earlier then, of course, it would have been different.'

'Typical lawyer, weasel-word bullshit.' Simon had calmed down a little and was back to his usual chippy self. 'So, what are you going to do?'

'Whatever I can, basically. I've been working with the Serious Fraud Office for the past six weeks to try to help them to nail the parent company. In return, they've promised me I won't go to jail.'

'So, you'll be OK then?'

'No, I'm still completely fucked. I'll be struck off by the Institute of Chartered Accountants, barred from being a director for years, and I'm looking at some sort of compensation penalty north of a hundred thousand quid. Oh, and I'll have a criminal record for fraud.' I can hear my voice cracking with built-up emotion as I lay out the full extent of the disaster and my attempt at a brave smile feels creepy and sickly on my lips. 'So, on balance, could be better.'

'Bloody hell, mate,' Simon gives me a full-blown man-hug. 'I'm really sorry.'

'Cheers,' I am struggling to speak again. 'Appreciated.' Our embrace breaks apart in the awkward untangling involved in any man-hug of longer than three seconds.

'Have you told Fiona?' says Simon, deepening his voice by half an octave which was another compulsory response to over-lengthy physical contact.

'Not yet. And you need to promise me you won't tell a soul about this. Especially not her. I need to square a few things away over the next week or so and then I'll find the right opportunity.'

'Are you crazy? She's worried about you enough as it is. When she finds out you've been covering this up, you're toast.'

'I know, I know. It's just ... well I've got my reasons and I'll deal with the flak when it happens.'

'Whatever, mate. It's your call but, trust me, you're gonna be neck deep ...'

It is getting dark as we make our way back up to the house. Neither of us says a thing.

2017 - Jim

I love Saturday nights. The main reason is because Saturday days are over and they can be a bit of a pain.

In the season, Sally and I go out to a restaurant on the coast just along from Theoule about once a month. It's called l'Air du Temps; the menu is a bit pricey for us, but the food is great and the best tables sit on the rocks overlooking the Med, with the Bay of Cannes stretching out and decorating the terrace like a painting. The lights of the town shimmer in a perfect arc and the dying sun warms up the pumpkin-orange rocks of the Esterel. You have to get your priorities right in life and sitting here, together with someone you love, and a glass of good wine, takes a lot of beating.

Sally is so different from anyone else I've ever met and I count my blessings every day I'm with her. I haven't gone quite so far as to start believing in God but I do increasingly feel a need to give thanks to someone or something. I guess it comes with age. I could never have imagined I might end up with someone like her and, before I met her, would not have believed I could find this kind of happiness again.

She is quite a bit younger than me, but that's not really the thing. She's "fresh" as in "a breath of fresh air". It's the best way I can find to explain her. Most people I know have some sort of built-in reserve or cautiousness, an inner filter which moderates what they say and do. Sally doesn't have one of those filters; she is who she is, take it or leave it.

This pure honesty isn't the bluntness verging on rudeness which some people have, nor is it a stubborn, self-satisfied pride in being a plain-speaking person. It is rather a reflection of her natural openness and an almost buddhist ability to focus on the here and now.

But that's not because she's stupid or naive. Sally didn't have it easy growing up and has certainly learned to look after herself. In spite of that, she's somehow managed to hold on to this fresh vitality and, being around her, it rubs off.

She's unusually quiet this evening. We've finished our food and are sitting enjoying the view and the last two glasses of Bandol. Provence isn't generally rated for its red wine, but there are definitely some exceptions and most of them come from the tiny Bandol region a few kilometres east of Marseille.

'Penny for them, Sal.' I kick her foot gently under the table. 'What's on your mind?'

Sally smiles. 'Not so much really. I was just wondering what happens next.'

'How do you mean, next?' I say. 'Next, as in "do we go home or out to a club" or what? I think I'm too old for clubs though and, let's face it, the ones round here are overpriced, posy dumps.'

'No, not that "what next?" although it's an interesting thought,' she says, appearing to find the idea of taking me to a nightclub amusing for some reason. 'What next for the business? We can cope with the number of villas we've got right now without taking on any staff, but we're at the limit and we keep getting asked to take on new properties. What should we do?'

'Well, we get asked to take on more properties because we do a good job and our owners recommend us to other owners. It doesn't mean we have to say yes though.'

'But what if we lose five or six when Brexit goes through? No-one knows what's going to happen to the market.'

'Well, it's not going to change overnight,' I say. 'If the market gets tough, owners will have to sit it out anyway. It won't be worse than 2008.'

The number of properties we manage is the reason why Saturdays are a bit of a pain. We're up to fifteen now and, in the season, around two-thirds of them will have a changeover on a Saturday. They're high-end villas, with demanding customers who want to check out late, or check in early, or can't find the place, or all arrive at the same time, or whatever. The list of new ways they can find to make our lives difficult goes on and on.

'Fair enough. And I know what you think about taking on staff,' she says, 'but I do wonder if we're missing a trick. We had another juicy one come through this morning. Up in Eze. It looks perfect. A bit far to go but a nice bit of business, and it wouldn't hurt to have a safety margin.'

'I know. I saw the email,' I say. 'Let's have a look at it on Monday and we can have a general chat about the future then if you want. We could probably manage one more without help anyway. But, right now, I'd much rather talk about something else. We're off the clock, let's enjoy the wine and the sunset.'

Sally reaches across the table and gives my hand a squeeze. 'You're right. Sorry ...'

Sunday mornings are my second favourite time of the week. I don't get involved with any work things at all; Sally deals with anything which can't wait until Monday.

We live in Vence, which is in the hills about half an hour from Nice airport. Not the prettiest town in the region; it's overdeveloped but, if you're not a tourist, it's also a "real" place to live and possibly the best option if you want to be away from the coast.

I've been a member of the Cyclo Club de Vence for seven or eight years and very rarely miss a Sunday morning ride. We're training for a race in a few weeks and today we plan to do a dry run on La Vencoise which is a 133km ride with some serious climbs (over 2,600m in total). It's not quite the Tour de France but still proper cycling. I'm hoping for a time somewhere under five and a half hours, which would put me about an hour behind the frontrunners, but hopefully within the top ten for the 60-65 age class.

I love cycling, and cycling in France is the best of all. Even groups of amateur cyclists get a cheer when they go past a bar or a market and the notoriously arrogant and lunatic French drivers are almost all completely respectful of "le peloton".

The start is opposite the Bricorama DIY store and I meet the others there just before eight. There are thirty of us riding today, a good turn out and, as usual, there is a lot of pre-ride banter. I get more than my share as I'm the only "rosbif" in the club but my French is plenty fluent enough to give as good as I get, and I've even developed a solid Provencal accent to go with it.

We need to get the banter out of the way as we won't want to waste our breath over the coming hours, especially over the first 42km, which are almost all climbing.

We set off in a single group with a little good-natured jostling for position – although we all know our place more or less. Most of us will probably stay together for the duration, with the smaller group of serious competitors pushing ahead after a kilometre or two. It's a glorious June day and you can see why this part of Southern France was a mecca for so many painters; the light gives an inner radiance to everything it touches.

The Cote d'Azur is all a bit crowded now, with modern white-painted concrete villas everywhere you look. The cypress trees dotted around are too few to compensate for the sharp man-made angles and nature appears to be fighting a losing battle in this part of the world. Most of the larger trees have been gone for years. Forest fires are regular events and the ancient forests are now only a memory.

Traffic is also a big issue even out of season which is another great thing about cycling. Our route will take us away from all of that, up into and behind the huge limestone massifs, which dominate everything here. The two nearest outcrops, which are dear to the hearts of all Vencois, are the Baou des Blancs and the Baou des Noirs named after the Penitent Brotherhoods which were popular here in the seventeenth century. They had different factions who wore either black or white robes and who wandered about doing good works as well as building chapels on the rocks, giving them their names.

After about five kilometres of climbing uphill, I find myself slipping into the rhythm, separating mind and body and leaving most of the pain behind with the body. On the steepest climbs I'm not experienced enough to insulate myself from the agony of screaming lungs and stabbing, lactic acid knives, but for most sections, I'm comfortable enough in my cadence-induced trance.

I first started coming down here when I was a kid. My parents used to have a place not too far away, which they bought when property prices were much lower than they are now. There were several English families with villas in the village, they all had children of the same age and we'd come down in July for four or five weeks every year and run riot, a happy mob of nut-brown savages bombing each other from diving boards and flitting from kitchen to kitchen like locusts. If we timed it right, we could manage three lunches a day. We ended up being in a group which was about half English and half French and I'm sure we invented speaking Franglais well before the word became well known.

It all began to change as we became teenagers and the mob began to break up. Kids up to a certain age seem to be able to get on regardless of gender, nationality, age gaps and character, but from about twelve or thirteen, they become more picky and start to develop their own social framework – I like this type of person, but not that type. It's a shame really as that kind of divisiveness only gets worse as we get older.

I remember a particular time when I was just fifteen. It was the last summer when we were all together as a group, a few of the other parents had already sold their villas and I could sense that something was ending; there was a desperation in the way we did everything, trying to burn the memories into our skins, each experience touched with urgent, bright colours and packed with adolescent hormones.

Isobel was a "froggie", a word which had to be said with an outrageous French accent like the taunting French Guard on the wall in Monty Python and the Holy Grail, which was definitely the film of choice. 'I'm French. Why do you think I have this outrageous accent, you silly king?' It still makes me laugh. Isobel was the sister of one of the guys in our inner circle, a couple of years older than us and usually doing her own thing.

We were all standing by the pool in our villa's garden one evening, drinking those baby bottles of 1664, smoking Camel cigarettes and generally trying to look as cool as possible, when Isobel appeared next to me. She had her long, dark hair tied back in a single braid and she smelt of woman. More than a girl, she'd moved on and developed that sophisticated, coquettish style which French girls are trained in from an early age. Oozing glamorous, unobtainable sex.

'*Ca va, mon petit?*'

'*Ouai, ca va.*' I did my best to appear as cool as I could, brain hamster-wheeling frantically and trying to understand why she was bothering to talk to me.

'We go for *pique-nique* tomorrow, yes?' She rested her hand on my arm, just a touch of her fingertips. I had no idea what was going on. It was probably some sort of humiliating joke she was playing with her friends, but I wasn't planning on playing hard-to-get to protect my ego.

'*Pique-nique. Demain. Super,*' I replied, suspecting that forming complete, coherent sentences in either language was beyond me.

'OK. I bring food, you bring *biere. Je viens te chercher a midi.* I come at twelve, yes?'

Although Isobel was only two or three years older than me, I felt like the Dustin Hoffman character in The Graduate and I was only ever going to do what I was told. 'That sounds great, Isobel. *A demain,*' I mumbled as she wandered off leaving me dazed and swaying slightly like a boxer who's taken one punch too many.

And so it was. The next day, she arrived on her moped – at about twelve-thirty of course – I hopped on the back and we were away. We dropped down to the rocky coast road, the Corniche D'Or, which runs right next to the sea, and drove for half an hour, winding in and out of the hairpin bends. I had one arm wrapped around Isobel's flat belly, pressed against her, warm salt air lifting our hair. I can't remember whether I was actually laughing out loud but I certainly was inside. It was the perfect teenage fantasy. It had to go wrong, but I fully intended to enjoy it for as long as I could.

Isobel knew a special place apparently and, a few hundred metres the other side of Le Trayas, we pulled over into a small gravel lay-by, took the backpack with the food and beers and started walking down a stony, scrubby slope through the maquis and towards the sea. I really don't remember anything that was said that day or whether we spoke at all, although I suppose we did.

After fifty yards or so, the track got steeper and we needed to half-climb down using our hands as well. The cliff dropped to sea level and there was a narrow channel, about twenty yards across, separating us from a small rocky island. Isobel quickly stripped to her bikini and made a bundle of her clothes. I followed suit and we swam across to the island, holding clothes and backpack out of the water with one hand.

It was a tiny island but, once we had climbed up the other side and walked around, we were completely isolated by a massive rock which towered over a smooth, stone shelf, sun-warmed and sheltered from the breeze. The view was panoramic and the wine-dark sea stretched out all around, dotted with a smattering of light turquoise in amongst the rocks below us. We weren't overlooked from anywhere. It was our own private island and we might as well have been Aristotle Onassis and Jackie Kennedy.

We had all day, which was lucky as it turned out. It was perhaps not such a surprise that I didn't cover myself with glory on my first time out. Apart from the obvious issues of clumsiness and ignorance, the combined effect of all of my fantasies being rolled into one and suddenly presented to me on a plate, was far too much for my testosterone-riddled body and I was mortified by my complete lack of self-control.

'Sorry. I didn't mean to ...' I doubt I lasted thirty seconds.

Luckily, Isobel didn't seem too worried. It wasn't her first time.

'*Ne t'inquiètes pas, mon petit. On a du temp.* We have time, yes?'

And we did have time. The whole afternoon lay in front of us and, by the time we swam back across the channel, the sun was about to dip below the horizon. It was still early days, but I'd definitely started to feel that I was getting the hang of it.

I have no idea why Isobel picked me, but that day, and the weeks which followed were incredible. Apart from the undeniable pleasures of discovering sex, I could feel myself growing in confidence and self-belief. The French have an expression to be "comfortable in your skin" and that was what was happening to me. In a few short weeks, I left childhood behind me. I grew up.

We went to parties as a couple which did wonders for my ego and my reputation in our group. I smoked my first joint. Isobel even took pity on my clumsy English feet and taught me to dance French rock and roll like a pro.

We also went back to our island many times and, despite being so close to the road, I never saw a sign of anyone else having been there. It was our own paradise, a sacred grove dedicated to us and, although I knew better, I found myself falling deeper and deeper in love with Isobel.

Leaving to go home was horrible and is one of the few moments from my youth where I can still remember exactly what I felt at the time, both emotionally and physically. It was the biggest loss of my life until that point.

Isobel and I made all of the usual promises to keep in touch and meet in London or Paris, but neither of us had any delusions about what it had been. Wonderful, amazing, transformational perhaps, but that was it. It was over.

I was taking the train to join my parents in Aix and Isobel drove me to the station in her sister's car. I stood like a zombie watching the small, battered Renault pull out of the car park, tyres screeching on the baking tarmac. The afternoon sun burned in a familiar eggshell sky and stripped every feature from the concrete platform, leaving it grey and sterile.

I was twenty minutes early and stood alone in front of the tracks, dirty green rucksack bulging at my feet. Even in town, the sound of the cicadas was overwhelming; it had been the soundtrack of my life for almost two months and I struggled to imagine living without it.

In the hills above the town, the looming rocks of the Esterel were already glowing orange and ochre and I imagined the scents of oregano and thyme drifting down to me through the empty streets.

Every last ounce of my self control had been used to say my goodbyes without breaking down completely; meanwhile the aching emptiness inside me had slowly filled to overflowing with trapped tears.

Nothing could ever match the unique joy and excitement of those months; I knew with a sad and terrifying certainty that I was passing a turning point in my life. Whatever the coming years had in store, each future experience would fall a little short in comparison.

The train glistened in the distance like a mirage and it was only once I heard the certainty of its arrival thrumming through the tracks that I believed I wasn't imagining it.

But I wasn't. Carriage number nine stopped silently in front of me and then, as though someone had thrown a switch, the platform was filled with people and noise: doors slamming open, suitcases scraping on rough concrete and cries of welcome and farewell.

I can still remember feeling the heavy bag biting into my shoulder as I took a step forward and onto the train.

By the time I eventually got into my parents' car and we started the long drive north, I wasn't crying visibly but still couldn't trust myself to speak for over an hour.

Looking back today, I suppose my parents were probably watching me work through my pain, smiling wryly to themselves and remembering their own first loves and losses. After all, it's only part of the big Lion King Circle of Life.

It wasn't, as it turns out, the high point of my life – there have been plenty of other contenders – but it is a sweet memory, covered a lot of "firsts" and is definitely up there in my top ten.

My happy memories are interrupted by the first big downhill of the day. We get up to fifty kilometres per hour on this section and it requires total concentration. It was only after I got to France and started cycling properly that I learned why cyclists shave their legs. It's not to make you more streamlined or so you can wear silk stockings in your secret life. It's so the medical services can patch you up more easily when you take a fall, which you will sooner or later.

Taking a fall here would probably result in something not so easy to patch up; the barriers on the side of the road would stop the bike dead, but most likely catapult you over the top. It's a long, long way down, the sort of drop which features in all of the best cinema car chases where the baddies' cars fall for ten or twenty gut-wrenching seconds before they bounce and explode, or like the one in the Italian Job where they are left perched half-on and half-off the cliff with all of the gold at the wrong end of the bus.

That's when Michael Caine says, 'Hang on a minute, lads – I've got a great idea', and the film ends. I've always wondered what his idea was.

I'm sitting quite comfortably in the middle of the main pack and no one is fighting for position changes on the downhill today. It's not a race and there's no point in taking crazy risks. We are down the six-kilometre descent in no time and settle in to the second, and last, big climb of the day up to the Col de Bleine. Back into the groove and I can return to my daydreams.

This is one of the aspects of cycling I love most, the opportunity to be alone with your thoughts and to take the time to put things in perspective. I could try yoga and meditation I suppose – they work for Sally – but it's probably best to stick to what I know.

1995 - Fiona

Simon and Alastair had been outrageously drunk at the Easter party. The two of them were giggling like little schoolboys when they came back from the river. Giggling, reeking of cigars, and with alcohol oozing from their pores. In other circumstances, Fiona might have found it vaguely amusing, but nothing about Alastair had been charming or funny for a long time.

That had been the only positive side of Alastair's behaviour over the past few months; he was generally drinking less. Fiona liked a glass of wine herself, and it wasn't as though Alastair had a problem, but the demon drink had a way of encouraging poor judgement and it had been the root cause of many arguments over the years.

She wasn't going to take any risks on that particular Sunday and, as soon as she'd seen them stagger up, she'd grabbed Maggie and Hamish, said her goodbyes to Jane, Mike and the others and made her escape. Fiona hadn't seen Alastair since. He'd stayed over with his parents that night and had been up in town in "important meetings" for the past couple of days.

She decided to walk into town for her lunch with Elaine rather than drive, as she fancied a few glasses of wine and had no issues indulging in a bit of alcohol-related hypocrisy. What the hell! She deserved it.

Elaine never needed an excuse and, by the time the main courses arrived, they were both in full flow. Elaine, in particular, had a wicked sense of humour and apparently no sense of political correctness whatsoever.

'... So Suzanne's son has come out,' said Elaine. 'No surprises there. Having a ballbreaker like her as a mother would put anyone off women for life.'

Suzanne was one of their closest friends and Fiona might have pretended to be a tiny bit shocked on any other day, but she was feeling exceptionally wicked herself and just laughed. 'You're such a cow,' she said. 'Anyway, how do you know he's come out? I've not heard anything.'

'Suzanne told me last night. Apparently, John's not taking it very well. I mean what does it matter, anyway? What would Alastair say if Hamish turned out to be gay? Would he get all caveman about it?'

'I don't know,' said Fiona. 'He'd probably be OK with it. To tell you the truth, I've not got a clue what Alastair thinks about anything these days.'

If she'd had the right muscles, Elaine would have pricked up her ears like a dog or a horse, but she had to make do with leaning forward and raising one eyebrow. 'Things not so rosy in Casa Johnson?' she asked. 'About bloody time the two of you got off your pedestal for a bit.'

'Thanks for the love, sympathy and sisterly tenderness,' said Fiona, expecting nothing less from Elaine. She was among the world's worst people to confide in.

'Sorry, dear friend.' Elaine covered her mouth with her hand and dipped her head. 'I'm devastated to hear things aren't going well. Is there anything I can do to help?' She grinned at Fiona, perfect white teeth on full display. 'Any better?'

'Much,' said Fiona, laughing. 'For a moment there, I was worried you might actually be a total bitch who took pleasure from her friend's suffering.'

'Moi? Well, maybe a teeny, tiny bit ... and only sometimes ... and that's only human isn't it?' She leant forwards, both hands flat on the table. 'Anyway, what's up with you and Mr Perfect?'

The best part of a bottle of Pinot Grigio had done its job and Fiona desperately needed to talk to someone. 'It's difficult,' she mumbled. 'It's like I don't know him any more. He's got so nervous and secretive.' She took a deep gulp of her lukewarm wine before looking up at Elaine. 'It's not like him.'

Fiona was beginning to become frightened by how much Alastair had changed. Not only was he working all of the time, but even when he wasn't, he was twitchy and compulsive. A couple of times over the previous week, she'd walked into his home office to say something, and he'd snapped the lid of his laptop closed, covering it with both arms, the defensive accusation in his eyes making him look like a cornered animal.

'So, an affair then?' said Elaine. 'Sound like a classic case. Someone at work, I'll bet.'

'You are so stunningly predictable,' said Fiona, 'but I don't think so. I'm not that thick and he's not that clever.' She'd already spent many lonely hours running through possible clues in her mind, always coming to the same conclusion. 'I'm sure I'd know. It's more like he's lost his balance in some way and is actually becoming unhinged, but he won't talk to me about it. He just avoids the issue.'

'I take your point, but you'd be amazed what people can get away with, trust me,' said Elaine, winking extravagantly. 'That being said, it doesn't sound like he's doing a brilliant job of hiding it, whatever it is. If we were talking about anyone else, I'd ask if you've suggested he see someone.'

'What, someone as in a shrink or something?' Fiona was genuinely shocked. 'Alastair? Can you imagine it?'

'Not really,' admitted Elaine. 'His feet are so firmly planted on the ground, he's probably growing roots.'

Fiona didn't know how to describe the changes in Alastair. He hadn't turned into a raving, wife-beating monster, he simply wasn't her Alastair any more; whatever cold fire was burning inside of him was methodically and clinically cauterising each of the threads of intimacy and tenderness which defined them as a couple.

But she wanted to try. It was as if saying these things out loud would suddenly make everything clear in a sky-splitting flash. 'It's so difficult to explain,' she said. 'It's as though he's not there any more. As though the real Alastair's been taken away in the night with no warning and no explanation: locked away; thrown out of an airplane; boxed up and shipped to a hidden warehouse in deepest, darkest Peru. I have no idea what's happened, and I'm terrified I'll never find out.'

Fiona looked down and pretended to be reading the menu while she used her napkin to dab at her eyes. She'd not allowed herself to address these emotions until that moment. It might have been the wine talking, but she could feel the sadness welling uncontrollably upwards from her core, as strong a sense of loss as she'd felt when Arabella had been taken away from them. At least then, Fiona had been given an explanation which she could understand.

Now, the saliva was sticking callously to the back of her throat as she realised what it was she felt most strongly of all. She was lonely – desperately lonely – and she didn't know what to do about it. Her cheeks were wet and she tried to tell Elaine she was sorry, but the words wouldn't come.

Elaine, unusually, had nothing to say either. She pulled her chair around to be next to Fiona, waved the waitress away, and sat quietly with her arm round her friend, allowing the tears to flow.

1995 - Alastair

Going to the office is becoming an increasingly surreal experience. I need to put on a brave face and pretend everything is normal, while the rest of my life has turned into a cold war spy thriller; secret meetings and phone conversations, smuggled confidential documents and need-to-know protocols are all inextricably mixed and muddled with my guilty feelings of betrayal and double-cross.

My secretary, Jackie, has taken the brunt of my bad behaviour over the past few months, but still manages a cheery smile when I walk in, half an hour late.

'Good morning,' she says, putting a welcome mug of coffee in front of me. 'How was the famous Easter Party? Recovered yet?'

'Just about,' I reply. 'Yesterday was a bit of a blur though. Any calls?'

'Nothing important,' she says, 'but Jack and Peter have been hovering outside for twenty minutes wanting to talk about the Zykan trademark dispute. They say it's urgent.'

'For fucks sake.' This was the third time in a week. 'Tell them to fucking wait will you. Can't anyone just get on with doing their bloody job?'

I slam my coffee mug down hard, sending brown splatters all over the papers on my desk, and forcing Jackie to jump backwards and out of the way. God, my fuse is getting shorter and shorter every day. I need to get a grip.

I look up at her as she stands in front of me, her arms crossed and her morning smile now turned upside down. I manage a feeble grin. 'I'm sorry Jackie,' I say. 'It's not your fault they're idiots. Please ask them to wait while I get done with my emails ... and if you could find me a cloth or something to wipe this up, that would be great.'

As I plough through my messages, calls and morning meetings, some of the ideas and thoughts I have been having for the past few weeks are becoming clearer and better formed. Talking with Simon must have helped. It's as though a velvet theatre curtain is being pulled back, inch-by-inch, to gradually reveal the floodlit stage behind. Until now, I have been able to peer around the edge a little, but it is only once the curtain is fully open that I can see everything.

I don't like my job. That's it. It's really that simple. The only part of what I do which gives me pleasure is the fact that I'm good at it, but that's not enough and recent events would suggest that it's not even true.

I don't like being an accountant and I don't like the people and the system which surround me. I don't share their values, nor their obsession with money – having lots and getting more. I like the freedom which money gives me and accept that there is always a price to pay, but I don't need as much as I have, and I certainly don't want to pay as big a price as I've been paying.

I am actually feeling light headed. It is a huge step to take on board a controversial idea like this, to accept that it's real. That acceptance has somehow crystallised the loose strands which have been floating around in my head, forming them into solid, hard-edged shapes that won't be ignored.

Did I genuinely feel this way? I was clearly very stressed but, even so, I couldn't find anything wrong with the basic premise. I don't like my job. The conclusion is so blindingly obvious that I can't understand how I could have hidden from the truth for so long?

I think about my colleagues and friends in the city. They aren't bad people, or at least most aren't, but they've all somehow bought into the system. Thick skinned and driven by Darwinist impulses, they've all learned, as have I, to rationalise and justify. They carry around terms like "fiduciary duty", "wealth creation" and "restructuring" like Templar shields which protect them from real human consequences while they proudly march after the cross of Mammon. Both dinner party conversations and boys' nights in the pub, all stay true to the party line. It seems medieval. Haven't we moved beyond that as a culture? Not even a little?

My judgement is probably being distorted by everything else which is going on in my life at the moment, but I don't actually think these thoughts are coming from that. My impending doom may be the reason why the curtains are finally being pulled back, but the revelation itself is true.

It is a shame I couldn't have had this epiphany a couple of years ago as it comes too late to help me right now but, if I feel the same way in a few months time, I will need to think very carefully about the future.

As always, I'm flustered and out of breath by the time I arrive at the small, but richly furnished, room on the first floor of a white stucco terrace at 27a Wigmore Street.

'Hello Alastair,' says Julia, holding the door for me and looking at her watch. 'Is there no way you can plan to leave a bit earlier for our meetings? Being late and stressed is never a great way to start.'

'I know and I'm sorry ... Again,' I reply. 'I'm doing the best I can, but these days I'm like one of those plate spinners they used to have on seventies talent shows, running around like a loonie trying to keep everything going.'

'Interesting way of putting it,' she says, laughing. 'Come in, have a glass of water, and take a few moments to calm down. You can leave the spinning plates outside. They'll be fine on their own.'

'Thank you.' I sink into the welcome embrace of a soft armchair. This is the fifth or sixth time I've been to see Julia, but I still feel like a fraud. She's trying to help me to understand my issues but I don't need anyone to do that. I understand them well enough myself. I simply want someone I can talk to. Someone protected by the veil of doctor-patient confidentiality.

'So, how have you been?' she says, sitting opposite me on a low, black leather footstool. 'Anything new? How are you getting on with controlling your temper outbursts?'

'Nothing new, really. Life is still pretty shitty, but I knew it was going to be and I can't say I'm any less angry about the cards I've been dealt. The reality is that it can only start to get better once this is all over.'

'I'm not sure that's such a constructive way to look at things,' says Julia. 'If our solutions are always around the corner, they have a tendency to keep slipping around the next corner, and the next, and so on. Will it ever, actually be over?'

It's unfortunate that Julia feels the need to state the obvious so often, although she's young and pretty and her voice is wonderfully soothing. All-in-all, it's remarkably pleasant to spend a few precious minutes with her, cocooned in here with the whole world left outside.

'I get that,' I say, leaning forward in my chair. 'And I'm not pushing all of my problems off to the never-never. I've got my final meeting with the Serious Fraud Office on Thursday. I just need to keep the plates spinning until then.'

'All right. It's only a couple of days. What happens at that meeting?'

'They'll confirm the details of my settlement offer and I'll sign off on it. No more hiding, no more uncertainty, and the whole disaster will go public a few weeks later.' I lean back into the soft chair, imagining for a few seconds the body-sagging relief that will come once the cork is pulled and the evil genie is out of the bottle.

'And you're confident everything will go as you expect?'

'As confident as I can be. I won't go to prison and we'll be OK. I'll probably struggle to find work for a while, but we should have enough left over after paying any penalties to manage for a year or two. Once I'm through this, I'll find a way to make things work.'

'Good,' she says. 'That will be a big step taken, but I'm still not sure your negotiations with the Serious Fraud Office are the underlying problem.' She gives me her best psychiatrist look over the top of her black-framed glasses. 'Have you spoken with Fiona yet? Your parents?'

'No, not yet. I've been advised by my lawyer to wait until after I've signed the agreement.'

I can see from her face and posture that she isn't going to drop the subject. I wouldn't be surprised if she actually decided to wag her finger at me. 'Well, personally I think your lawyer is wrong,' she continues. 'From how you've described Fiona to me, she won't be at all happy to be presented with a fait accompli without having been informed or consulted. And neither will the rest of your family.'

She's right on the money, of course, but rocks and hard places spring to mind. 'Fair enough,' I say. 'But, let's face it. She's not going to be happy one way or the other, and she's going to think I'm a total idiot. But it's only a few days now; I'll tell Fiona straight after the meeting and it's really got nothing to do with the rest of my family.'

'Make sure you do,' says Julia. 'Because I believe that telling her is your biggest fear and, until you actually face up to it, you will continue to struggle, your anger won't go away and the headaches will get worse.'

'Maybe you're right,' I say. 'But it's only a few days ...'

Julia hasn't finished. '... And you don't actually believe it has nothing to do with the rest of your family do you? From what you've described to me, this is likely to become a high profile scandal with you right in the middle of it. It's going to affect them all.'

This is why I struggle with the whole idea of counselling. I'm fine. I've got some issues I need to deal with, and I'm dealing with them. My headaches are only headaches. I'm very stressed. Of course it's affecting me physically, and of course I'm angry. But why does it need to be dragged down into the cliché of my relationship with my wife and parents? It seems so predictable and pointless. That being said, she does have a point about the scandal.

'Well, we can agree to differ on that,' I say. 'In any case, it's still a moot point as I'll tell them in a few days as well. As for the scandal part, you're completely right. It will affect them and I'm not ignoring that.' I take a few seconds to calm myself. 'I actually think it's going to be even worse than I previously thought, so I've decided I need to make myself scarce for a few months.'

'Scarce? How do you mean?' says Julia, arching her eyebrows.

'I'll go abroad for a while – probably to France – keep my head down, and wait for the worst of it to blow over. Hopefully, if I'm not around, it'll take most of the heat off my family and the media will focus on the real guilty parties in the American head office.'

'Oh,' she says.' That makes some sense I suppose, but are you sure you know what you're doing? It may take you longer than you think to recover from this experience and the idea of you going off alone for several months worries me.' Julia gives me her serious over-the-top-of-the-glasses look again. 'It's my job to see beyond actions and events to human consequences and I believe this process has affected you deeply. You're a confident man, used to success and being in control of your environment. You still believe you can control upcoming events but, if things don't work to plan, they may prove too much for even you to deal with. Whatever you may think and feel about yourself and your abilities, you must remember that everyone has a breaking point. Everyone.'

'Thank you, Julia,' I say. 'I do understand that this is your job, and I wouldn't have come to you if I wasn't confident that you are good at it. But you shouldn't worry. When I found out about this, it was a huge shock and I know it will be an absolute disaster for me professionally, but I actually don't really care about that. I never waste time on what might have been and I've got my mind around it now. Who knows? It might turn out to be all for the best in some way.'

2017 - Fiona

Fiona hadn't seen much of her children over the previous few months. Hamish was travelling a lot and Maggie was head down with wedding preparations. Fiona struggled to get her mind around the fact that her daughter would be married in a few weeks. She must be getting old.

They met, as they did every year, at the OXO Towerrasserie on the South Bank. It was easy enough for Fiona to get into London and it suited both of the kids. Hamish worked in Canary Wharf and Maggie was in the West End.

Some people didn't care about birthdays, but Fiona did. She expected to be taken out for lunch and to be given presents and cards. It had been a standing joke in the family for years. Her view was simple – a birthday only comes once a year and it is a shame to waste the opportunity to be the centre of attention, even if only for a day.

When she arrived, Hamish was already there; he was a proper gentleman and knew it was wrong for a lady to have to wait alone. Just like his father.

They greeted each other with hugs and kisses. 'Getting old, Mum,' said Hamish with a grin. 'How's tricks?'

'Cheeky bugger,' said Fiona. 'We're all good. Nothing new or exciting to report. My life's actually getting more and more boring. The high points are swimming, shopping, cooking, gardening and pilates. Simon's at work all day and I don't get any sense that he's planning on retiring. I know I shouldn't complain but ...'

'I agree. You probably shouldn't,' said Hamish. 'It sounds like you've got it pretty good and, trust me, work's not everything it's cracked up to be. If you're so bored, you could always get a job or do some volunteer work.'

Fiona laughed, but it wasn't really funny. 'What would I do? It's not so easy. All I ever knew was how to be a lawyer and that was thirty years ago. I suppose I could train to be a swimming instructor, but can you imagine what that would be like? Lots of little fat people wallowing about in the shallow end and shaking their blubber around. I don't think I'd last a day.'

'Mum,' said Hamish sharply. 'You really can't say things like that. When did you start to become so intolerant?'

'Trust me, darling. Middle age and Sevenoaks will do that to you. Anyway, enough about my boring life. It's making me sad, and it's my birthday, after all.' Fiona generally tried to avoid thinking too deeply about how her life had turned out, 'What about you guys? Can I expect to be a grannie any time soon?'

Hamish laughed. 'Well, how long did that take? Three minutes? Four? You know you're becoming totally predictable, don't you?' He looked at his watch to change the subject. 'Where has Maggie got to? I've got to be back in the office by two.'

Fiona looked up and saw her daughter come through the door. 'Here she is. Great way to avoid the question by the way. Do you think I was born yesterday?'

'Nope, I think you were born fifty-eight years ago today and that's why we're here,' replied Hamish, his puerile, unfunny retort falling on habitually deaf ears.

Fiona gave Maggie a big hug and looked her up and down. 'Looking good, Bridezilla,' she said, 'you'll be the most gorgeous woman in the church.'

'Thanks Mum,' said Maggie, blushing. 'I'm so nervous. I've lost three kilos in the last couple of weeks. So, anyway. What were you guys talking about?'

'Hamish was just about to tell me when I can expect to be a grandmother,' said Fiona, grinning.

'Excellent,' said Maggie. 'I'm excited about becoming Auntie Maggs too.'

'What is it with you people?' Hamish was still smiling, but his eyes told a different story. 'Give me a break. We'll produce more little Johnsons in our own time and not to order.'

Maggie turned to her mother as they all sat down. 'Men,' she said. 'They actually seem to believe their own bullshit. It's incredible.'

'More to the point,' said Fiona. 'Could we agree not to mention my actual age again, please. Once was more than enough and a general 'Happy Birthday' will do fine from now on.'

Fiona saw that Hamish was grateful for the change of subject and wondered for a second whether he and Susan were actually trying for kids but having problems, but her attention was swiftly snatched away as he produced a small, but beautifully wrapped package and placed it on the table in front of her. 'Present time!' he exclaimed. 'I've ordered the food. Our usuals. Now, who's for a glass of bubbly?'

Fiona's birthday ritual followed a very predictable pattern. The food was the same every year; they had scallops with black pig ham and blood orange jelly, followed by monkfish, clams and piquillo pepper and the whole thing was topped off by a Valrhona chocolate fondant served with whatever ice cream was currently fashionable. This year it was salted caramel. Fiona always chose the wine. She'd become quite an expert.

She looked forward to the lunch for weeks in advance. It wasn't because of the food – she ate out in nice restaurants most weeks – but it was one of the rare occasions when she was able to spend some quiet time with her children without one of their partners being around. She was happy enough with their life choices and everyone got on well, but it wasn't the same as it was with only the three of them.

After Alastair had left – bloody hell, it was well over twenty years now – they had bonded even more tightly than before, each of them protecting the others in one way or another. She was still in awe of the way that small children were able to show such strong empathy. They had an amazing ability to know when another child, or adult, was in need of consideration or tenderness; this was despite the fact that they managed to be such little monsters at other times.

It appeared that empathy, like many other skills and

characteristics, was innate and was then unlearned steadily as life progressed. That didn't make any sense from a Darwinist perspective. What was the point of evolution singling out these qualities over thousands of generations, if they were then discarded before they became really useful?

She worried the absence of a father had affected them more than she could see, especially Hamish who'd been an unusually serious and quiet boy until he was about thirteen or fourteen. His love of team sports, especially rugby, was the catalyst which had changed that and helped him to develop a good extrovert character and strong social skills, but she suspected there was something locked away inside of him which would be better off exposed to the light of day and dealt with. Everyone had some sort of issue though, and it was all to easy to apportion blame to obvious factors such as broken marriages.

Fiona hadn't been brought up in a world where everyone rushed off to see a psychiatrist every ten minutes and, despite counselling and psychoanalysis seeming to be as humdrum these days as having your hair done, she felt that people were generally better off getting on with things and not dwelling too much on bitterness or regrets about paths not taken. God knows, Alastair disappearing had been no picnic for her either. Was it really almost twenty-two years? Could it be that long?

Hamish had Simon as a stepfather, of course. Well, both Hamish and Maggie had, but it had never quite worked for either of them for all sorts of reasons. On the face of it, Simon had made the effort to pick up the role and had tried hard; it's possible he'd tried too hard but, in the beginning at least, he had tried.

Unfortunately Simon was terrible at accepting any kind of criticism, and with children of that age, any incoming step parent is bound to need to deal with a lot of rejection. It takes empathy, gentleness and patience to build a trusting relationship with small children, and Simon wasn't really playing to his strengths. Anyway, whatever the reason was, there was never any real affection between either of them and Simon and the relationships had quickly become formal diplomatic ententes of almost Victorian politeness and distance.

She'd always tried to prevent Hamish and Maggie from being angry with Alastair, which may not have helped. Apart from the fact that criticising their father was negative and wouldn't achieve anything, she was still confused about what had happened herself. When you have spent so much of your life with someone and have got that close to them, you need to believe you know them and understand how they will behave when things are difficult.

She knew Alastair wasn't a coward or a liar, so there must have been something else going on that she hadn't known about. There must have been something, because the only alternative was that she hadn't known him at all, and that would have dealt a catastrophic blow to her self-esteem.

The decision to give Alastair some benefit of the doubt had led her to add another ritual to her birthday lunch. Before the champagne was finished, she raised her glass. 'To your father. Wherever he is, and whatever he's doing. Slàinte!'

Hamish and Maggie joined the toast. 'To Dad.'

All three of them were quiet for a moment and Fiona saw that Maggie's eyes were glistening. 'Are you all right, darling?' she said. 'What's wrong?' She reached over and stroked Maggie's shoulder.

'I'm all right, Mum,' Maggie replied. 'Really, I'm fine.'

She didn't look fine to Fiona. She looked as though she was about to burst into tears.

'Come on Maggs,' said Hamish. 'Something's obviously wrong. What is it?'

'It's Mum's birthday,' said Maggie. 'I don't want to ruin it with my issues ...'

'... Don't be so silly,' Fiona jumped in. 'It's only a silly birthday. I'll have another one next year. What's wrong?'

Maggie waited a few seconds before replying. 'Well, it sounds a bit idiotic saying it out loud but, you know you've always tried to stop us being angry with Dad for leaving?'

'Yes,' said Fiona. 'I know it's difficult but I felt it was for the best ...'

'... And I have generally always tagged along and not had a

problem with it. Much less than Hamish in fact.' Fiona watched the two of them exchange looks and the tight smile on Hamish's face spoke volumes. 'It's just that now, as I get closer to the wedding and realise that it's really happening, I keep thinking about the fact that he's not going to be there to walk me down the aisle. He probably doesn't even know I'm getting married.' Maggie put both hands on the table, fists clenched, and leant forwards. 'I'm sorry Mum, but I am angry. I'm so unbelievably pissed off with him. I'm sad too but, right now, mostly angry and I can't forgive him for this, I really can't. I'm sorry.'

Hamish put an arm around his sister and hugged her.

Fiona looked at her two beautiful children. 'Maggie, you're a grown woman and I'm well past believing I can tell you how to feel. Let's face it, I probably never could. Maybe he does deserve our resentment and anger. Maybe he actually was being a selfish, cowardly bastard. I don't want to believe it, and I don't want you to see him that way, because I want you to believe your father's a good man, but I can't always manage to convince myself either. I've had plenty of moments when I've cursed him to high heaven for what he did, and I'm sure I'll have plenty more. How about we change the toast this year?' She picked up her glass. 'To your father. The selfish, cowardly bastard!'

Hamish laughed, and lifted his glass high. 'Screw him. To the three of us.'

There were no more emotional moments and rest of the lunch had continued with the normal, familiar banter which always gave her so much pleasure. Hamish and Maggie made their excuses before rushing back to their already-overdue meetings while Fiona, who was in no hurry, was able to take her time and enjoy one more coffee before leaving. She had always hated to rush off after a good meal and, after all, today was her birthday.

She took the watch off her wrist and examined it carefully, rolling it between her fingers. It was a Breitling Transocean which Simon had given her that morning for her birthday and it was truly beautiful, very smart but not too girlie. She shuddered when she thought about how much it must have cost and also when she remembered how many beautiful watches she already had. The problem was that Simon was always so generous and it was easy to become addicted to beautiful, luxurious things, especially as he had such exceptionally good taste. She had never been able to figure out quite where all the money came from but it seemed as though, outside work, he was quite the expert at buying and selling fine wines in his own right.

One of the things which Maggie had said over lunch was niggling away at her. The implication that Hamish, even more than Maggie, was harbouring deep-seated anger towards his father, was something she had not really appreciated. He had clearly been very disturbed by Alastair leaving and, for the first few months, had frequently gone into inconsolable tantrums which lasted for hours at a time. They'd started in the weeks leading up to Alastair's departure but really kicked off on the day Fiona had sat them both down and explained the situation.

Maggie had always called it "going Hamish crazy" and Fiona had decided at the time that the best thing to do was to wait for a while and see if things improved. That phase lasted less than six months, and the rages simply stopped one day and never came back. Fiona remembered feeling so grateful the attacks had stopped that she never considered whether there would be long-lasting effects, or indeed what lay behind them in the first place.

Thinking back, she wondered whether she had actually been a fit parent in those first few months. She'd been grieving in her own way, as she'd understood deep down that Alastair wouldn't be coming back. It was also possible that she may have listened too much to advice from Simon who, she had to say, was not the world's greatest parenting guru. Fiona suspected Simon had never really liked children which, in many ways, made the sacrifices he'd made even more admirable. It wasn't entirely his fault that he was a rubbish stepfather. At least he'd tried. It was her responsibility to protect her babies, not his.

Had she possibly relied on Hamish's apparent maturity too much during that period and treated him as older than his years? She'd focused so much attention on little Maggie, who was having frequent panic attacks, that she was now afraid she might have missed some important tell-tales about Hamish's problems. He was only nine at the time. Who knew what had been going on in his mind?

She thought back to the frequent jokes she made about when she would be a grandparent and the way he always responded. Could he be delaying having children deliberately? He and Susan were still young but the way he looked when she brought up the subject was genuinely distressed. How terrible it would be if her neglect had made him somehow phobic towards the idea of having, and raising, children.

Hopefully, she was overthinking things, but Fiona knew something wasn't quite right. She wouldn't do anything until after the wedding, but then she would sit down with Hamish and get him to open up, however painful that might turn out to be.

1995 - Girl in Casino

I wasn't planning to come back here but, since Thailand, my confidence has been completely shot and I need to be surrounded by familiar places and things. My dreams of living the perfect life on a sunny island somewhere exotic are on hold, and rainy, dreary London will have to do for now.

After finishing Uni, I decided I deserved a break, and me and my mate, Nicki, took a gap year travelling round South America and Asia. We ended up in Thailand, on an island called Koh Samui, which was basically no more than a few huts on a beach at the time.

It's getting more popular now, but back then, it felt like we were living in a Bounty advert or something. It was paradise. We had our own straw hut nestled between the white sand beach and the palm trees, there were a few totally-chilled bars and restaurants, and the sun shone all of the time. Almost everyone there was in their twenties, taking a gap year or two, finding themselves, losing themselves, in between jobs, basically whatever took their fancy. Real life was on hold and no-one was in any hurry to leave.

You could live well, eat well and drink well for five or six dollars a day and life seemed too good to be true. It was, of course; there's always a catch in paradise, always a snake of some sort, waiting for willing suckers to be charmed into making stupid decisions.

My snake was called Anders, a gorgeous Swedish hunk who was the coolest, most chilled person I'd ever met. I mean, nothing ever fazed him. Not ever.

Anders showed up on the island one day a couple of months after we got there. He knew a couple of Danish girls who lived about ten huts down the beach from us and it didn't take long for him to surround himself with a small harem, which included me and Nicki. You'd have thought the other guys would have been jealous but not even that. They were under his spell too.

He played amazing guitar and knew every song, which he sang in his husky troubadour voice, the faintest trace of a sing-song Swedish lilt slipping seductively in between the odd word. He rolled the best joints, swam like Tarzan and threw a frisbee like Hercules at the Olympics. You name it, he did it best. It was as if a little god had come down to earth to grace us with his presence.

All of the girls on the island found their way into his bed at some point or other but, after a month or so, he and I became more and more of an item and I moved into his hut. This was quite well timed as I was almost out of cash and, although the huts cost half of diddly-squat to rent, it was still more than I'd have been able to afford for much longer.

So, one day, Anders says he's going to Bangkok on a bit of business and asks if I want to tag along. He tells me there might be some work in it for me as well.

Let's face it, I was always going to agree. I was twenty-three and totally in awe of the guy. You know how it is when you get into that state of hero worship where you can't see the wood for the trees and every time your sensible angel pops up and whispers in your ear, you move into full denial and decide the angel is just jealous because you're having all of the fun? Well, maybe you don't know, but that's how it was with me and Anders.

When we get to Bangkok, we go to the red light district and end up down this back alley behind the Japanese street in Patpong – the one where all of the salarymen go to get their jollies. We go down to the end of the alley and dip into a small bar, still full of girls but with no clients, or at least no Western clients.

It's the first time I've seen Anders even slightly on edge, but I'm still not smart enough to make for the exit. Anders nods to a Thai man who's sitting at the far end of the bar. He's small and slight, but looks super fit, like a kickboxer; his ebony-black eyes sitting flat in his deeply pockmarked face like buttons on a rag doll, no depth, no emotion. Not someone you'd ever want to be on the wrong side of.

'This is Sitthichai,' says Anders, managing to recover a bit of his swagger. 'He's the main man around here.'

The slightest of nods – a blink and I'd have missed it – and my presence is acknowledged. I put on my bravest smile, wondering exactly how much trouble I'm in.

'You'll be helping us on a little trip,' Anders tells me, putting an arm around me either protectively or proprietorially, I couldn't tell. He turns to his Thai friend and grins, 'She's cool and she's got a British passport, so there won't be any problems.'

Sitthichai stands up and takes a step towards me, handing me a brown paper parcel. He oozes the scent of sweaty cloves from Indonesian kretek cigarettes, and the sickly smell makes my stomach lurch. 'You take good care of this, pretty lady,' he says, clamping one hand on my wrist and transfixing me with his button eyes. 'It very important to me. You understand?'

I nod frantically, still not sure exactly what I am promising to do.

He lets go of my arm and turns to Anders. 'You too, big boy. No mistakes. OK?'

In spite of my churning bowels and aching wrist, I am still impressed with Anders. He manages to keep his cool, even though I think I know him well enough to guess he's shitting himself inside too. He may not be quite out of his depth but, big boy or not, he's definitely needing to stand on tiptoes to keep his nose above water.

I start to breathe again as we get back to busier streets, but still don't know what to say to Anders. We take a tuk-tuk into the centre of town and I'm certain we're being followed the whole way. Maybe people are listening to us? Anders tells the tuk-tuk to wait while we go up to our hotel room. Once we're inside the room, he opens up the parcel and takes out a large, full wash bag. It's a garish pink and made of that nasty shiny plastic. Not something I'd be seen dead with.

'Put this in your backpack and let's get going,' he says. 'You're taking a little trip. I need you to buy me some tasty Swedish herring.'

I shouldn't have been surprised to find out that Anders was involved in the drugs business, nor that I'd been cast in the role of sacrificial lamb. But it was all going to be OK, they'd done this thirty times before, it was only half a kilo, it was sealed inside the lining of the wash bag so the sniffer dogs wouldn't smell it, no-one would think of stopping a sweet young thing like me. Nothing to worry about.

All I had to do was fly to Stockholm, meet a guy, give him the wash bag and come back a week later with a few jars of pickled herring and some akevit for Anders. For this trivial task, I'd get two thousand quid, enough to keep me on the island for another year at least.

So I just follow along like a little puppy, or a puppet, or a muppet or whatever other kind of idiot blindly does what they're told without thinking, all the way to the airport. Anders drops me outside – you need to have a ticket to go into the hall – and gives me a kiss. 'Just chill, girl. It'll all be sweet. I'll see you next week.'

Inside the terminal, I'm suddenly back in the real world, myself again. Staring at all of the soldiers, police, dogs, guns everywhere. The music from Midnight Express is pounding in my head; it's forty-five degrees but I'm in a cold sweat. I realise I'm going throw up and run to the nearest toilets. Shit, shit, shit – what am I doing? How did I get here?

I come out of the stall, wash my face and look at the person in the mirror. I don't recognise her; I don't remember who I used to be. I'm lost. One thing's for fucking sure though, I'm not going to spend the rest of my life in a Thai jail.

Once I get back out and start to go through immigration, I feel as though I'm floating along like in a film, above and outside reality. I know what will happen before it happens. My bag is, of course, pulled aside by the customs police. A senior guy with a sharp, crisp uniform and too many teeth who speaks perfect public school English.

'Do you mind if we have a look in your bag, Miss Richards?' He has already started unzipping it. 'It's only a routine check.'

'No problem. Go ahead,' says my disembodied voice.

As the customs guy pulls everything out of the bag, his right eye starts twitching and his hands become scrabbling crab claws looking for scraps in the small pile of sun-bleached cotton which is my wardrobe. 'Where is your wash bag, Miss Richards?' he snaps. 'That's not normal for a young lady. Where do you keep your makeup?'

'I left it behind,' I reply. 'I've finished almost everything anyway and thought I'd get more in Stockholm.'

He stares at me for a few seconds and then goes through the contents of my bag carefully one more time, lips now set in a thin, straight line. He looks upset and annoyed, but I don't think he blames me. Someone has given him a bad tip. 'Thank you, Miss Richards. Have a good flight,' he mumbles eventually, ramming my clothes back into the bag and pushing it towards me before turning sharply and stalking off.

When I get to Stockholm, I manage to scrape together the money for a ferry back to the UK and here I am. I worry that Anders or his Thai friend will still be looking for me and I can't put the whole episode behind me. "What if" images run circles in my head whenever I'm alone and have time to think. I was so close to doing it – minutes away – but for once, my sensible angel shouted loudly enough and I thank her on a daily basis.

I can't remember what my future dreams used to be and certainly don't feel up to doing anything about them. For now, I can't manage anything more than to keep my head down and kill time.

1995 - Alastair

I wander down High Holborn like a zombie in a suit. It's almost lunchtime, soft rain is falling and everyone has somewhere to be. The tube yawns – a hungry, gaping cyclops-mouth sucking passers-by into its rumbling innards and spitting out the leftovers. The queue at the fruit stall blocks the pavement, adding to the chaos.

I really don't want to be underground and fight my way past, left down Kingsway, crowds thinning as the road widens and the grey buildings loom high above me.

Unlike everyone else, I have nowhere to go and no idea where I am going. My mind no longer functions, it spins in pointless circles and my feet follow an invisible trail that only they know.

The strange thing is that I have stopped being angry.

I have been angry forever. Such a long time where every little thing has set off another uncontrolled – and uncontrollable – surge of fury. Trivial, insignificant things. Dropping my keys, toast stuck in the toaster, kids too noisy, kids too quiet, train late, the tiniest pinprick enough to tear open my balloon of rage and indignation at the injustice of life.

I'd even got to the point of swearing out loud when I was alone. Really cursing, using language I would never use normally. The world was closing in, conspiring against me. Fate was my biggest enemy. Lady Luck was a preening, thankless whore.

When I wasn't angry, I was wallowing in self-pity. 'Why me?' I would think, or even say out loud. 'What have I done to deserve this?'

I can hear my shoes flapping on the damp pavement, a weak, pathetic sound, echoing across the suddenly-empty street, a suitable soundtrack for my weak pathetic thoughts. I have always despised self-pity – that's something which is drummed into you from Day One if you've got a father who's an officer in the Marines – and I can't understand how I've allowed myself to sink so deeply into this black hole.

My flapping feet turn right on to Aldwych and we make our way together down towards the river.

Angry, self-pitying and generally a complete pain in the arse; it must have been hell putting up with me for the past while. The kids are probably too young to have noticed, but Fiona certainly has. We have had some nasty fights recently and they have all been my fault.

Strangely, it appears as though the anger is done with now; a door has closed somewhere inside me, just like that. There is no more uncertainty, no more hope that "something will turn up". I feel strangely calm and in control for the first time in ages. I don't know how much my sessions with Julia have helped me to deal with setbacks calmly, but I suspect they've achieved something; there might be something behind all of the psychobabble after all.

Before I finished my final session with her on Tuesday, she spent some time talking about the five stages of grief: Denial and Isolation; Anger; Bargaining; Depression and Acceptance. Although these "rules" are normally aimed at people who have lost a loved one, they can be extended to other scenarios. Julia also explained that the stages don't need to come in that sequence and some may never materialise at all. I didn't really understand the bargaining stage – apparently, we tend to secretly try to make a deal with God, fate or some other higher power in an attempt to postpone the inevitable – but the rest make total sense.

In any case, my days of bargaining are over.

As I get to Charing Cross pier, I see a neat row of fading flowers stacked against the iron railing, left in memory of the Marchioness disaster. This was the place where everyone had embarked and memories were still fresh even five years later. Fifty-one dead and all because they took a boat trip on the river to celebrate someone's birthday. It puts my own problems into perspective. One of my colleagues died when the Marchioness sank. Not a very close friend, but a friend nonetheless.

I walk down to the bank and find an empty bench to sit on. The Thames does look menacing from close up, a thing to fear and respect. The waters are slate-grey, roiling under the arches of Charing Cross Bridge and I imagine what it must have been like for the passengers that night.

Singing, dancing, drinking and then a sharp, metallic, grinding, wrenching screech, the lights go out and the world turns upside down. Everyone would have been screaming, lashing out, trying to hold on, and clueless as to what was happening. Some lucky ones may have been knocked unconscious as the ship turned, others would have begun to understand as the water rushed in, cold and dark. How long would it have taken after that? How long would they have struggled on with no idea which way was up, which way was out?

I stand up and go to the railing, not really sure why I'm here. The meeting I've just come from ended up being much worse than I expected it to be, a very long way from the dramatic Death Row reprieve I had been foolishly allowing myself to hope for. It is terrifying how we are so influenced by American movies. I wasn't in America, I wasn't on Death Row, and there were no miracles coming. Why waste precious minutes with vain hopes?

We met earlier that morning at the offices of my lawyers on High Holborn: the same two officers from the Serious Fraud Office who had been "debriefing" me over the previous months; their boss, a sharply dressed woman in her mid-forties; my lawyer, John Gilbert, and me. It was clear who was in charge of the meeting and she walked straight over to introduce herself as soon as I entered the room.

'Good morning, Mr Johnson. I'm Stella Clarke, senior case officer for the SFO and I'm in charge of bringing together the various elements of our investigation into Polaris LLC and in this particular case, formalising any arrangements we will be making with yourself.' She took an official-looking document from her briefcase and laid it down in front of her, giving it a couple of tiny tweaks to align it perfectly with the edge of the table.

'Good morning, Ms Clarke,' I replied. 'Very pleased to meet you.' I couldn't resist emphasising the "Ms", she looked so uptight.

I wasn't, of course, even slightly pleased to meet her and was dreading what she might have to say. I also still had my anger bubble well inflated and the misuse of the word "yourself" was something which was guaranteed to get under my skin. Pompous, ignorant cow. She wouldn't be making arrangements with "myself", she'd be making them with "me". Why not just speak bloody English?

Ms Clarke continued, clearly loving the sound of her own voice. 'While the SFO recognises the contribution ... seriousness of your offences ... set an example ...' She must have droned on for twenty minutes without saying anything substantial before she got to the point. Having duly satisfied her ego and having dazzled us all with her ability to waffle endlessly in smug, pompous bureaucratese, she picked up the letter and started to read.

'In light of your co-operation and, as an alternative to formal legal proceedings, the Attorney General has agreed to the following:

'Firstly, you will receive the mandatory minimum custodial sentence for an offence of this severity which is five years. This will, however, be a suspended sentence and you will not therefore be required to go to prison at this time. You will however have a criminal record.'

I remember breathing a huge sigh of relief at that. I'm not sure I would do well in prison and, although I had been assured it was unlikely that I'd go, you never know until the fat lady sings.

'Secondly, you will be required to resign immediately from any, and all, positions, directorships and other employments within the Polaris group. You will also agree to waive any notice periods to which you may normally be entitled and will not be entitled to compensation of any form. You will, however, retain any pension rights which you currently have.'

So, no notice pay, no accrued holiday pay, no nothing. Fat lot of good the pension rights would be unless they somehow managed to get the Americans to make whole the pension funds.

'Thirdly, your ICAEW practicing certificate will be revoked and you will not be permitted to hold any company directorships within the European Union for the next ten years.'

I had expected this also. John had told me it was inevitable. It meant that I was now almost completely blocked from finding a job of any sort in finance. Maybe something with one of the big consulting firms but, most likely, they would run a mile when they figured out who I was and what I had been part of.

'Finally, in order to complete this compromise agreement, you will be required to pay a penalty of three hundred and seventy-five thousand pounds which will be placed into a support fund for the affected pensioners. This sum to be payable within thirty days of today's date.'

That was the moment when my life came to an unexpected end, but there were no flashing lights, fireworks or fanfares. Nothing at all to mark the moment.

Ms Clarke put the letter carefully back into position and added a few kind words of her own. 'The terms of this offer are not negotiable and you have until close of business today to confirm your agreement. If you haven't confirmed your agreement by that time, the Attorney General will be obliged to pursue this matter through the courts. On the basis that you agree to the proposed terms, these discussions will remain confidential until the fine has been paid.'

She straightened the letter one more time, sat up straight and looked across at me. 'I think those terms are extremely fair in the circumstances. You should be grateful to Mr Gilbert. He's done an excellent job for you.'

As I lean out over the water, I realise it was at that moment, as she crossed her arms primly in front of her, that my anger evaporated. What's the point in being angry? Or self-pitying? Neither of them will get me anywhere. I am well and truly fucked and that is something that nobody can deny. I don't have a job, no future job prospects apart from maybe working in a pub, and I certainly don't have three hundred and seventy-five thousand pounds of cash floating around. The penalty is so much bigger than

I'd been expecting. We will lose the house, have to pull the kids out of school, cash in all of our ISAs, sell the cars and it still won't be enough. This was not what Fiona signed up for. I know that for sure.

Everything has happened so fast. I've gone from hero to zero – as the bloody Americans would say – in less than four months, and I remind myself that neither Fiona, nor anyone else in my family, knows anything about it yet. That isn't going to play well. This is now as much their problem as it is mine. How can I have kept it to myself? What have I been thinking?

Until that moment, I suppose I was genuinely holding on to a small nugget of belief that a solution would miraculously appear and I would be able to escape. After all, I genuinely hadn't been complicit in the plans to rip off the pension funds. I had been stitched up like a kipper and someone would surely see that at the last minute, tell me they understood everything, and exonerate me completely.

Let's face it, I was being childish and naive. That's not how the world works and I realised that as I sat in John's office listening to my doom being read out, blow by blow.

I didn't say anything once Ms Clarke had finished her little performance. I sat without moving, allowing the silence to grow, and watching everyone else shift and fidget in their chairs. After twenty or thirty painful seconds, John stood up and ushered the lovely Ms Clarke out of the room together with her two sidekicks, thanking them for coming and explaining that he would discuss this with his client and get back to them later in the day.

He closed the door behind him and sat down across the table from me. 'I'm sorry,' he said. 'I had no idea the penalty would be so large. They're obviously thinking about how much press this is going to get, and they can't afford to be pulled apart by the Guardian for being soft on white-collar crime. Are you OK?'

'Yes, I'm fine, thank you.' My voice came from somewhere else, oddly distant and formal. 'This changes everything. I haven't got that sort of money. Is there no room for negotiation?'

'I'm sorry, but none,' he replied. 'We've been negotiating for six weeks now. This is their take-it-or-leave-it offer. If you go to court, you'll lose, the penalty will be as big, the legal fees much, much bigger and you're probably looking at a minimum of two years of actual jail time.'

'Well, what happens if I take the deal and can't pay all of the money in time? Will I go to prison then?'

'Almost certainly.' He was confident. 'The deal is conditional on you fulfilling all of the agreed terms. If you don't pay the full penalty on time, they will almost certainly take you to court and you can't expect any goodwill from the SFO if you make them look like idiots.'

'So, lose-lose then?'

'I'm afraid that's about it. You took on some serious responsibilities, and the attitudes around fraud and corporate governance have got much stronger since Maxwell. Everyone will say that a man of your experience should have been on top of this much earlier which, as you know, I tend to agree with. It's your signature on all of the key documents. I don't think you have any options at this stage. You need to find the money from somewhere.'

'OK, OK, I get it,' I say, standing and picking up my briefcase. 'I don't know how I managed to be so blind either. Assume I'll sign, and prepare the signature copies please. I need some air. I'll be back by four.'

And so, I stand by the side of Old Father Thames, watching the water flow by. The river is a true reflection of life itself; once it's passed by, that's it. It won't flow back, you can't ever recapture the lost moment and undo your mistakes. This dirty ribbon of water writes time's passage for ever in a sweep of a giant calligraphy pen.

Not so far, maybe half an hour downstream, the water reaches the North Sea, with no more banks leading it along a predictable path. Its nature changes there, revealing infinite uncertainties and possibilities, deep dark places where it's no longer possible to see the future, to plan, to control.

Maybe not so much like life itself for most people, most of the time, but seemingly a perfect mirror of my current bleak future.

How would I be able to protect and support my family now? An archaic concept but, for me, it is visceral, as much a part of me as breathing. It's just what you do. And now I wouldn't be able to.

My generation grew up in what could be defined as a post-feminist era. So many of the ideals and principles of equality were simply accepted as normal by everyone I knew. We all understood there was a lot of work still to be done if we were to achieve a truly equal society, but the basic principles had been carved out deeply enough.

There are some gender roles though which appear to be more a part of our animal selves and haven't changed so much – or at least not yet. The need to hunt, to fight, to support, to protect. Both sexes have those drives, but they still show themselves differently. I have never questioned the idea that I will support and protect my family. Provide a house, put food on the table, pay for schooling, healthcare, whatever was needed. In my world these are "normal" expectations and, although there are many exceptions, it is amazing how little has changed in that respect. The ability to provide is as key to my self-image as a man as the ability to procreate or to be a good lover.

The ringing of my new mobile phone snaps me alert. It's John.

'You said you were going to be here by four.' He is clearly not happy. 'The papers are all printed and ready for signature and I've already had the SFO on the phone twice.'

'Oh shit.' I look at my watch. It's quarter past five. 'I'll be with you in fifteen minutes. Sorry.'

'OK. I'll see you then. Don't be late.'

I decide I still can't face the Tube and set off briskly up Villiers Street. I can get there in a quarter of an hour on foot if I push it.

Much as I can't see a way out of this mess at the moment, I'm not ready to give up without a fight – another of those basic instincts. The waters of the Thames behind me might only take half an hour to reach the sea but I have thirty days to find a solution and I owe it to everyone to give it a try.

The first step to rebuilding my manhood is probably going to be the hardest. I need to tell Fiona and my family what has happened and let them have a say in what happens next. The cold sweat on my palms reminds me all too clearly of how frightened I am of that conversation. I know Fiona will see this whole fiasco in a single light – complete betrayal.

But the first thing to do is to sign that bloody compromise agreement and draw a line in the sand.

2017 - Sally

It's been an interesting day.

We've had this new villa owner approach us asking if we can take on his property management. A few holiday rentals but everything else as well – pool cleaning, gardening, housekeeper, security, the works. It looks like a nice property and the owner sounded sensible enough on the phone. It's also right on the edge of Eze which is about as pricey a location as you can find round here and average house prices aren't exactly low. Not a huge villa, but big enough, and a great location.

The thing about Eze is that, not only is it a beautiful medieval village, hanging off the cliffs overlooking the Med, but it's also very close to Monaco. This means that, if you're very rich and not totally brainless, you can set yourself up as a Monaco resident and pay no taxes, but live in France, which is much better because Monaco is a pointless crowded shithole full of smug idiots. Eze is ideal for those people, which is why property values have gone through the roof. I'm not saying the people who buy there aren't also smug, but at least they're smart enough to not live in Monaco.

Anyway, I didn't have anything better to do, so I thought I'd go over and check it out. It's a great drive and we have the roof off our battered, little Suzuki jeep from April to October so it's the same as cruising in a soft top Merc or Aston apart from the speed bit ... and the handling ... and the noise and ... Who cares? It's great fun and I love it.

I took the Grande Corniche out of Nice, which has to be one of the most amazing roads in the world. It's been in loads of films and is the definitive winding mountain road, snaking along the edge of the cliffs with precious little between you and eternity. Grace Kelly died driving along it and it gives me a bit of a shiver each time I drive past the crash site. There are still always fresh flowers at the memorial. I've often wondered who puts them there, it's been over thirty years since she died.

As I got closer to the address I'd been given, I began to get the sense I'd been here before. When Jim and I first moved here, almost fifteen years ago, he showed me the villa where he'd spent time as a kid and I was convinced this was on the same street.

Well, it wasn't only the same street as it turned out – it was the same villa. I remembered the unusual, wrought iron gates. What are the odds of that? I had a quick look around from outside to be sure and made my way back home.

So here I am, wondering what to do. I have to tell Jim – he knows about the enquiry – but I know it's going to upset him and dredge up too many memories. He doesn't like talking about his family at the best of times, but something must have happened recently and it's getting to him more than usual. Maybe someone died? He's been on Facebook a lot and he's not sleeping well. I can't imagine hearing about the Villa Eugenie is going to help.

Jim and me, we get on well at every level, we're companions, mates, lovers, supporters, the whole enchilada, but there's nothing sticky or demanding about our relationship. It's like that poem by Khalil Gibran 'On Marriage' – which I love, by the way. It talks about being close, but giving one another space to be individual people. Well, Jim and me do that. We don't keep secrets from each other, but we allow the other to have the time and space to share their private thoughts and issues in their own way and in their own time.

Until Jim, I'd never understood this was possible. All my relationships before were intense, all consuming and ultimately messy, mutually abusive and eventually painful. With Jim, life has been completely different. I've found my soulmate. I never thought I'd be so lucky.

Well, there's no point in worrying about it. I'm going to have to tell him about the villa and we'll see how it pans out. Maybe I've got it wrong and there won't be a problem. I bet I'm not though.

It can wait until tomorrow, he'll be knackered when he gets back from his cycling and it'll be shower, supper and an early night. I've made some potato gnocchi, which will go very nicely with a fresh tomato and basil sauce.

One day at a time.

1995 - Fiona

Fiona had completely forgotten she'd agreed to meet Simon for lunch and was about to go around to a friend's house when the phone rang. It was, of course, Simon.

'I've booked us a table at Julie's for one o'clock. I hope that works?' He rattled off the words in a single burst, not leaving Fiona any escape hatch to wriggle through.

'Sounds great,' she replied. 'Looking forward to it.'

'Excellent. I'll see you then.'

And that was that. She wondered afterwards if she had known even then where this was taking her. Possibly? To be honest, she no longer really cared. Anything was better than where she was. Luckily she didn't see much of Alastair these days, seeing him only made it worse.

Things had changed between them, and she couldn't quite put her finger on when it had started really going downhill; it was at least six months, although everything had become much more difficult after Christmas.

They'd had a great Christmas and New Year sailing in the Caribbean. Fiona had put her foot down and insisted they have a family holiday and that it be somewhere where they couldn't be tracked down. She had already been close to breaking point.

The four of them went cruising on a forty-four foot Oceanis yacht in the British Virgin Islands. The weather was stunning with good wind, but not too much, and it had been wonderful for them to spend time together. Hamish and Maggie were still young enough to enjoy being with their parents and both she and Alastair had enough yachting experience to keep the sailing controlled and relaxed.

Alastair had already been working much too hard for much too long by that stage and was looking exceptionally fat and pasty when they first arrived. He was also completely exhausted – maybe more than she had realised – and basically did nothing but sleep for the first two days after they landed in Tortola. They had been forced to stay in harbour waiting for him to surface.

She and the kids had been on the edge of mutiny when he did come up for air. It was just in time, as Tortola marina is not a great place to spend a holiday. A couple of expensive yachtie restaurants and bars, boats everywhere and lots of people coming and going, but that was it.

But surface he did, and he was a different man, transformed into his old self in a flash. Still pasty and flabby but nothing sun, salt and sea air couldn't change.

'Come on, you lazy landlubbers,' he'd announced in the most ridiculous Captain Birdseye voice. 'We're booked for Christmas Day at Foxy's on Jost van Dyke. It's a two-day sail so we need to get going. Avast me hearties!'

And off they went. He'd locked his phone in the safe and hadn't given anyone at work details of where they were. That was the deal and he'd stuck to it, or rather clutched on to it like the lifeline it was.

Looking back, it had been almost perfect. Like a second honeymoon, except for the kids who did make onboard romance slightly challenging. It wasn't such a big boat, after all. Luckily, Alastair had another surprise in his back pocket. He had an old university friend with a holiday house on Tortola who was down for New Year and had who kids of similar ages to Hamish and Maggie. A couple of calls from the Marina office and, smooth as butter, they dropped Maggie and Hamish off and had three days alone on the boat over New Year. Wonderful times.

Fiona could feel the muscles in her jaw tighten as she remembered that those wonderful times were now over three months in the past and they hadn't made love since. By far the longest time they had been without sex. Even after the birth of the children, the break had been shorter. Yes, things had become even worse after they got back, and she didn't understand why. He wouldn't talk to her, avoided any attempts to have a serious conversation, and was just shrinking into himself.

Apart from that holiday, she couldn't even remember the last time they'd had any fun together. She was only thirty-six and still in her prime. They'd both contributed to building a comfortable, secure life with a rosy future and then, for no apparent reason, he had abandoned her to a grey, mundane and lonely existence which was absolutely not what she'd expected. She knew her attitude was that of a spoilt child, but she didn't care; she'd had enough.

As it was always impossible to park anywhere near Notting Hill, she took the tube to Marble Arch and walked from there. There was a light drizzle but she had an umbrella and plenty of time; the walk would take less than forty minutes and it was a part of London which had always fascinated her. A strange mix of posh and seedy, from the brothels on Sussex Gardens to some of the most expensive apartments in the world overlooking Hyde Park. Each time she was in the area, she would follow a slightly different route and there was always something new to discover.

Fiona was nervous. Excited. Having lunch with Simon felt somehow illicit. It was only lunch for Christ's sake! She needed to calm down. It was only lunch, but there had always been something else with Simon, hiding in the shadows out of sight. She remembered that one time in France about seven years earlier when she was pregnant with Maggie. The "something else" had shocked her by sidling into plain view for a moment before slipping away again.

Jane and Mike had decided to sell their villa in Provence and the whole family, including Simon, had gone down together on a farewell trip. Most of the time Fiona had been stuck like a beached whale, either trying to keep out of the sun or to look after Hamish who had just started to run about like a Duracell bunny.

Alastair had tried half-heartedly to help but struggled to resist the temptations of tennis with Simon, or messing about on the springboard, and both lunch and dinner turned out to be typically boozy for everyone apart from her.

There had been one night after dinner, a little breeze had taken the edge off the temperature although waves of heat were still rolling out from the walls and stone tiles. Fiona was standing by the pool in the moonlight, listening to the cicadas and stretching her aching back when she heard someone come up behind her. It was Simon.

She had felt his hand on her shoulder and then he had gently pulled her around and kissed her. Not a friend's kiss, it was a deep, full kiss, passionate and tender. She had been too shocked to react for a few seconds and, by then, Simon had turned and walked off into the darkness. They had never spoken of it.

The rain was easing as she arrived at Julie's and, although she was five minutes early, she could see he was already there, standing just inside the reception, laughing and chatting with the manager – Simon probably supplied the restaurant with wine. He looked relaxed and poised. Certainly not as nervous as Fiona felt.

Simon had always been a good looking guy, with that slight curl to his hair which allowed him to wear it a little too long and flopping forward over his brow. He was dark, but not swarthy, and they had been around enough swimming pools together for her to know he was slim, muscular and generally well proportioned.

It was strange that he never had girls around when they saw him. With the exception of those months with Jenny which had really not worked out, Fiona had never met one of his girlfriends. A bit of a mystery, as he was undoubtedly a very attractive man.

He was dressed smartly, jacket but no tie and Fiona realised that, somewhat subconsciously, she had also made an effort. She couldn't hold back the feeling that this lunch was more like a date than anything else.

'Fiona.' He had spotted her and stepped out of the restaurant towards her. 'You look lovely.'

She couldn't help herself. 'Well, you certainly look a lot better than you did on Sunday evening. The pair of you were completely shit-faced.'

He lifted his hands in mock surrender. 'Guilty as charged, Milady. If I remember correctly though, it was you who told me to take Alastair for a few drinks, wasn't it?'

'A good point, but there are limits.' Fiona was laughing now. She had been relatively sober on Sunday as she'd had to drive and it now amused her to picture the pair of them swaying and giggling as they arrived back from their walk. She doubted they remembered any of it.

'Come on, let's sit down. I'm starving,' said Simon, holding the door for her and ushering her into the restaurant, where they were instantly greeted by the manager and led through to a secluded corner table, framed by thin, black swatches of twigs and festooned with fairy lights. All of this set in an arch of rough plaster, painted Barbie pink. Somehow it worked perfectly.

Fiona was suitably impressed. 'What an amazing place. I've heard about it, of course, but it's my first time.'

Simon smiled at her while the waiter gave them menus, unfolded their napkins and poured two glasses of champagne from the bottle on the table. 'Well, luckily there's a first time for everything. I thought Cristal might be a good plan. I hope you don't mind?'

'Not even slightly. If I'd had it more than twice in my life before, I might go so far as to tell you it's my favourite.'

'There are some advantages to being in the trade, I suppose. Cheers. Great to see you.'

They both raised their glasses and took a first sip. The champagne was absolutely delicious. Fiona didn't know a lot about wine but she knew enough to be able to tell when something was special, and this was exceptional. She felt the first bubbles popping in her head almost as soon as the sharp crispness hit the back of her throat.

Simon was very much at home but Fiona knew he did a lot of this as part of his job, so it wasn't such a surprise. When she'd first lived in London, she had struggled to make ends meet and then, by the time the money started to come in, she'd found herself up to her neck in nappies. She'd almost totally missed the young, rich and single phase that everyone raved about. It seemed a bit unfair.

'Shall we get the ordering bit out of the way?' he said, picking up his menu. 'If you're happy to take pot luck, I can ask the chef to do us two three-course lunches with whatever he thinks is best today. That's what I tend to do here.'

'Sounds great, said Fiona. 'I always find ordering is such a pain and I love surprises. Will you excuse me just for a moment? I'll just be a tick.' She stood up and made her way to the Ladies, leaving Simon to order the food.

As she looked in the mirror, adjusting her make up, she asked herself yet again what she was doing there. It was only lunch, but there was the nagging sense that Simon didn't see it that way and what was even more worrying was the fact that she didn't care.

She walked slowly back through the crowded restaurant, half-recognising someone at almost every table. As she sat down again, she saw that the menus were gone and there was already a small amuse bouche in front of her, in the shape of a tiny espresso cup filled with Jerusalem artichoke velouté. She straightened her napkin across her skirt and took a delicate sip. It was slightly frothy, with a rich, smooth tang. Absolutely delicious.

'So, what did Alastair have to say for himself?' She had been waiting to ask from the moment she arrived. 'Did you find out anything useful?'

Simon shifted around in his chair. 'Can we talk about something else please?' he said, looking into the bottom of his soup cup. 'We did discuss a few things but I promised I wouldn't say anything. Even to you.' He looked up at Fiona and shrugged his shoulders. 'I know you really want to understand what's going on but please don't push me. He promised me he will talk to you this week and, if he doesn't, I'll tell you what I know, promise or no promise. Can you live with that?'

Fiona felt the disappointment like a cold weight settling inside her, but realised it wasn't worth pushing harder. One way or the other, it was just a few more days, but she was more convinced than ever that there was something serious going on.

'OK, I won't ask you to break your Cub's honour,' she said, holding her glass out and smiling. 'On one condition. That you give me a bit more of that glorious champagne.'

'Thank you,' said Simon, topping up her glass. 'It's a deal.'

The rest of the meal passed in a blur. Superb food, superb wine, although way too much, and Fiona felt that, once the elephant in the room – Alastair and his issues – had been pushed aside, they were free to simply be two people having lunch together. They shared thoughts and ideas, compared snippets of their daily lives and future dreams, all of this happened naturally and without complications.

As the waiter arrived to offer them coffee, Simon leant forward. 'Why don't we go back to my place for coffee? It's around the corner and I've got a new Gaggia coffee machine I'm dying to show off.'

'Is that the nineties' version of etchings?' said Fiona who was enjoying herself and was in no hurry to get back to real life. 'Why not?' she said. 'The only issue is that Anita is expecting me back by five-thirty.' Anita was the au pair, a sweet twenty-year-old Danish girl who the kids absolutely adored.

'Call her from my flat and tell her you'll be back a bit late. She's picking up the kids from school anyway, I suppose?'

'She normally does but they're still on holiday and they've been going to a full-time tennis camp. I'll give her a call when we get back to yours and see what she says. She should still be at home.'

The bill paid itself by magic and a few moments later they were standing at the restaurant door being helped into their coats. God, Simon was a smooth operator. Fiona felt as though she was being swept along on a raft in the middle of a huge river, spinning in slow, inevitable circles, miraculously avoiding all obstacles but always too far from the bank to get off.

The flat really was just around the corner. A smart white-stucco terrace with black railings, all in true Upstairs-Downstairs style. Simon was on the second floor.

'The phone's just there. I'll get the coffee going. Make yourself at home.' Simon was already on his way to the kitchen.

She made her call and followed Simon. The kitchen, like the rest of the flat, was very slick and modern, bachelor-minimalist, black, chrome and glass everywhere.

Standing out in glaring contrast was the large painting looming over the breakfast table. It was a mess of loose, half-melted human figures in blacks, reds, ochres and umbers, presided over by some sort of king. They were all angry – fighting, grappling and struggling for survival in a burnt-out world. It reminded her of one of those medieval paintings of the circles of hell but it was different, much more modern and, somehow, much more disturbing.

'What the hell is that?' She stepped closer to look at the painting. 'I've never seen anything like it outside a gallery. It looks like an original.'

'If only.' Simon's eyes shone as he looked at the picture. 'Unfortunately, it's only a reproduction. The original is in Australia. You know I went over a couple of years ago to visit some of our clients?' Fiona nodded, still transfixed by the painting, which must have been one of the most striking pieces of art she had ever seen. 'Well, while I was there, an old friend took me to see an exhibition just outside Melbourne and this painting was there.

'It's called The Mockers, and was painted by a guy called Arthur Boyd after he left the army in 1948. He pulls all sorts of ideas from the religious paintings of Bosch and Breughel and combines those with his war experiences and everything else that was coming out about the concentration camps back then.' Simon paused for a few moments. 'I just think it says "never forget" better than any words.' He turned back to the ridiculous steampunk coffee contraption he was fiddling with. To hide his tears? Fiona thought so.

She knew most of Simon's parents' family had died in the Holocaust, although he never talked about it, and she felt a wave of affection wash over her. He had always been lonely in some way. Despite having lots of friends and an adopted second family at Alastair's home, she'd always understood that Simon remained a solitary soul with a need for affirmation. Predictably, the more he needed that affirmation, the less likely he was to get it, especially amongst his peers. Even the nicest people had cruel and bullying streaks when they sensed weakness and need.

She found herself standing behind him and wrapping her arms around his chest. Neither of them said anything. They stood silently as the coffee machine hissed softly, joining the rhythm of their breathing and swaying in time. He smelt so wonderful. No added scent, cologne or aftershave, just a nutty, manly smell. He smelt safe.

She still had nothing to say as he turned, took her face in both hands and kissed her, first on the tip of her nose and then on her lips. The kiss could almost have been chaste but the electric shiver which followed told a different story.

Simon pulled back slightly, looking deep into her eyes. 'Fiona, you are gorgeous. Simply gorgeous.'

She couldn't pretend any more. She wanted this, she wanted him, she didn't care if it was right or wrong, justified or not, it was no longer about choice. She pulled him close, lips crushing against lips, hungry tongues seeking and searching, their bodies pressed together. He was hard already and Fiona felt the deep glow of her own arousal.

They found their way to the bedroom and out of their clothes in a blur of fumbling limbs and tearing buttons. He was in as good shape as she remembered, broad, muscular chest with just enough hair, smooth flat stomach and there was no doubt that he was turned on ...

She pushed him back onto the bed and straddled him, bearing down as slowly as she could, trying to control her hunger to have him inside her, fighting to make that first moment last as long as possible. She could tell he was facing the same battle but it was too much for him, he reached forwards, pulling her hips down hard, arching up and thrusting deep. He held her tightly for an age, not moving and fighting to bring himself under control before moving his hands to her breasts and leaving her to set the pace.

It couldn't last, they both knew it, and, as Fiona felt herself pass the point of no return, she reached behind her running her fingers up his thighs, breaking down any resistance he had left.

She had always enjoyed sex but this was different. More intense than ever and she had felt something tear open in her head as she reached orgasm, followed by a rush of freedom and release. She didn't know whether to laugh or to cry and managed a combination of both as she collapsed onto the bed next to him.

They didn't talk much afterwards. It wasn't especially awkward or difficult but Fiona sensed that they both felt there was a real risk that it might become so. She needed to get back to prepare supper for Maggie and Hamish and left after about half an hour.

On her way out, she went back into the kitchen and looked at the painting again. 'Why would anyone want something like that in their kitchen?' she asked herself. Luckily it was a rhetorical question, because she really didn't have an answer.

2017 - Jane

Going to see that house with Jenny had set her mind spinning in sad, sinking spirals. On the one hand, she was delighted to see Jenny and Danno so happy and Natalie had turned out to be a lovely young girl – sharp, witty and very pretty. Jane wasn't sure she approved of the nose ring and had told her so, but that probably wasn't a surprise to anybody; old age definitely bestowed on its victims the right, or obligation, to disapprove and she saw no reason not to use it.

They all got on very well and the conversation had been touched with the kind of mischievous, good-humoured repartee which had always given Jane such pleasure. However, the problem was that, for the past few years, no pleasure was unalloyed; there was always something else lurking behind, a taint, an impurity, a nagging, persistent doubt in the darkness.

It didn't take much to make her sad these days. For most of her life, she had managed to maintain a wholly positive attitude to existence. You made your choices and you lived with them. Regrets were pointless indulgences. Edith Piaf had it spot on with "Moi, je ne regrette rien!" Jane tried to remember where she had mislaid that positivity and spent more and more time rummaging in the jumble of her thoughts to find it, to recover the motivation to pull herself up by the shoelaces and get on with the day.

The problem was that she hadn't made all of the choices; she hadn't had control over the events which had changed her life. They had happened without her knowledge and against her wishes. However hard she tried, she couldn't stop herself from thinking – no, not thinking, but knowing – that she did have regrets, and those regrets sullied everything beautiful and joyful with the smear of greasy fingers. Aches and pains were par for the course, but what was the point of life if you could no longer rejoice in the good things?

Jane missed Alastair. He was her first-born, her only son and she had loved him with a fierce and protective love from the moment he was born. Mike, and later Fiona and Jenny, had always teased her about the fact that, in her eyes, Alastair could do no wrong. She had always denied it, but was fully aware that it was true; she was missing all objectivity where he was concerned.

After twenty-two years, she still couldn't understand how she had let him go. Nothing is so important that it should be able to drive a wedge between mother and son and there was nothing she could see in the events surrounding his departure which even came close to justifying their separation.

Sadly, there wasn't a thing she could do about it, as she had no idea where he was, or how she could contact him. She knew he wasn't dead, mostly because her heart told her so, but there had also been the business of the flowers. A few days after Mike had died, she had received a beautiful bouquet of spring flowers, not a funeral bouquet, but her favourites, white, papery anemones with rich, blue centres.

Anemones were associated with death but not funerals and the Greek legends said the anemone was born from the tears of Aphrodite as she mourned the loss of Adonis. The usual European meaning of the flowers was "forsaken" although in Eastern traditions, the anemone was also said to be filled with the spirit of anticipation, something close to your heart that you wish for.

There had been a card, but no sender's name and address. The card had said simply 'Thinking of you'. She knew straight away that they were from Alastair. He knew how much she loved anemones and he also knew how superstitious she was about flowers and their meanings. It had to have been him.

After Jenny dropped her home to The Old Orchard, she walked around in the garden for a while, deadheading a few roses and absent-mindedly planning the next week's gardening tasks, hoping all the while to clean out her mind and live in the moment. Being "mindful" and living in the here-and-now appeared to be the overriding philosophy of the day, as preached by every newspaper, magazine and the racks of self-help books which swamped bookshops these days.

It didn't work. Mindfulness was not only over-marketed, but Jane felt the whole concept was a bit flawed. On one hand, it was obvious that enjoying the moment was a good thing. Any fool could work that out for themselves without a degree in psychology or rocket science. On the other hand, it was easy to say, but really difficult to do. The desire paths of her mind were deep-tracked and worn irrevocably in place. However hard she tried, the moments she lived in more than any others were the moments leading up to, and following, Alastair's disappearance.

She made her way into Mike's study, sat down at the walnut roll-top desk and opened the black document box in front of her. She had collected everything she could find around the Polaris scandal and Alastair's disappearance and reviewed the file most days to try to make sense of everything.

It was full to overflowing with yellowing newspaper cuttings, mostly from 1995, but a few more recent. The early cuttings followed a consistent pattern: *Polaris Missile wipes out 6,000 pensions overnight! Did Polaris Pension Chair, Alastair Johnson have his fingers in the till? Serious Fraud Office to prosecute Alastair Johnson 'in absentia'. Where is Alastair Johnson now? Family of Polaris pension chairman claim no knowledge of events. Chairman of the Polaris Pension Fund still missing* ...

Mike had called it her "Obsession" and been very dismissive, but he had already made his mind up once and for all, hadn't he? And far be it for Mike to ever question his own decisions.

She turned to the most well-thumbed page and read the offending paragraph, which was in an interview given by Mike to the Daily Telegraph. He had been so angry and she'd known it would be a mistake for him to do the interview, but he wouldn't listen to her even when she asked him, and subsequently pleaded with him, to delay it by a few more days. A few days to give them time to find out a bit more and to have time to think.

It had been the only time in their marriage when she had felt physically afraid of Mike; he had become a trapped animal, hurling himself against the bars of his cage but with no way out, a snarling bear suddenly and inexplicably finding himself toothless. Behind all of the loud anger and frustration, however, she had occasionally spotted a glimmer of fear, which was not something which Mike was wired to cope with.

'My wife, Jane, and I are both extremely disappointed in Alastair. We brought him up to have high moral standards and to take responsibility seriously. Not only has he failed in his professional duties leading to thousands of decent hard-working people suffering financial hardship, but he has also abandoned his family and left them to face the anger, shame and outrage alone. We will, of course do everything we can to help our daughter-in-law and grandchildren in these difficult times, but we can never forgive Alastair for his cowardice and the shame he has brought on our family. He has run away and, as far as we are concerned, he should stay away.'

Fiona and Simon had turned up a few days after Alastair had disappeared and had explained what had happened. Jane couldn't believe Alastair would behave like that but the facts were self-explanatory and extremely damning. Mike had given the interview to the Telegraph the next day. He had been so self-righteous and sure of himself and she had been forced to leave the room.

Despite the overwhelming evidence of Alastair's shameful behaviour – even Jenny was taking her father's side – Jane had always felt there was something that wasn't right. It was as though she was the only one who could see that the final jigsaw piece didn't fit.

She knew her son; he wasn't, of course, as perfect as she often pretended, but that didn't mean he would behave like that. The only explanation she could possibly accept was that he'd had a breakdown, that the stress and shame had broken him mentally in some way.

Thinking like that hadn't helped at all, it had only snared her just like Mike; she imagined Alastair lost, confused and alone, robbed of his usual confidence and resourcefulness, vulnerable and afraid, while she was caught, bound tightly and unable to do anything to help him.

This vision had stayed with her ever since and took on many forms around the common theme, the images still came to her both as vivid dreams and at random moments throughout the day. Every day.

When she'd first seen the article in print, she'd been completely stunned. It was a part of a long and detailed article, summarising all of the facts and looking very authoritative but there was that one paragraph quoting Mike; he'd had the audacity to imply to the journalist that he was speaking for both of them. How dare he? That was when the teapot had been broken. Jane remembered how disappointed she'd been that it had missed Mike's head and shattered on the tiled floor. It had been a beautiful teapot, the same one they'd used every day for thirty years, but it would have been worth the sacrifice if only her aim had been true.

She wrote to the Telegraph the next day, demanding a retraction and an apology for the implication that she shared Mike's feelings about Alastair, but got nowhere. The newspaper's response was formal and legalistic, almost certainly composed of a number of standard pre-prepared paragraphs, and explained how, as long as the words were correctly quoted, they had done nothing wrong and she should consider taking up whatever libel action she believed appropriate, directly with the individual quoted. Fat lot of use that was. Had they imagined she would sue her husband?

Her day- and nightmares took on many forms. Alastair might be sitting on a bench at a poorly lit railway station, shivering against the winter cold, other times he was walking through the poorer suburbs of some Mediterranean city or other, face leathery and parched from relentless heat – her imagination had endless depths to draw from.

There were a few things in common. He was never smiling or laughing, always alone and the dreams always ended the same way: Alastair is reading intently, his dark eyes shining, wide and glistening with nascent tears, the newspaper drops to the ground from slack fingers, his shoulders slump and he turns silently and walks away.

1995 - Alastair

I am getting annoyed and in need of a second pint when Piers saunters into the pub half an hour late. The Chapel is absolutely heaving, as it is every night after about half past six. It's probably the only decent pub within shouting distance of Paddington and it does great food as well. The only downside is that it's almost impossible to hear yourself think.

After my final meeting with John, where I signed my life away and started the thirty-day clock ticking, I called home wanting to make sure Fiona didn't have plans; I was ready to sit down with her and tell her everything. When Anita said she was in London and was coming home a bit later, I convinced myself she would be exhausted after a day's shopping and that gave me enough of an excuse to put the conversation off for another day. I asked Anita to tell Fiona I was staying in town again tonight and I would call her in the morning.

I hope she understood the message. Quite how Fiona managed to find a Scandinavian au pair who was both unattractive and didn't speak English, completely escapes me.

Luckily Piers was free for a couple of pints and something to eat, which meant I could kill two birds with one stone – I didn't want to be alone and Piers is my personal financial advisor. I need to know how much cash I can raise in thirty days.

Piers is dressed in full Cotswolds-in-the-City uniform including those fucking ridiculous red cords he thinks are so cool. He really is a fine representative of a deservedly dying aristocracy. Upper class twit of the year it has to be said.

Still, he's a good mate, and we've stayed friends since school even to the extent of being best men at each other's weddings and godparents to our mutual offspring. Also, the important thing about Piers is that he knows he's a total idiot and it doesn't faze him in the least.

'Sorry I'm late. Awful bloody traffic and absolutely nowhere to park.' Another thing about Piers is that he drives everywhere, in whatever state he happens to find himself. In his view, the constabulary are only there to look after him and his friends. Mundane laws and regulations don't apply to him. Somehow, he manages to get away with it. God knows how.

'You're a useless git, but at least you're predictable. Grolsch?'

'Don't mind if I do. Get some of those crunchy, hot, spicy things as well, would you? I'm famished.' He sits down at the table and I go up to the bar for the drinks. Everyone is very thirsty at this time in the evening and it takes an age to get served. I get some attention eventually and weave my way back through the throng, carefully balancing a bowl of the crunchy, spicy things on top of one of the pint glasses.

Piers grabs his pint and takes a big mouthful. 'Excellent. Cheers mate.'

'Good to see you. Cheers.'

'How's the delicious Fiona and the kids?' he says. 'Still as sexy as ever? Fiona that is, not the kids.'

'Last time I looked, she was definitely as sexy as ever, and the kids are both well. Hamish has started rugby and your favourite goddaughter is still as cute as ever. To tell you the truth, I'm working so much that I hardly see them these days.'

'That's not good,' he says, wagging his finger theatrically. 'Family comes first. Always remember that.'

'You do talk a load of bollocks, don't you?' I reply. 'With everything you get up to. Doesn't it hurt to be such a hypocrite?'

'No. No. No. You're missing the point completely,' he says, lecture mode fully engaged. 'You always do. A little dalliance here or there has nothing to do with it. That's nothing more than harmless fun. Family is a completely different thing. I lose count of the number of times, I've tried to explain this to you, but it just doesn't go in for some reason.'

'Of course. It's my fault for being so thick. I should have known. And I suppose Pippa understands and agrees with your reasonable and rational moral values.'

'Funny you should mention my dear wife,' says Piers, shifting the mock pomposity up several gears. 'I would say she's on the point of coming round to my point of view but, how shall I put it? ... It's work in progress. Yes, that's about it. Work in progress.'

We eyeball each other while trying to keep hold of our serious faces, but it's no good. Piers splutters out a mouthful of beer and we both crease up with laughter. I should see him much more often. He's good for me.

'Now tell me about the healthcare industry,' he says, having wiped most of the beer from his jacket. 'I hear there's all sorts of interesting deals going down in Biotech. You guys are set to make a big killing. That's what I'm being told.'

'You know I can't comment on that,' I say, wondering exactly what he's heard, and from whom. He's probably just fishing.

'OK, fair enough, old chap. Always worth a try. You'd be surprised what people will let slip after a couple of pints.'

'It'll take more than a couple to loosen my tongue and you know it,' I say. 'Why don't you try again later?'

'Maybe I will,' he says. 'Anyway, what is this about you wanting to liquidate as much of your portfolio as you can in the next few weeks? Why? It's really not a great time for the markets, and you know you'll kick in a lot of early redemption penalties if you do that. I'm sure I explained it to you when we started.' He is looking carefully at me and, if I didn't know him better, I could swear he actually looks, and sounds, like a competent, professional financial advisor. I brush aside the ridiculous idea. Piers? I don't think so.

'Yes, you did tell me. And I read the paperwork myself before I signed anything.' A few penalties here or there weren't going to make much difference to me in my current situation, but I had no intention of sharing that with Piers. 'I can't tell you why, Piers. I'm sorry, but it's confidential. Let's just say I have an "opportunity".'

'Fair enough, old man.' Piers is such a cliché. 'Mum's the word.'

He pulls a slim folder from his briefcase. 'Well, let's get to it before we get too pissed.' He pushes the folder across to me. 'You'll find everything in there. All at today's rates. The numbers will vary a bit depending on when you start the process but I wouldn't expect too much to change over the next couple of weeks. In a nutshell, you're in good shape as far as I can see. You've got Peps, ISAs and Tessas worth a total of a hundred and twenty thousand or thereabouts, and your share portfolio is running at a little over eighty-thousand at today's prices. You put another hundred thousand into an offshore trust for the kid's school fees, but you can't touch that as it's assigned to them personally.'

It's not enough. I knew it wouldn't be. 'What about the mortgage?' I say. 'It's in joint names, right? Do I have insurance? What would happen if I went bankrupt?'

'Bloody hell, who said anything about bankrupt?' Piers is definitely feeling uncomfortable now. 'It depends on a lot of things. The mortgage company still want to be paid their normal monthly interest but as long as they get that, they don't really care. If you have equity value in the property, which you do, and the Official Receiver can't pay off all of your debts from other assets, they have the right to take it out of your share of the value of the house.'

'Take it out of the value of the house, how would that work? They can't just take money from the value of a house.'

'I'm afraid they can. They would offer Fiona the opportunity to buy your share of the equity value. If she didn't, or couldn't, then they would probably put the property up for sale.'

'But that's crazy. Surely they wouldn't be allowed to force a family out onto the streets?'

'Their job is to recover the money for their creditors. They're not interested in what happens to you and your family. The courts will almost always rule in their favour in cases like these.' Piers finishes his beer and gets up. 'Same again? Any more nibbles?'

'Indeed. No nibbles for me though.' I don't know why I'm not hungry as I haven't eaten all day.

Piers has managed to jump the queue at the bar and is busy chatting up the girl serving him. Nice looking. A few too many tattoos for my liking, but definitely attractive. She laughs and touches Piers on the hand as she hands him his change. I don't know how he does it. He's always found it so easy to pull.

He brings the beers back over. 'Now, that little lady is most definitely a hottie.' He smiles wolfishly. 'Shame I'm married. Still, who knows how married I'll be after a few more of these? Cheers.'

'Piers, you're a total slut, you do know that?' I'm not at all sure he's joking. '... And a philandering shit as well.'

'Guilty as charged,' he admits. 'It's in my DNA. But anyway, getting back to you. It's not a gambling debt is it, Alastair? That would be quite classy. Some of my best friends have gone down that road. Although, to be fair, they've always been bailed out by Daddy in the end.'

He swills down a quarter of his pint and continues. 'Did you hear about the guy from one of the big newspapers who took everything he owned, walked into a casino and put the lot on red. He was an ordinary bloke, but he sold his house, his car, even most of his clothes. Married with three kids too. Can you imagine what his wife said? 'Oh darling, I'd just like to gamble our entire life savings and security on a fifty-fifty bet because I feel it's something I have to do. Is that OK?' 'Yes, that's fine, sweetie, you go ahead. Whatever you want.' Piers is, of course doing the voices and hamming the whole thing up. He can be very entertaining when he turns his mind to it.

I wasn't impressed with casino man. 'What a selfish moron,' I say. 'No, Piers, it's not a gambling debt. Nothing so exotic, I'm afraid. I'm really not allowed to tell you what it is, but I do need you to free up as much money as you can, as soon as you can. Looking at what you've given me, I'll net around two hundred thousand after penalties, tax and the rest.'

Piers nodded. 'That sounds about right. I'll email you tomorrow with a full schedule and timings.'

'Thanks. I appreciate you getting on top of this so quickly and know it was short notice.' I need at least twice that to pay off the fine and the lawyers but there's nothing Piers can do about that.

'Anyway, enough boring shit.' Piers has moved on. 'I haven't seen you in decades. What else is occurring? Is that creep, Simon, still sniffing around your little sister?'

I could never figure out why Piers had such a problem with Simon. There was no rational reason I could see but it had always been there. He didn't trust him and seemed to have decided he was some sort of parasitic gold digger. That didn't make sense anyway. My parents were well off but nothing special. It didn't make sense and I was stuck with the nagging doubt that it must be based on pure snobbery or, even worse, anti-Semitism.

They'd had quite a nasty fight when we were school kids but that was years ago, everyone was totally pissed and I never found out how it had kicked off. Whenever I'd tried to get to the bottom of it, Piers had always behaved very strangely – evasive and clearly uncomfortable – which was not like him at all. Once, when we were very drunk, he'd mumbled something about having promised he wouldn't say anything, but then he wouldn't even tell me who he'd made the promise to. After a few attempts, I gave up and decided to accept that it was one of those things. The trick was to never invite Piers and Simon to the same event, which we managed most of the time.

We got past the family catch up and a few more beers and the conversation was beginning to degenerate predictably into the repetitive, self-congratulatory drivel that only two blokes, catching up over a few-too-many pints can achieve. The easy familiarity between us, when combined with the alcohol, had allowed me to forget all about my impending doom.

Around half past ten, I can tell Piers thinks he's "on a promise" following his repeated visits to the bar and I decide that it's time to make myself scarce. In any case, I need something approaching a clear head for my conversation with Fiona tomorrow.

'So what happened?' I ask him.

'What happened about what?'

'What happened to the bloke in the casino?'

'Oh him. He made his bet, doubled his money and promised he wouldn't ever do it again. Apparently they're making a TV show about him. It's called Red or Black or something like that. The guy had balls but was, as you say, clearly a total twat.'

2017 - Fiona

'Could you do my zip please, darling.' Fiona was wearing a stunning deep-sea blue dress cut to the knee and set off perfectly by the string of iridescent abalone pearls which she'd been given for her fiftieth birthday. Her rich dark – with a little help – hair was set up and finished with tiny, white roses.

'You won't fit into that soon if you're not careful,' Simon said, as he stood behind her. 'Better go carefully with the champagne and canapés.' She was never quite sure when he was joking and when there was a little more edge. She knew better than to react, but surely he could give her a break today, of all days.

He looked immaculate in his grey tails. There was no surprise there. He was sixty but looked at least ten years younger, still in great shape, and the passing years made him more good looking rather than less. It really was incredibly unfair that men tended to age much better than women. Fiona suspected he actually kept a picture in an attic somewhere.

They sat quietly in the car on the way to church, each lost in their own thoughts.

Maggie hadn't wanted Simon to walk her down the aisle. She and Fiona had argued about it for hours. 'He's not my Dad. Why should he get to give me away?' Maggie had shouted, stamping her foot like a ten-year-old. 'Someone else can do it. What about Danno? He cares much more about me than Simon does.' Fiona could remember how much she'd wanted to simply give her daughter a hug, but Maggie had been too angry to allow it. A whining note of pleading had crept into Maggie's voice as she'd continued. 'If Granddad was still alive he could do it. What about Granny? She'd be up for it.'

Fiona had struggled to calm her down. 'Of course Simon cares about you, darling. He's looked after you since you were seven.'

But Maggie hadn't paused for breath. 'Oh come on, he never really wanted us, he only ever wanted you, and we came along as part of the package. Auntie Jen says he's always wanted anything that belonged to Dad, because he's so jealous of him.'

Fiona had almost slapped her. 'Did Jenny really say that? What a horrible, bitchy thing to say.'

'Yes, Mum, and you know it's true.'

'I know nothing of the sort, young lady and I won't have you saying things like that.'

'Don't be ridiculous Mum. I'm twenty-nine years old and I'm about to get married. You can't tell me what to say or think.'

The argument had quickly degenerated into familiar mother-daughter bickering, the back-and-forth accusations reminiscent of other arguments about boyfriends, coming home late, smoking, drinking, riding on the back of motorbikes ... The core tactics and language were identical.

Fiona could still remember the point in the argument when she had felt all of the fight puff out of her like a collapsing hot air balloon. She'd hugged Maggie as though she was about to be dragged off by white slave traders. 'I don't want to fight with you darling, especially not now and not about this. I know you and Simon don't get along and I'm sorry, but I can't turn back time. It's going to be your special day and you're going to need to decide this yourself, but you must at least try to understand other people's points of view. Apart from anything else, and I don't want to be crass, he is paying for everything. It's not my money. Can you imagine his reaction if I go to him and say you want someone else to walk you down the aisle? I can't make you change your mind about him but I can ask you, for me, as a favour to me, to do this one thing. Please darling.'

They were still hugging each other tightly and Maggie took a while to reply. 'Of course I will Mum. It's no big deal. I do understand.' She'd started crying, breathing in and out in gentle sobs,

'I still don't understand why Dad left us. What did we do wrong?'

As she and Simon arrived at the church, a soft rain was falling. Fiona sighed with relief thinking that they had originally thought about having a marquee wedding in the garden, but decided against it. The forecast was good for later on though, and everything was set for a lovely day.

Simon had agreed to meet Maggie and the bridal car just down the road and he dropped Fiona off outside the church. Hamish was an usher and ready with his umbrella. God, he looked like Alastair, it was uncanny. Tall, slim and comfortable in his morning suit, a son to be proud of. She wondered if he and Susan would ever decide to get married. Probably not. It didn't seem to mean so much to them.

Since her birthday lunch, Fiona had been thinking a lot about Hamish and her fears that she hadn't been as good a mother to him as she should have been after Alastair left. If his own experiences as a child had really put him off the idea of having a family, it would be tragic and she reminded herself again to have that talk with him as soon as possible. But not today. Today was all about Maggie and anyone who thought any different was in for a rude awakening.

As she entered the churchyard, she realised she was actually nervous. It had been ages since she had seen Jane and she didn't see a reason for anything to have changed between them. The last time had been four years previously at Mike's funeral, but she and Simon hadn't gone back for the reception so there had been no real conversation beyond the formalities. While Hamish and Maggie were still small, she had driven them to their grandparents from time to time and had always been invited in for a frosty cup of tea. It had been dreadful and Simon had inevitably found an excuse not to join her.

Fiona and Jane had been good friends before. They had similar interests and shared the same sense of humour. She had known Jane and Mike would disapprove of her and Simon getting together. It had been "o'erhasty" to say the least and, with hindsight, any fool could have worked out that their relationship must have pre-dated Alastair's disappearance, even without that bloody busybody journalist sticking his nose into their private business. Mike and Jane, especially Jane, weren't fools.

Easy to say now, but that whole time had been like living in a crazy dream. Fiona had never considered the possibility of Alastair walking away and leaving them with nothing, and it had shocked her to the core. She'd been fragile and vulnerable and Simon had been on hand to pick up the pieces. Maybe she should have taken more time to think, but she hadn't, and that was that. It was very easy to judge from a distance, but people rarely try hard enough to understand how things might look from the other side of the mirror.

The church was beautiful. It was a small Norman church, simple stone and wood with minimal ornamentation and just the right amount of flower decoration to set off its austere spirituality and to add a touch of festivity. The theme of white and peach roses worked perfectly. She was reminded yet again that Simon had always been very generous and, especially where making things beautiful was concerned, he had such a clever eye for detail.

Hamish walked her down to the front row. Jane was already sitting in the second row with Jenny, Danno and Natalie. Funny how Danno had turned out to be the most successful one of all of them. Simon still had no time for him and called him a 'cheap, tacky tunesmith' but Fiona had always liked Danno and would have made the effort to keep in touch with both him and Jenny if the option had been there. She would have expected Jenny to be more understanding of the situation, but because of her history with Simon, that was never going to happen. In any case, the Johnson family were a tight unit and, when things got tough, they knew how to circle the wagons and stick together.

She was surprised at how pleased she was to see them all. Whatever their personal differences and disagreements, there was something special about generations of family coming together at a wedding. It marked a continuity, demonstrated that the human race could be above petty squabbles, and that people and society were hardwired to endure and to build the future. Everyone smiled and shook hands warmly. They were in public after all.

Fiona looked across the aisle at Jeremy, Maggie's husband-to-be, and smiled at him. He looked anxious, and so he should. She was about to give him Maggie's hand and had made it absolutely clear he had better look after her daughter. Simon might be walking Maggie down the aisle, but Jeremy knew exactly who to be afraid of.

They were both anxious. An imaginary clock ticked the loud seconds slowly away for them both, as they waited for Maggie to appear. It was a cruel ritual. Everyone knew how it would almost-certainly end but there were enough exceptions, enough grooms left standing at the altar, to leave a little doubt and to twist the knife. Most people had seen or read Far from the Madding Crowd, and that didn't work out well for anyone.

Fiona's heart was in her mouth and her eyes were prickling from the moment the processional music started. It was actually happening, her little girl was getting married.

With the light-filled arch framing the bridal party in a hazy silhouette, it was easy to imagine Alastair was walking Maggie into the church. Where the hell was he? Did he actually not care that his daughter was getting married?

The organ grew louder, "Here Comes the Bride" filling the small church with its throaty rhythm as they came on into the nave. It wasn't Alastair of course, but it didn't matter. Maggie looked absolutely radiant and so happy and Simon looked dashing as always. Fiona felt Hamish's hand on her shoulder, the physical contact acting as a conduit for their shared emotions.

Bursting with love and pride, mixed with relief, she looked at Maggie, now standing next to Jeremy, and reflected that she hadn't screwed everything up. The most important job for a parent is to give your children what they need to be prepared for their own lives and, looking at them both, she hadn't done such a bad job.

1995 - Girl in Casino

Some punters are a bit different from the rest and you do hope things will go differently for them. There was a guy came in last night. Quite pissed, just a normal bloke, but he had this strange look in his eyes, a dark emptiness, like you could look in and keep on looking. Totally freaked me out.

Do you remember the picture they used to have on the front of a packet of Camel cigarettes back in the day? Especially in Paris when you went on a school trip and everyone was trolling around looking for smokes, beer and those little red Chinese bangers that were illegal in the UK and had like a two-second fuse. Oh, and flick knives and gawking at whores on the rue St Denis, and any opportunity for a snog or a grope. I expect they took us to some amazing buildings and taught us all sorts of important cultural things, but I'll bet I'm not the only one who doesn't remember a single thing about all of that.

Still, back to this bloke and the picture on the front of the Camel packets. It was a drawing of a camel, smoking a Camel of course, with his head pushing out through the packet, tearing it open, big lips sucking on the cigarette and one huge black eye just watching you. There was a reflection of a window glinting in the eye but everything else was just deep black, coal black. You looked at that eye and you kept on looking forever, into the camel's soul. This bloke's eyes were the same, but everything else about him was very normal.

He was forty-ish, wearing a nice grey suit, nothing too fancy, probably Boss or something, not new, not old. No tie though. He looked like someone who would normally have a tie.

Probably quite decent looking in his day but running to flab and generally worn like most of these city commuter types are; a few months doing some real work on a farm or something would do them all a world of good. Fat chance of that happening though. Even with the podgy, pasty look going on, I still liked the look of him for some reason. Must've been the eyes.

I've always had a bit of a thing for older men. No idea why, it's just one of those things I've had since I was in my teens. I'm going to have to deal with it at some point. I'm twenty-five now and if I keep liking blokes ten or fifteen years older than me, it could become a bit of an issue. At some point, I'll need to go and visit nursing homes on the pull.

My last disastrous relationship finished a couple of months ago after dragging on for ages; God knows how it lasted so long. I met him at this health centre out by Heathrow where we go after work sometimes. We get membership as a perk, but only from midnight until six in the morning. He was one of the trainers in the gym, mid-thirties, in great shape obviously and very charming in a smooth-talking bar steward sort of way.

We saw each other quite a bit for a while, always at my flat, but it just went nowhere. After a few weeks, I realised I'd seen all he had, seen it all when I first met him. There actually wasn't any more. No hidden depths to plumb in late-night drunken conversations, no surprise history or interests in common, absolutely nothing.

The same well-rehearsed, charming and witty lines came up again and again, the same boyish smile, which I actually once caught him practising in front of a mirror. He could rabbit on passionately about body mass, nutrition supplements and the advantages of lighter weights and more repetitions, but nothing else.

I don't understand why I didn't move on, because he had actually turned out to be the most boring bloke in the world, but I guess I didn't have anything better at the time and at least he was fit and quite tasty. Eventually one of the girls who worked at the club decided to put me out of my misery and told me I was one of three relationships he was juggling at the time. He never had less than two women on the go and often as many as four. Apparently, he was famous for it.

I didn't even bother with the screaming showdown, he wasn't worth it.

Now, Camel Eyes wouldn't behave like that. There was a lot more to him – including a wedding ring as it happens – but, to be fair, that's never stopped me before. I kept catching him looking at me, but I don't think it was because he fancied me. He had this far-away look, mouth slightly open, almost like he was in a trance.

I had a proper trance experience when I was travelling, a few months before we got to Thailand, so I've got a bit of an idea of what people look like when they're away with the fairies. We were in Peru and everyone had been talking about going to the Amazonian rainforest and doing this natural psychedelic drug called ayahuasca. It wasn't only drinking the ayahuasca, there was this whole traditional ceremony tied in with it, and you had your own shaman to look after you.

The Lonely Planet guide had loads on ayahuasca ceremonies and it was high on the list of must-do, once-in-a-lifetime experiences. The locals called it the vine of the soul. There were plenty of scare stories but everyone said you'd be fine if you went to a good shaman. I was totally up for it. I was actually up for pretty much everything those days if the truth be told.

Nicki didn't want to do it because she'd had a bad time on ecstasy at a rave a few years before, and wasn't risking that again. She said she'd come along though, and be around to keep an eye on me while I was under. The actual trance was supposed to only last a couple of hours but apparently there were on-going effects and some other travellers had told us the whole ceremony could take days.

Anyway, a guy we met in a bar in Cuzco recommended this shaman, they call them curanderas, called Reyna Luz Edery Flores about two hours downriver from Puerto Maldonado and so we decided to try and find her. Apart from anything else, with a name like that, she had to be great. The bar we were in was called the Pisco Factory and was one of the best bars I've ever been to, but that's a whole different story. Just remember to try the coca sours if ever you're there.

I'd never seen anything like the rainforest and the sudden change from the high, dry mountains up around Cuzco blew me away. It was proper jungle with every exotic jungle cliché you could imagine. Not only beautiful things like macaws, parrots, butterflies, etc., but also armies of soldier ants as long as your thumb, crocodiles, piranhas, jaguars, who luckily kept themselves to themselves, and every kind of snake there was: huge, tiny, poisonous, crushy, the lot. As you can probably guess, I'm not so keen on snakes.

The journey upriver through the rainforest by motorised canoe was like a scene from one of those Werner Herzog films, with Klaus Kinski sitting in a boat staring at you with those crazy eyes. When you looked at him, you knew he wasn't acting. Some important screws actually had come loose and were bouncing around in his skull.

I don't talk about what happened in the trance and, to be honest, I don't think I'd do it again. They say you should only go ahead if you're in a good mental place and I get that now. Everything opens up, both inside your body and everywhere else, and you can see your tiny little place in nature and the universe. You end up having lots of different trips all at the same time which is totally weird and very unsettling.

For me, and for lots of people, not all of it is good, because you open yourself up to all those hidden, covered up feelings, fears and regrets. We've all got them and, let's face it, they're usually not pretty. The main trance might only last for a couple of hours but it feels like days and, for me at least, it took days to recover.

Reyna had been born a few kilometres up the road and had spent most of her life learning about plants and nature in the rainforest. I'll bet she knew more about botany than any of those scientists who do shows on TV, but at the same time, she was like the local mayor for her village and community and everyone seemed to really look up to her. I'd have placed her age at anywhere between forty and eighty, you just couldn't tell.

She had this great singing voice and seemed to know exactly what she was doing all the time. She could even manage your trance while you were in it. There was one time when I lost it a bit and I started dropping down and down into a dark tunnel and then she started chanting. The chanting seemed to wrap around me like a rope and to pull me back up again. I can still remember how relieved and grateful I felt as, at the time, I was pretty sure going down that tunnel would be a one way journey and not going anywhere good.

I wouldn't do it again, but I'm glad I did it. It was definitely a top ten experience and, although it sounds a bit poncey, it gave me a better sense of my place in the world. Small and insignificant for sure, but on the other hand, as important as any of the other small, insignificant things which make up the universe. By stepping outside myself, I got a bit of perspective which is never a bad thing.

I don't think Camel Eyes was on any sort of drugs, apart from a hefty dose of alcohol, but there was something in his face which reminded me of the other people I saw in trances while I was there. A sort of remote, disconnected blankness.

I've got this feeling he'll be in again, but I won't actually be able to meet him or get to know him personally. The rules are pretty strict and we need to keep our distance from the clients for all the obvious reasons. I'd have to report any sort of contact outside the purely professional and I might lose my job even if I did. Still, it'll be interesting to see if I'm right and he does come back.

2017 - Jim

The Chapelle de Rosaire is almost certainly the most famous landmark in Vence and it's only half a kilometre down the hill from our small rented villa. It's an amazing place – the entire building was designed by Matisse – and I go there whenever I feel like a bit of inspiration. Usually full of tourists but, if you live nearby, it's easy enough to pick a quiet time, either at the beginning or the end of the day. I'm planning on going there after breakfast once I've stretched out my aches from yesterday's ride. It doesn't get any easier as I get older.

Our villa is typical for around here, making the best possible use of a small, hilly plot of land. We've got two bedrooms – one is the office – a "cosy" living room and a cramped, old-fashioned kitchen. There's room to park a car, a sort of lean-to utility room where I keep my bikes, and a tiny garden that gets the afternoon sun and is just big enough for a small table, a hammock and Sally's beloved herb garden. We've also got a great little gas barbie/grill out there which we use for almost all of our cooking.

It was built about eighty years ago, which gives it big advantages over some of the more modern houses. Our little home might be small, dark and poky but, for most of the year, we're outside the whole time anyway. The difference comes in the winter. Modern villas tend to be larger with lots of windows, sliding French doors and marble everywhere. That's great from May to September, but all of the architects and builders seemed to have forgotten how cold it can get out of season.

After moving here, we spent the first two years living in a modern duplex, which we were caretaking for an American family. I've never been so cold in my life. However good the double-glazing is, and whatever you do to try to heat the place up, you're fighting a losing battle; the cold always sneaks in somehow and eats into your bones. The first winter was the worst. I had a bad flu bug and was running a high temperature; I can remember coughing like I had pneumonia or TB.

I've been guilty of man flu like all of us, but this was the real thing. I couldn't lie down in bed because it made me cough too much and I would sit on the sofa fully dressed, wearing a coat and wrapped in a duvet. It didn't help. The cold was everywhere and got everywhere, seeping off the marble and working its way through every chink in my padded armour. It was miserable.

Not the same with these older stone-built houses; they used local Provencal building techniques which evolved over thousands of years to match the climate and – surprise, surprise – they work and it makes a huge difference. Still cold, but a wood fire in the small living room is enough to create a warm nest to creep into, even when an icy, seven-day mistral is rattling the shutters.

Winters are short, though, and even in January, the odds are high that there'll be blue skies and sunshine during the day. One of the things I love most about living here and my job, is that, for ten months of the year, I get up in the morning, put on a pair of shorts and a T-shirt, and I'm dressed for work. We generally leave the canvas roof off our little jeep; it's got a couple of rubber bungs in the footwells and, once you've taken them out, any rain flows straight through. We park it anywhere and don't worry about theft or damage – it's worth almost nothing and my one concession to security is that I've welded in the radio. I'd like to see some punk try and get that out in a hurry.

Sally told me more about the Villa Eugenie enquiry last night – I'm still struggling to get my mind around the fact that it's our old holiday home. Apparently it's just been bought by some famous musician, Daniel Morris. The name rings a bell, but I can't remember which band he's in. One for Google if I ever get around to it.

The coincidence is too strong and I can't help feeling this is some kind of message. I understand that the decision to live here in the first place wasn't totally random; we're always drawn back to the familiar, and some of the best memories of my life are associated with this region. But someone has now approached us to look after the actual villa where I spent so many happy holidays. That seems too unlikely to be pure chance. There are tens of thousands of villas in the region and Eze is actually a bit outside our catchment area. We only manage fifteen properties which are all either in Vence or much closer. There's something about this enquiry which is making my skin tingle.

I never used to be one for mysticism; I have always dismissed the whole idea of astrology, fate and divine intervention as complete mumbo-jumbo claptrap. As the years have passed, however, I've had a few things happen in my life that I can't explain by logic or reasoning. I wouldn't say it's turned me into a believer, but I'm a lot more receptive than I used to be. Some of the spiritual ideas and thinking Sally learns and practices in her yoga also make much more sense to me than they would have done years ago. Maybe that's why most gurus and monks are so old; it takes a long lifetime to figure these things out.

One of the experiences which chopped a wedge out of my cynicism was the time when Sally and I got together. I'd met her once before, but only briefly and I didn't even know her name. The string of random events which led to us meeting again was so unlikely that I can't really believe it was pure chance. I was so lucky to find her and can only believe that, soppy as it sounds, we were "meant to be".

Sally has gone out to deal with the bank this morning. Our business is registered in her name and she has the joy of dealing with all of the paperwork. There are many wonderful, positive things about France but they are almost outweighed by the bureaucracy; the mindless, byzantine, labyrinthine webs of the banking, social and fiscal systems which are designed to suck the marrow from the bones of anyone who has to deal with them. I am certain most of Kafka's writing must have been about France, especially The Trial.

I help where I can, but most things require the "responsable" in person so I can't do much. I'll make it up to her later by cooking something special for lunch.

There is a little cafe on the corner of our street and I have time for a quick coffee before the chapel opens. I have taken to drinking a "noisette", an espresso with a touch of warm milk on top. I used to prefer a short, single espresso, but the dab of milk does add something – as long as it's only a dab.

Le Vencois is a typical French bar/cafe and is set back from the main road keeping it free from tourists. People down here like tourists well enough, and many of us make our livings from them, but that doesn't mean we want to drink with them when we're not working.

When I first met Sally, I was working in a bar on a Greek island which was quite different. It may have been because I was a lot younger, but I think it was mostly because of the place; it was a total party town, reasonably upmarket, but still outrageously uninhibited and pretty damn crazy. Unlike here, there was very little separation between the tourists and the people who worked in tourism.

For most of us, we would work when we had to, but the rest of the time was dedicated to one big alcohol-fuelled, Dionysian frenzy. The tourists only needed to keep up the pace for a week or two, but for us it lasted months. I was there for three years and don't know how I survived, or why I didn't get out earlier.

Thinking back, it was like one of those surfing videos which were always playing in the nightclubs in endless loops. You're on your board, on top of this massive fifty-foot wave, hurtling over jagged rocks and razor-sharp coral. It's great, it's exhilarating, but one thing dominates the whole experience. You can't choose when to get off, you're on the wave for the duration or you're dead. That was how I felt back then.

The conversation in Le Vencois was all about Brexit and the prevailing opinion was one of "good riddance". If the bloody rosbifs didn't want to be part of the club, then they should leave with their tails between their legs, but not until they'd been made to suffer and pay handsomely for the insult. I could swear I heard someone mention Agincourt, which wouldn't have been such a surprise as it comes up in conversation here more than you would believe.

I do sometimes despair about the ways that people can twist so much into a matter of national pride – Agincourt was six hundred years ago, but the shame still lingers. How ridiculous is that? What is national pride worth anyway? I'm Scottish and, I suppose, proud of being Scottish, but that doesn't mean that I think that the continuous attempts to create an independent Scotland are great steps forward for either Scotland or the UK. Let's face it, for most Scots, national pride has its roots in a Hollywood film about William Wallace, developed and starred in by a half-mad Australian.

That's the only good thing about Brexit I can think of. It seems to have put the idea of Scottish independence on hold for the time being. I'm not planning on joining the debate though. The people in the bar are Pascal, the owner, two or three of his regulars who I know in passing, and a couple of pensioners sitting in the corner. As I've got older, I've learnt that there are many times when it is best to keep your mouth shut, and this is one of those times. We are, after all, in a region where local elections usually involve a neck and neck battle between the National Front and the Union of the Right and I'm certain none of the other customers want to hear my views on any of this.

Before long the conversation moves seamlessly along to whether President Macron's older wife is hot or not, and it is really time to make myself scarce.

To get to the chapel, you drop down some steps from a normal main road, which runs through the centre of town. It's not at the end of some cypress-lined boulevard in the country like most of these places; Rosaire is set in the middle of a normal residential area. I get there just as it's opening and I'm the first one in, which is how I planned it.

I'm not religious at all, but this place isn't about religion, at least not for me. It's about light and the graceful simplicity which is unique to Matisse. I don't think he was even slightly religious, but he wanted to build this chapel in gratitude to a woman called Monique Bourgeois who had been his carer for several years and who had decided to become a nun. A celebration of human relationships, rather than religious subservience.

Every time I go into the chapel, I'm immediately struck by the clinical starkness of the building, which is quite different from most religious buildings. Everything is made up of white, rectangular spaces with the exception of the dark wood of the simple, spartan chairs and the light flooding in from the large stained glass windows. Classic Matisse scissor-shapes made up of three primary colours – the blue of the sea, the green of nature and the yellow of both sunshine and ripe corn – combine to send kaleidoscopic shards of light across the floor and onto the white-tiled, hand-engraved walls.

It's not calming and spiritual like an old church but more joyous and celebratory, filled with a raw passion for life and living. I would much rather aspire to Matisse's religion than to the dark and austere Protestantism which I grew up with.

I walk slowly, trying to get my mind around this whole villa coincidence. If there is some sort of meaning to it, I can't imagine what it might be. My parents sold the house years ago to pay back the loans they'd taken out for our school fees, and I'd not actually thought about it much since. Sally and I drove there a few months after we got here, just to see if I could remember the way, and for old-time's sake, but I've not been back since. The last time we were all there as a family was almost thirty years ago. They were good times but they've definitely been relegated to the past.

Sally has obviously noticed I've had something on my mind for the last few weeks, and is worried that going to see the old villa might open up old wounds. She told me she'd be happy to tell them we weren't interested if I wanted, and we agreed that I'd have a think and we could decide later.

I really can't think of any reason not to take it on though. It's only a house and I must admit to being fascinated with the idea of seeing it again. The musician is coming down with his wife next week and I'll tell Sally to set up a time for us to go over and see them. If they're not total losers and they're happy with the fees, we might as well take it on.

I know why she's worried, but the villa thing doesn't have any impact on what's been bothering me for the past few weeks. I will tell her about that at some point, but I haven't yet got my thoughts straight and don't feel ready to have a discussion with anyone, even Sally.

1995 - Fiona

By the time Fiona got home, it was about six-thirty. Sevenoaks was only twenty-five minutes from central London on the train and the walk from the station took less than quarter of an hour. If anyone had asked her to describe anything about the journey, she would have drawn a complete blank.

The strange thing was that she didn't feel guilty at all. At least not to begin with. In fact, she was almost proud of herself for doing something to get out of the corner she and Alastair had painted their life into. A bit like those stories where someone cuts off their arm or leg with a knife to get out from under a fallen rock. Well, maybe not quite like that, but she had taken a positive step to move out from under her "rock" (and managed to hang on to all her limbs as well, which was a bonus).

And the sex had been really, really good. Short, yes, but sweet, passionate and fulfilling. Fiona hadn't felt that kind of blind lust for many years. She knew that the next time – there was going to be a next time, then – would allow them to take it slowly, and she was confident that wouldn't be disappointing either.

Thinking back, there actually was something she remembered about the train journey home. She'd been smiling the whole way.

Walking up the drive, however, the smile was wiped from her face as she thought about seeing Alastair and trying to mask her guilt. Her face would betray her, she knew it would. She'd always been a poor liar and it wasn't as though she had any previous experience of adultery to draw on. Was this actually adultery? That sounded much too serious.

Hamish and Maggie were upstairs doing their homework and

Fiona was deeply relieved when Anita told her Alastair wouldn't be coming home until the next day. She would have a chance to collect her thoughts, and to sober up. One thing was for sure, she wasn't going to tell him anything about Simon, it was all too fresh and uncertain.

Having navigated the usual evening routine without incident, Fiona went to bed before eleven and was out for the count. She didn't dream.

The next morning passed without incident until Alastair phoned at around eleven. He sounded very calm and serious, told her they needed to talk, and that he had a lot to explain to her. He would be home in an hour and they could walk over to their favourite pub for lunch.

Fiona had no idea what Alastair was planning to tell her and the possibilities bubbled up one-by-one in her head like sulphur gas escaping from a volcanic mud pool – slow, steady and processional, with some definitely smelling worse than others. She had no new information, no basis for new conclusions and she had been through the identical process hundreds of times over the past months. There was no point in going over it all again, but despite the fact that she had a good, logical mind, she couldn't resist the pointless, repetitive cycle.

While she was waiting for him, the phone rang three times. She knew it would be Simon and didn't answer. One thing at a time. He didn't leave a message.

When Alastair arrived, he appeared to be in good spirits, less worn and crumpled than he had been for the past few weeks. He gave her a hug and a kiss. 'I'm sorry I've been so useless for the past couple of months,' he said. 'There are reasons and I think you'll understand when I explain.'

She could see that he was on the verge of tears, and she held him for a few moments, stroking his hair. 'Don't worry. It'll be all right. Everything's going to be OK.'

He lifted his head and looked at her, now back in control of himself. 'You're not going to agree that I've been right to keep everything to myself for the past couple of months, but I had to. I don't know why exactly, but I felt I had to. In any case, I'll tell you everything now.'

Fiona wasn't sure why, but Alastair was frightening her. They weren't talking like husband and wife. There was no warmth, no sense of shared history and experiences. In spite of yesterday, she knew it wasn't her problem. Alastair had changed; he was switching back and forth between his old self and this cold, driven and focused stranger. Bright, slightly evangelical eyes and talking a little mechanically. Like a Stepford Husband.

'Come on,' she said. 'Put your boots on, and we'll talk on the way.'

The way to the pub took them along bridlepaths and footpaths. Ancient, overgrown cart tracks, with high banks on both sides and hawthorn arches spilling white blossoms over clouds of cow parsley. Fiona loved cow parsley, it was probably her favourite plant. A hazy spring sun was enough to add a little warmth and to send a few shards of light through the arches, picking out the colours and the contrasts of the hedgerows.

Alastair stopped in the middle of the arched walkway and turned her to face him. He looked in her eyes and told her he needed to say something before he explained about the mess he was in. Fiona didn't know what to think until she realised that it was her old Alastair talking; at least for a moment, he was back with her – his voice, his face, his smile, everything as it was supposed to be.

He told her how much he loved her, how sorry he was and how much he hoped they could put this terrible period behind them. Her heart stopped dead as the events of the previous day came rushing back. What had she done? How could she have betrayed him so easily? And with his best friend? Whatever he'd done, he didn't deserve that.

When he asked her if she still loved him, she felt the enormity of her betrayal flood over her. Of course she told him she loved him – it was true after all – but she couldn't look him in the face while she said it. She knew he would see the truth in her eyes – a flashing neon sign advertising her guilt in lurid pink. All she could do was to say the words and then press him to move on with his overdue explanation.

They started walking again. Alastair switched seamlessly back to Stepford Husband and brought her up to speed with clinical precision. He could almost have been running through a PowerPoint presentation, he was so structured. They started at the beginning and went through the entire process starting with his appointment to the Chairman role, through to the point where he found out how the funds had been transferred and on to the last six weeks of discussions with the Serious Fraud Office.

Fiona kept quiet and listened although she was growing increasingly anxious with each moment. As a former barrister, she found it natural to see the issues in terms of the law rather than her personal views of right and wrong, fair and unfair. From a personal view, it seemed clear that Alastair was, at least partly, a victim. A negligent one admittedly, but a victim all the same.

The legal perspective was quite different though, and Fiona thought it was clear cut. She knew his lawyer, John, who was very competent, and she would have been surprised if he had missed anything material. Alastair would remain legally responsible for the fraud unless they were able to extradite some of his bosses and she didn't see that happening any time soon.

Eventually, Alastair got to the details of his meeting and the compromise agreement he had signed.

'The thing is,' he said, the strain showing in his hoarse, scratchy voice, 'everything was exactly as John said it would be. Losing my license, no notice period, the director's ban. It was all as expected until they got to the penalty. John had told me all along it would be a hundred, maybe a hundred and fifty thousand quid, and I knew we could manage that with something to spare. That's one of the reasons why I didn't say anything before. I was certain we would have enough put aside for the next year or two.'

Alastair stopped and turned to her. He suddenly looked old. Shrunken, withered and drawn. 'But it was worse than John had told me,' he said. 'Much, much worse.'

'How much worse?' asked Fiona, feeling the wind building and storm clouds gathering overhead.

'I have to pay them a penalty of three hundred and seventy-five thousand pounds.'

Fiona turned away from him to look over the fields, trying to control her breathing, to stay calm and to put her thoughts in order.

It didn't work. Not even slightly. 'You fucking idiot,' she screamed at Alastair. 'You complete and utter moron. What were you thinking? It's only been three or four years since Maxwell. How could you let this happen?'

'I don't know,' Alastair spat back at her. 'I really don't know what happened. Too much work, too much ego, not smart enough to see what was being done to me. I don't know.'

'Three hundred and seventy-five thousand fucking pounds. I don't believe you've done this. We don't have that sort of money? What does it mean for us? Will we lose the house?'

'You're right, we don't have enough. I saw Piers last night and he reckons we can get together around two hundred thousand without selling the house. We can take out another fifty-thousand on the mortgage loan account but it's not enough.' Alastair took her by the shoulders and looked at her for several moments, not blinking. 'I will sort this out though. I'll find a way.'

Fiona slapped his arms away. 'You'll find a way. How will you find a way? Magic beans? Tell me what you're going to do to fix this, then.'

'I can't tell you now. I'm sorry. I need a few days to sort things out before I tell you.'

'I do not fucking believe it. You can't be serious.' Fiona turned and stomped on up the hill, with Alastair trailing behind like a beaten dog. She'd known something was wrong but had never imagined anything like this. All of the foundations which gave some structure to her life, gave her security, comfort, the confidence that she would be able to look after her kids. All of these had crumbled to dust in a few short minutes. She had given up a decent career for Alastair and the children. There was no chance of getting that back on track now.

'I'm sorry, Fiona. I'm really sorry. I don't know what else to say.'

As she turned and looked at her husband, standing still, hands by his sides and palms open, a dam broke inside her and she burst into tears. She felt Alastair's arms around her as she sobbed uncontrollably, great wracking sobs. 'What are we going to do, Alastair? I don't know what to do? What about the children? Will they have to change schools?'

'It will all be OK, darling. I got us into this and I'm going to get us out of it. The kids' school fees are safe. No-one can touch the trust fund even if I go bankrupt.'

'Well, I suppose that's a small mercy. What about the house? Will we have to move?'

'I hope not. Certainly not if my plan works.'

'How can you be so sure?'

'I don't know. I just am. I'm going to make this right.'

They walked on, arms-length apart. Fiona was mostly calm again. This was a problem they needed to find a way past. It wasn't the worst thing that could have happened by a long way; they had been through tougher times together and managed to survive. Even when Arabella had died, the tragedy had tested their relationship but, in the end, it had made them stronger as a couple.

She thought about Arabella every day, it was no longer painful to remember her, only a little bittersweet and somehow important not to relegate her completely to the past. These shared experiences were surely what gave a couple resilience?

Alastair broke the silence. 'There's one big thing we need to talk about. Maybe the biggest thing.'

'What? Is there something else you haven't told me?' Fiona snapped, realising her sense of calm was nothing more than a thin layer of dross floating on the surface of her anger. The slightest disturbance exposed the white-hot, molten steel beneath.

'No. No. Take it easy,' said Alastair. 'It's nothing like that. It's just that, even though Maxwell died before any of the shit hit the fan, it was still a nightmare for his sons and their family. Thousands of honest, hardworking people, stripped of their pensions. A scandal like this is a perfect recipe for a media witch hunt and, let's face it, they've got a point.'

'But it's not your company. You're only an employee. Stupid, useless and incompetent, I grant you, but an employee nonetheless.'

Alastair didn't smile. 'I'm afraid that's not going to be how the press will see it. They will need the company to have a face and that face will be me. Once this becomes public in less than a month, I'll be hung out to dry and I doubt my family will escape either. The American head office will be unreachable and that just leaves me. I've been talking to some PR people and they told me that, if I don't actually "do a Maxwell", then I should consider some sort of personal security. People are going to be very pissed off.'

Fiona began to feel the true enormity of the situation bearing down on her. 'But surely there must be some kind of government protection. A pot which compensates people who've lost out through fraud?'

'Nope. There's nothing. They've been talking about doing something since Maxwell, but it could be years before anything actually happens. The SFO might get something out of Polaris eventually, but that's going to take years as well.'

Fiona understood that Alastair had spent a lot of time thinking this through. Dealing with money was one thing. There was normally a way to manage – they had always had so much more than they actually needed anyway. Even if he couldn't find another "proper" job, he would find something and so would she. If they had to sell the house, they'd cope, somehow. She was leaving the "Simon factor" on the side for the time being. That wasn't real. Not yet, at least.

Scandal was different though, much more caustic. It would eat away at their support network as well. Friends, family, the kids' friends, everyone would have an opinion and make judgements. Those nice, easy judgements made after a couple of glasses of wine and with the minimum of knowledge or understanding. 'Did you hear about Fiona's husband? Ran off with a hundred million pounds. He stole it from his company's pension fund and now thousands of normal, hard-working people have lost their pensions.'. 'Yes, I heard. Terrible isn't it. Those poor people, and he seemed like such a decent man. It just goes to show ...'.

'OK, Alastair. Point taken,' she said, suddenly feeling very tired.

'That is actually the most fucked-up bit of a royally fucked-up situation. What can we do though? It's going to be completely out of our hands.'

Alastair stopped and turned to her. 'Well, I think that, whatever happens, I need to disappear for a while.'

2017 - Jane

Jane half expected to be stuck on a B-list table with a few other relics and tedious people. It would all depend on who had made the seating plan. As it turned out, it must have been Maggie because she'd been given a great view of the top table and was seated between Danno and one of Maggie's work friends, a delightful young man called Toby.

She was surprised to see all of the men dressed in tails, including the youngsters, but Toby explained how, as there were so many weddings going on, all of their friends had bought their own morning suits. It worked out much cheaper that way.

Maggie worked for a technical publisher, which produced a huge number of business and scientific magazines; Toby was an editor in charge of twenty monthly publications. His specialisation was in distribution technology and Jane was pleasantly surprised to discover how he was able to make such a dull subject appear interesting.

We live in this unbelievably complicated and interlinked world, Toby had explained, using the analogy of a giant ants nest, which can only function if there is enough structure and process to make sense of it all. Different types of ant have the jobs of either sourcing, transporting or processing the food and materials needed by the nest. Without the transport ants knowing what to take where, and when, the whole thing falls over.

Jane had certainly never thought about how physical objects moved around, about how the fresh strawberries got to Waitrose, or how the shampoo got onto her hairdresser's shelves. When Jenny drove her to see that house the other day, there had been a lorry in front of them with big writing on the back of it. 'Too much traffic?

Why not stop buying so much?'. It didn't really click at the time but after Toby had given her a crash course in how the ants were trained to do what they had to at the right time, it all became clearer and actually quite fascinating.

The world had been a lot simpler when most people's universe was the village or town they lived in and a few neighbouring towns, but civilisation had moved so far beyond that, and society now appeared to be out of control, a snowball rolling downhill, getting bigger and gathering speed. What was going to happen when it got to the bottom?

Still, Jane reflected, that was unlikely to be her problem.

The wedding had been beautiful and Jane was, for the most part, focused on how happy she was for Maggie. She looked absolutely stunning and there had been a collective intake of breath through craned necks as she'd appeared in the arched doorway. Jane had lost that happy focus for a few moments, however, as they got closer and she had seen Simon's smug face.

She could consider forgiving Fiona for her poor choices – she had been through a very difficult period after all – and Alastair was to blame for most of that stress and strain. Fiona had been, in Jane's opinion, weak and foolish, but she was quite happy to accept that most people, including herself, were weak and foolish from time to time.

Simon, however, was a different story and she had no intention of ever giving him the benefit of the doubt. Mike had had his doubts about Simon from the very beginning, and she remembered how uncharacteristically anxious he'd been for that short period when Jenny and Simon had been going out together. Mike hadn't trusted Simon, but Jenny had been besotted with him for a while, and even Mike was smart enough to know that trying to interfere would have been completely counter-productive.

Mike had been a proud, stubborn idiot but he had loved his children and had tried to look after them in his own way. Now that he was gone, Jane found herself thinking about him more kindly than she had for many years before his death. He had been spot on about Simon as it turned out, and luckily it hadn't taken Jenny too long to figure things out on her own. It did seem that Simon's behaviour had always been driven by a warped jealousy of Alastair. How strange?

It was also strange that, despite all of the time Simon had spent with them, both at home and on numerous holidays together, they never really found out much about him and had never met his family, even though they'd only lived a few miles away at the time. It seemed as though Simon was ashamed of his parents, afraid they weren't good enough to be introduced.

She knew his grandfather had brought the family to the UK from Germany in the thirties but not much more than that. There was something about a sister who had got into some sort of trouble and been sent to live with relations in London, but that was about it.

She and Mike were nothing but welcoming to Simon from the start and Alastair had been a good and loyal friend. She could understand how Simon might have been a bit envious of everything they had if he was coming from a less advantaged background, but could see no reason why that should manifest itself as jealousy and resentment of the people who had been so kind to him.

She thought back to the time when Fiona and Simon had visited after Alastair had left. Had they really imagined she, Mike and Jenny were so naive that they wouldn't be able to see that the affair had already started? Jane never found out how long it had actually been going on but Simon and Fiona were certainly in close cahoots at the Easter party and she hadn't been at all surprised when that journalist did a big exposé of their relationship.

Alastair saw the best in people and had always defended Simon and trusted him. Even when Alastair was away at boarding school, Simon would still come around to the house; he'd looked lost and lonely and you could see the first glimmers of resentment even then. When Alastair brought friends from school home, they would often be cruel to Simon and she, like Alastair, had always taken Simon's side. She wouldn't tolerate bullying, particularly when it was driven by that kind of puerile snobbishness. Maybe, in Simon's case, she should have left them to it.

She realised her mind had been wandering while Danno was telling her about Natalie's summer plans before university. 'I'm so sorry Daniel,' she said. 'I was miles away. You said she was going to South America?'

'Yeah. She's well excited about it,' he said. 'She flies to Lima on Monday with two girlfriends. They've got three weeks there, doing the Inca Trail and a whole bunch of other stuff, then down to Chile for a month and finishing with a month in Argentina. She's been working all hours to save up enough for the trip. Me and Jen are helping with the flights but the rest is on her. Nat's an impressive young lady. A bit like you when you were her age, I'll bet.' Danno gave her a cheeky smile.

Danno had always known how to charm Jane. In the early years, he hadn't come across as such an ideal prospect for her Jenny. Two years younger, no real job, long hair, beard, nose ring and probably all sorts of other bad habits. As it transpired, however, he had turned out very well indeed. He'd always been devoted to Jenny and Jane had seen from the start that he was a kind person who would be a good husband and father. What neither she nor Mike could have known was how successful a songwriter he would turn out to be, and how much money could be made from writing songs.

'Daniel, you're incorrigible. You do know that don't you?'

'No law against it, is there, Mrs J?'

'I suppose not,' Jane replied. 'It appears you can't help yourself. What do you and Jenny think about Natalie travelling? You must be nervous?'

'Jenny's terrified,' said Danno. 'And, to tell you the truth, I'm not much better myself. Nat's only nineteen. We won't be sleeping a lot for the next three months is my guess. She's my little girl, it's a long way, and I've no idea what it'll be like out there. You read all of these stories, but I never travelled myself, so I don't really have much of a clue. I was always so into my music that I didn't find the time, and it never actually interested me much anyway. I had lots of friends who did something, InterRail or whatever, but it wasn't my thing.'

'She'll be fine,' said Jane. 'She's confident, resourceful and smart and she's very lucky to have the opportunity to do something like this. You should both be very proud.' Jane rested her fingers gently on Danno's arm. 'And you should be very pleased with yourself for Maggie's song. She'll remember that all of her life. Such a special wedding gift.'

Danno had composed a song for Maggie and arranged for one of his friends, a professional backing singer, to perform it in the church while the immediate family were signing the register. It was a beautiful piece of music and Maggie had clearly loved it, rushing up to hug Danno as soon as they were out of the church.

'It seemed to make sense,' said Danno. 'It's the best thing I have to give, and the music felt right as soon as I started it.'

'Ladies and Gentlemen.' Jane looked up and saw Jeremy's best man standing. 'I am delighted to introduce to you ... the Mother of the Bride.'

Jane leant over to Danno and whispered into his ear. 'I'm so glad Maggie insisted that Fiona did this speech rather than Simon. I don't think I could have coped with that.'

Danno nodded his head slowly three times. 'I hear you, Mrs J. I totally hear you.'

Fiona stood to a wave of applause and waited, quietly smiling, until it faded. Jane had to admit she was looking very good for a fifty-eight-year-old. Alastair had chosen well.

Jane saw that Fiona was nervous, but her voice was clear and strong.

'Dear friends, I understand that it is unusual for me to be making this speech, but Maggie asked me to do it and, as you all know so well, I can't deny my daughter anything.

'I have a number of pleasurable responsibilities to fulfil, and the first is to welcome you all here today. It is fabulous to see so many old friends and family all together and to see all you young and beautiful people, dressed so beautifully. I keep expecting Hugh Grant to appear.' A ripple of laughter spread across the room. 'On behalf of the bride and groom and their families, I would like to welcome you all here on this truly special day.'

Fiona paused and looked down at her daughter. 'My next responsibility is to say a few words about Maggie. Those of you who know her well will realise that summing up this beautiful talented young lady in only a few words is quite a challenge, but I will do my best. In order to talk about the whole Maggie, I need to mention the time when her father left ...

'... Although she was only a child, and has had Simon to fill that role as she grew up, I know Alastair leaving was a key point in her life and was something she struggled with for many years.' Fiona had continued to look at Maggie as she said this but now turned to the room.

'Some people allow that kind of upset to weaken them, to make them bitter and resentful, but not Maggie. Some people close in on themselves and hide when things are difficult, but not Maggie. She was always a happy, laughing child and that difficult experience didn't change that, it just added a new dimension to her character. She became more thoughtful, considerate and loyal to everyone close to her.

'These characteristics have developed with her as she has grown into this beautiful young woman who sits here beside me. My daughter is now a wife and has brought a marvellous new addition into our family.' Fiona turned back to the bridal couple. 'Jeremy, I am delighted to be able to invite you into our family. You are a wonderful young man and I know you will continue to make Maggie happy. Welcome.' There were a few whoops and cheers from the tables at the back.

Fiona continued. 'The road from childhood to marriage wasn't, of course, totally smooth. There was a period, shall we call it "The Missing Years", when there were more rough cobblestones than tarmac. I promised Maggie I wouldn't say anything about a certain incident which happened when she was fifteen but, unfortunately for her, I lied.' Ripples of giggles and murmuring flowed back and forth. The audience wanted at least one good story about Maggie.

'She and Rebecca,' Fiona said, turning and smiling at Maggie's Maid of Honour, 'were both fifteen at the time. It was Rebecca's birthday party.' By now, Maggie was facedown on the table, head covered by her arms.

'Well, to cut a long story short, Rebecca really liked this boy, Tom, who fortunately isn't here today, and she had invited him to her party especially. She and Tom were getting on very well as the evening progressed and had disappeared to the bottom of the garden for some reason or other.' Fiona paused to allow the sniggers to die down. 'This was fine until Rebecca's ex-boyfriend, who was a few years older, turned up, stinking drunk and making a huge fuss. Rebecca's parents sent someone to find Rebecca to help them to deal with him and, after about an hour, they managed to calm him down. Drama over, Rebecca returned to the party to look for Tom but couldn't find him anywhere ...'

Fiona looked at Maggie who was glaring daggers at her from under her protecting arms. '...And where exactly was Tom, Maggie? Who was he with?' The room exploded with laughter and Fiona had to almost shout to finish. 'What a testament to true friendship that Rebecca is here today as Maggie's Maid of Honour. It was touch and go for a while though ...'

Fiona raised her glass and, as everyone settled down she brought the speech to an end. 'My final and most pleasurable task is to ask you all to stand and to join me in toasting my beautiful daughter Maggie and my wonderful new son-in-law, Jeremy. To the bride and groom!'

'To the bride and groom,' everyone chorused and Jane felt the unique warm tingle which comes when a group of people are all focused together on one positive, unselfish thought. A thought that tugs up the corners of your mouth into a beaming, joyful smile without bothering to go through your brain on the way. Weddings will do that.

Danno turned to Jane. 'Great speech,' he said. 'I think she got it just right. Simon looks pissed off though.'

Jane had always prided herself on being kind and tolerant and wishing everyone well. As she got older, however, she felt she had earned the right to a little latitude. She turned back to Danno.

'Good!' she said.

1995 - Alastair

I really don't know how Fiona is going to react. She's normally quite sensible, after some initial fireworks, but this situation is very different. It's been a tough few months already and I know she's going to feel totally betrayed. She definitely won't like my plan to borrow money from my parents. I know she won't. I think I'll save that for another time.

There's no one around as I walk up from the station. Sevenoaks is a ghost town, which is strange for a Friday morning. It's as though everyone has cleared the roads in readiness for my walk to Calvary. I'm not looking forward to this.

Whatever Fiona might think, the only way I am going to be able to find the money to pay the penalty is if my parents are able – and willing – to help us. I need almost two hundred thousand pounds more and I know they will have to take out a big additional mortgage to find that much. Christ, I've been dreading my conversation with Fiona, but I suspect it will be a picnic in comparison to speaking to my Dad and asking him to lend me that much money.

On my way back to my hotel last night after seeing Piers, I couldn't get the story about that casino bloke out of my head. What would it feel like to risk everything on the turn of a card, the flip of a coin or a spin of the wheel? Apparently, the guy hadn't needed to do it, he just wanted to. I suppose it was the sort of thing Homeric heroes might do, throwing your life and livelihood into the hands of the fates. Asking the biggest question of all. Do the Gods still favour me or will I die today?

Not something I could ever imagine doing. I suppose that's the accountant in me coming out. I understand the way probability works too well and know why most gambling businesses are very successful. The profit must be coming from somewhere, and it's obviously coming from all of the idiot gamblers who think they can beat the odds and take too long to figure out they can't.

It's not that I've got any great moral issues with gambling as such, I'll usually make a bet on the Grand National and have spent a bit of money in Las Vegas and Monte Carlo when I've been there on holiday, or for conferences. That's the way I've always seen it though, spending money, the same as paying for a meal in a nice restaurant. I would never let myself get caught into believing I was actually going to come out on top – that goes against everything I've ever learnt.

The only exception for me was in my late teens when I used to play three-card brag in the pub with friends. I was doing my A-levels and most of my village friends were already working. That meant they could afford to lose, which also meant that they usually did. Still, it kept me in beer and pork pies and it's very different when you don't have a "house" which has the odds in its favour.

Anyway, last night I was staying at the Mayfair Hotel on Piccadilly, still booked on the Polaris account but I guess for the last time. The Mayfair has an in-house casino called the Palm Beach and, after everything that had happened during the day, I couldn't imagine getting to sleep. I didn't feel like watching crap TV, so I decided to go downstairs for a nightcap.

If you're staying at the hotel, you're automatically a member of the casino and I only had to show my room key to get in. The venue is amazing, really old school. They've used the original Art Deco ballroom for the gaming area which is very classy. Everything oozed money, from the staff in immaculate dinner suits, to the fluted marble columns and Tiffany chandeliers, to the group of white-robed Saudis playing blackjack and surrounded by a flight of night butterflies resplendent in skimpy fishnet and sequins. The nectar came in the form of magnums of Dom Perignon and bottles of twenty-five year-old single malt, and God knows what sort of pollen would rub off later.

I had to have a Vodka Martini, shaken not stirred. It was that sort of place and I've been a big Bond fan ever since I was a kid. I've actually still got my metal Corgi model of the original Goldfinger Aston Martin DB5 with working ejector seat, bulletproof rear windscreen, revolving number plates and machine guns behind the headlights. Those were really quite different times.

Once I had my drink, I took a stroll over to the roulette tables, imagining what it would feel like to gamble everything you had on one spin of the wheel. I suppose it was only then that it hit me. I didn't actually have anything.

When I'd woken up that morning, I'd still had a job, a career, a house, savings, and money in the bank. The results of some lucky breaks, of course, but twenty years of hard work and sacrifice as well. And now, after signing one stupid bit of paper, I was in a worse situation than if I'd walked into the Palm Beach, put everything on red, and lost.

I remember standing still for several seconds with my eyes closed as the fight puffed out of me and the first tendrils of despair began to snake their way through my crumpled, sagging body. There was always a solution, There was always a way to fix things. But this time ...

There must have been seven or eight roulette tables and I found myself randomly walking around them in a daze, half-heartedly looking at how people were betting.

That was when I saw her for the first time.

I honestly don't understand what it was that struck me about her because the truth doesn't make any sense. What I remember is how she was surrounded by an aura, a real and visible silver-blue glow. I know it isn't possible of course; I am a rational educated person with a masters degree. I'm a qualified accountant, for Christ's sake. But, I did see it. I wasn't that drunk. I just can't explain it.

She was the croupier at the last table, closest to the VIP area. She wasn't drop dead gorgeous – pretty though, with a delicate, elfin face, sharp eyes and short, dark hair. She was very smartly dressed, like all of the staff, and the simple combination of dark trousers, cream blouse and dark waistcoat set off her slim figure well. If I'd had to guess, I would have put her at about twenty-eight, but I'm rubbish at guessing ages.

I must have looked like a village idiot or a pervert as I stood there for an age, just staring at her. Apart from the impossible glow, there were a couple of other things about her that I remember. I was sure she wasn't French but she had a surprisingly good French accent when she was calling the bets at the table. The other thing was her hands. She had the most beautiful hands I've ever seen and her movements were slick, confident and crisp as she raked and stacked the chips, time after time. She was like a Balinese dancer creating an entire performance only from gestures.

It was the strangest thing and not like me at all. I'm not without imagination but, on the other hand, I'm not a great romantic or a poet. I'm a pragmatic person, living in the here-and-now and, as I walked back up to my room later on, I easily convinced myself that I must have imagined the whole thing. It had been the worst day of my life, after all.

Fiona is waiting for me and opens the door while I'm still walking up the drive. She is looking lovely. More colour in her cheeks and somehow younger and more animated. I suppose she is excited and keen to find out what's going on.

I give her a brief hug and throw my overnight bag down in the hall. 'Let me get my boots on and I'm ready,' I say.

'OK. Let's go. I'll grab a coat.'

'I assume you got the message last night? I'm never quite sure whether Anita has understood a word I've said. Why doesn't her English get any better?'

'Yes, I got the message,' Fiona replies. 'And it is quite amazing how poor her English is. I think there are three of four Danish au pairs in Sevenoaks and they've all banded together. As far as I know, they don't have any English friends, so that might explain it.'

I decide against asking whether Anita's friends are all as unattractive as she is. It's maybe not the right time for that kind of humour. 'What about the kids? I've been so rubbish at spending any sort of quality time with them.'

'They're fine. They've been doing a tennis course all week and, what with that and seeing friends in the evenings, I've hardly seen them either.' Fiona's voice is bright and sharp and businesslike; she also avoids looking at me as she turns the key in the lock and we set off.

It's only a couple of hundred yards to the footpath and within five minutes we're in the middle of the countryside, walking across the fields towards the pub. I'm still feeling like a spineless idiot and I'm not quite ready to move away from the small talk and chitchat. 'Anita told me you were in town yesterday,' I say. 'Do anything interesting?'

'No. Nothing much,' she says. 'You know, the usual. A bit of shopping, popped into the National Portrait Gallery. Nothing special.' Fiona is being unusually abrupt and I realise that, unlike me, she is impatient to move away from the small talk.

I can't avoid this any longer. 'I know you're impatient to find out what's been going on with me over the past six months,' I say, stepping in front of Fiona and holding her still, my hands taking her shoulders and gently turning her to face me. 'And I'm going to explain now. But before I do that, there are a few things I need to say. It won't take long.'

'Of course,' she says. 'But, you're frightening me a little.'

'This part shouldn't frighten you at all,' I say. 'Quite the opposite in fact.' I take a deep breath and look into her eyes. 'I just want to tell you that I love you. I've always loved you, and will always love you. The last few months have been a nightmare and I know I've not been there for you, Hamish or Maggie. I need you to understand it has had nothing to do with how I feel about you all. Everything has been about work and the secrets I've had to keep.

'I'm afraid I've left this all too late, and I've lost you for ever. I hope that's not true and all I can do is to promise you that, once this is all over, I'll do whatever it takes to get our family back to normal.' She must be able to hear the truth in my voice but I can't tell what she's feeling. I plough on. 'We've had so many wonderful years together and I hope we can have many more. I don't want to give up and I'm almost afraid to ask. Do you feel the same way? Do you still see a future for us?'

She wraps her arms around me and hugs me, saying nothing to begin with. 'Of course I do,' she says, eventually. 'You know I do. Whatever has happened. Whatever it is. We'll find a way through it together. Knowing you still love me is all I need.'

'Thank you, darling,' I say, not entirely convinced. 'As you'll understand soon enough, the next few months are probably going to be even worse, and you'll almost certainly want to kill me when I explain things, but as long as I know there's hope, I'm certain we'll make it through to the other side.'

Fiona releases me and we start walking again. 'OK,' she says. 'I think it's about time you put me out of my misery, don't you?'

And so I begin. 'Well, it all started when I was made Chairman of the Pension fund at the end of last year ...'

As I talk, I can tell that Fiona wants to interrupt and ask questions, but she restrains herself. I know a part of her will be looking at the situation like a lawyer and I'm hoping she will see that I have only made foolish mistakes rather than being complicit in deliberate fraud.

It is going well enough until I get to the details of yesterday's meeting with the Serious Fraud Office. That definitely changes the mood. Fiona is incandescent. I think if she were holding a baseball bat, she would use it on me. If, of course, the bat didn't catch on fire first.

In amongst the screaming and shouting, she is asking some real questions and I'm trying to answer them as well as I can. I knew this was going to be bad, but it's so much worse than I expected. I'm very grateful there isn't anybody within a half a mile radius.

She is especially upset when I won't tell her about my plan to get the remaining money. I understand why, but I know she will think that it's totally wrong to ask my parents to help. They are retired and don't have piles of cash lying around. It will be much better to speak to them first and, hopefully, present her with a fait accompli. Fiona has always thought I take my parents for granted and that may be so. But isn't that what parents are for?

After a long while, she appears to have got her mind around the basics and I can tell from the furrows on her forehead that she is thinking methodically, trying to work out what it actually means for her, and for us. We haven't touched on what I think might be the biggest problem of all – the way I am likely to be vilified by the media – but that can wait.

We walk on in silence for a while, an invisible electromagnetic field humming and sparking between us. As I feared, every last droplet of goodwill and mutual love has boiled away to nothing, but I'm glad I said what I said anyway. It will hopefully pay off in the long term.

After about ten minutes, she stops and turns to face me. 'So what do we do now?' Her expression is set into her practical lawyer face. 'How will we manage? I can't see how you can ever get another decent job after this. Certainly not in the UK.'

'That's not for sure,' I reply. 'I might be able to get some consulting work, possibly advising people on how to avoid this kind of situation. The thing is that I'm not sure I have the stomach for it any more. I wonder if I'm really cut out for the corporate world. Leaving aside major fraud like this, everyday life is all about making questionable moral and ethical compromises. I think that each of them takes a little mouse-bite out of your soul.'

'Not so different from being a defence barrister,' countered Fiona, who couldn't stop herself from playing devil's advocate. 'There are always clients who you know in your heart are guilty, or expert witnesses who you need to coach to tell a very specific version of the truth to make a point. Lots of little moral and ethical compromises there. But you start by believing in the law and the right of each of us to a fair trial in accordance with the law. It may not always be perfect, but it's so much better than the alternatives.'

'Maybe so. Maybe it isn't so different, but I'm not quite convinced. The moral compromises you make in business don't have the same pure goal at their heart. You could try and argue that you start by believing in free market capitalism and the rest follows, but capitalism is a vague concept and is ring-fenced by huge numbers of laws and regulations designed to prevent the uncontrolled exploitation of the "have nots" by the "haves". The moral and ethical compromises which we see every day in the corporate world almost always involve ways to bypass or avoid those laws and regulations with the sole intent of helping the rich to become richer.'

'Bloody hell,' Fiona is clearly shocked. 'Where did that come from? I had no idea you felt like that.'

'Neither did I,' I say. 'Until very recently, neither did I.'

Another couple is approaching us along the bridle path, walking a couple of black labradors. We don't know them and we stop talking for a few minutes until we are past them and they are out of earshot.

'I don't understand why you haven't said anything before,' says Fiona. 'I always thought you loved your job. This makes it sound as though you have hated every minute of it and just suffered in silence to provide for us. Is that what you're trying to say?'

'No, it's nothing like that. The last thing I'm trying to do is blame you guys. I thought I enjoyed my work too. I don't really know where those ideas have come from. I think I'm losing it a bit. Everything has turned upside down and inside out and I can't find the way to get myself back on track. Let me do what I can to sort out the current mess and then we'll see.'

'OK.' Fiona stops and grabs my arm. 'But, as you refuse to tell me what you're going to do to fix things, I'm not quite sure what you expect me to do in the meantime.'

'Give me a few days. I only need a little time.' I hate the pleading, whinging note in my voice. 'What we need to do now is to talk about the part of the problem which I don't think can be fixed.'

'What else?' Fiona is getting fired up again. 'What haven't you told me? Are you bloody having an affair?'

'No, of course not,' I say, wondering where that idea sprung from. 'Don't be ridiculous, it's nothing like that, and it's not something I haven't told you. It's about the consequences of what I've already explained. When the media get hold of this at the end of the month, they're going to blow it up into a huge scandal. Don't you remember what happened to Maxwell's family? And he was dead before it went public.'

'But, surely they'll attack Polaris and not you? They're the guilty ones.'

'They'll try, but everyone involved is in the States and they'll all be locked away in their gated communities, impossible to reach. I'm the main fall guy over here and the press won't give up the story simply because they can only go after the second best option.'

'Oh, bloody hell,' she says. The penny has dropped. 'Does that mean we'll have journalists camped outside the house for the next six months? And at the kids' school?'

'I expect so. And, even worse, the employees and pensioners who've lost out will probably put together some sort of protest group and join them. It could get nasty.'

'But there are things we can do, right? You can get some sort of confidentiality agreement? Have your name hidden?'

'I tried that, it was a complete no-go. They want me to be hung out to dry.' I take a deep breath, looking down at the crumbling edges of the tractor ruts. 'That's why I need to disappear.'

'What do you mean, disappear?' Fiona clearly thought I was beginning to crack up. 'You can't just disappear.'

'Well, I think I have to, at least for a few months until it blows over. If I'm not around, they'll lose interest in you and the kids quickly enough.' I have no intention of telling her that, if I can't find a way to pay the fine, I will have to run or go to jail. That's my secret, and my problem.

'But, what will you do? Where will you go?'

'I don't know yet. If I avoid using credit cards and move around within the EU, I'll be quite difficult to find. I thought I might do some grape picking; it's cash-in-hand, free wine and I might work off some of this flab. Apart from that, I haven't really thought it through. There hasn't been time.'

Fiona's face is bright red and, for a moment, she looks as though she's going to explode, but she has always had this lawyer's ability to control her emotions at times like these. She will now take her time to process everything before Round Two. The electromagnetic field separating us hums back into life and we continue the walk in silence, both lost in our own thoughts.

1995 - Jane

Jane woke up early. The days were beginning to stretch out at both ends and the dawn chorus had been particularly energetic that morning, mostly as a result of a family of jackdaws which had decided to make its home in the unused part of the chimney stack. She didn't really mind, but they were a particularly chatty family and most of their conversations tended to develop quickly into loud arguments.

She lay in bed thinking about the strange telephone conversation she'd had with Alastair the previous night. He'd wanted to come down for lunch tomorrow, which was now today of course. This was strange in itself, as he'd only just been down to see them and he didn't visit that often. But he'd also sounded nervous on the phone and had said something about wanting to have an important discussion with Mike and her.

Mike had been muttering all week about something being wrong with Alastair, but whenever Jane asked him to explain why, he couldn't put his finger on anything specific, and stuck to making vague comments, 'I just know' or 'can't you see something isn't right?'.

Mike had never been a great communicator, which had always been an issue for Jane; she loved to talk, argue, debate, play devil's advocate, tease, gossip, the whole shebang. She'd met her match when she got married though. A brilliant and eloquently expressed train of thought could be instantly switched into a leafy, dead-end siding with a simple 'uh-huh' or 'hmnn' from Mike.

He simply didn't believe in talking for the sake of it. If you didn't have a specific goal in mind when you opened your mouth, it was better to close it again without speaking. When you did need to say something, you should always get your point across clearly and concisely with no unnecessary words to distract the listener. Where was the fun in that? And as for discussing emotions and feelings ...

It was the army's fault, of course. Even back when they first got married, most people didn't actually grasp what a full-time professional career in the armed forces really meant, both for the soldier and for his, or her, nearest and dearest.

During the last big war and in the difficult years which followed, they'd all had plenty of reasons to understand what it meant, but memories were short, and those who had the best reasons to remember did everything they could to forget.

Mike had passed out of the Royal Marines training centre at Lympstone as a young Second Lieutenant in 1954, and was assigned to 45 Commando, where he'd been promoted to Lieutenant eighteen months later. He was twenty-five years old and in charge of a troop of thirty marines, most of whom were older than him and all of whom were much more experienced.

Jane had met him at university a year earlier and they'd been officially dating since then. When he first joined the Marines, she was in awe of the idea that someone so young and fresh-faced could have the ability to maintain authority over tough, battle-hardened men, but he always seemed relaxed and comfortable and he explained that it was simple. If he wanted respect, he needed to be fitter and tougher than his men and to convince them he knew what he was doing, whether or not it was true.

She only saw him a few times in the year after university as he was based in Malta, but he visited her at her parents' home in Sussex as often as he could. On one particular Friday, she'd taken the bus into Tunbridge Wells to have her hair done before Mike arrived on the Saturday morning. She'd planned to see a friend, but came home early because her friend was down with the flu.

It was a dismal grey autumn day and the last few leaves were fighting a losing battle to stay aloft. She cut through the back garden by the side gate and was brought to a standstill by the sight of a

Royal Marines officer in full dress uniform walking out of the gravel drive and turning up the hill towards the station.

Was that Mike? What was he doing here? Jane could remember her feelings as though it were yesterday. For an instant, she'd had the terrible thought that it was one of Mike's fellow officers who'd come to tell them something bad had happened to Mike – they did all look so similar in full uniform after all. But it had been Mike – she'd been certain – and they always came in twos to give bad news didn't they?

He wasn't due down until the following day and there he was, dressed in full parade uniform. On top of that, he'd arrived when she was out and left before she got back. There could have only been one reason. Even so many years later, just thinking about that moment of delightful epiphany made Jane's stomach flip over again in a tingling, queasy spasm of girlish glee.

She'd been right, of course. Once she'd found her wits again, she'd known that for certain. The proposal came the next day and was suitably correct, formal and romantic. She'd rehearsed her "pretending to be surprised" routine and said 'yes', of course. They were married a year later, she was only twenty-two and, although it was forty years ago now, that frozen moment when she was stopped in her tracks – as though in a game of Grandmother's Footsteps – remained as intense and bright as it had ever been.

Mike never talked about his experiences as a soldier except for on one occasion, many years later, soon after Alastair and Fiona had lost their first child. He had been quite drunk. Actually, they had both had more to drink than they should have had, but Jane didn't believe it was the alcohol talking. Something wanted to come out and chose that particular moment to do it. It might have been the shock of Arabella's stillbirth or the fact that Mike was due to retire at the end of the year. Jane never really knew which.

'You know I've never talked about my life at the "office", have I?' He sat across the kitchen table from her, staring into his whisky.

'No, darling. But I realise you haven't wanted to, and that's fine,' Jane had replied. 'You have your reasons.'

'Well, I want to now,' he'd said, in a monotone. 'I don't know how to begin but there's one particular incident I want to tell you about. It happened before we got engaged. I'm not comfortable talking about this, it was over thirty years ago and it's a long story, but I think I have to tell it to you.'

Jane could still remember how her hands had started to shake under the table. 'I'm listening. Take as long as you want.'

'OK. Well, in late fifty-six, 45 Commando were assigned to take and hold Port Said during the Suez crisis in Egypt. The Israelis had already occupied the Sinai, and our paras and other marines companies had secured the beachhead and moved inland. We were landed by helicopter, which was the first time they'd tried it outside training and it ended up being a complete mess, but they eventually got us, and our gear, on the ground. Four assault cells from 45 with one hundred and twenty marines in each cell. Our task was to go street by street through the native quarter of Port Said and deal with the insurgents who were holding it. Everyone was on edge, of course, and this was made worse by the reports of hidden explosives and snipers which were coming in from the other troops who'd already engaged.

'It started badly. About half an hour after we started our advance, we were attacked from the air by friendly fire. Some idiot in the Navy or Air Force had given the wrong co-ordinates to a plane from one of the aircraft carriers offshore. Everyone in my troop was OK, but twelve marines were injured from other troops and another lieutenant, who'd been through training with me, was killed.'

'Was he a friend of yours?' Jane had reached across and taken Mike's hand.

'Not especially,' said Mike. 'But after everything you go through in the training and afterwards, you all become very close anyway. I knew him well enough.'

'I'm so sorry. That sounds awful.'

'I'm afraid that's not the difficult bit. We were invading another country, fighting against hundreds of thousands of soldiers defending their homeland. Casualties were inevitable, although it would have been better if the gunfire hadn't been coming from our own side. No, the worst of it came afterwards, once we were deep in the city, trying to make it safe.

'One of my newest recruits was shot in the chest by an Egyptian army sniper. His best mate, a young lad called Bulldog, who had trained with him, was standing right next to him when it happened. He tried to stop the bleeding, but there was nothing he could do. His friend died in less than a minute. My sergeant asked me what action to take and I told him to cover the body, log the location and to check that the other young marine was holding up OK. We were still under fire and deep within hostile territory; we needed to remain focused and move forwards.'

Jane shouldn't have been surprised or shocked. She'd seen enough films and read enough books to know that war wasn't pretty, but this was completely different. Her husband, the man she loved, was telling her about these terrible events. Events which actually happened, not products of some screenwriter's imagination. It was different.

'I was worried about the young marine, Bulldog, and asked my sergeant to check on him a couple more times, but he assured me he was fine. I should have checked myself, but didn't and I'll always regret that.

'It was only about ten minutes later that we came under fire again from the roof of some sort of restaurant or cafe. We returned fire and neutralised the threat. I then sent five men in to clear the building. A few seconds later, I heard two shots in rapid succession and, shortly afterwards, the corporal in charge came running out, ashen faced, saying, "Boss, you need to see this".

'When I went inside, Bulldog was standing in the middle of the room, his Lee-Enfield rifle on the floor beside him, facing away to the far corner. He was mumbling and stuttering again and again, "... there was a gun, I s-s-saw a gun, there was a gun ..." When I got to the corner, I saw a young woman in traditional dress crumpled in a heap. One of our medics was already there and, as he turned her over, I saw the small baby in her arms. Both were dead.'

'What happened? Was the marine court-martialled?'

'No. Once we had the area secure, my sergeant and I talked it over and then ran it past my commanding officer. It was decided that the incident should remain "internal". We found another reason to ensure Bulldog was removed from active duty, and everything was swept under the carpet. It was never reported officially and no one was ever sanctioned for it. It was only collateral damage and, in those days, there was no room for morale-busting scandals.'

'Oh, my God.' Jane had got up and walked around the table to Mike. 'What a terrible thing, and you've kept it inside of you for all of these years. You poor darling.' She had wrapped her arms around him and hugged him with all of her strength.

'You know what the worst of it was?' Mike had said after a few moments. 'It was all for nothing. The bloody politicians were already agreeing to pull out. We did everything they asked us to do and they then made us retreat after a week. All for nothing.'

Each time Jane thought about this experience, and almost certainly others he'd never talked about, it became clearer how much being a soldier must have affected Mike over the years. It was before they invented post-traumatic stress disorder but, aside from not having a name for it, he'd probably suffered from something similar. It explained his stiff and distant approach to fatherhood but, on the other hand, maybe he was more qualified to judge Alastair's behaviour than Jane was giving him credit for.

Whatever Mike thought about Alastair's state of mind, however, he had looked fine to Jane when they saw him at the weekend. OK, he had been outrageously drunk, but that wasn't the first time he and Simon had behaved like that. They were still boys at heart.

It was a little unusual that the pair of them had left so quickly in the morning. No time for breakfast and they barely managed to say goodbye but, what with his important job and everything, Jane was sure he was very busy.

Still, there was no point stewing over it, he would arrive around midday and they'd find out then. In the meantime, she needed to pop out to get some more eggs. She was making him a bacon quiche, which had always been his favourite.

2017 - Sally

I don't know whether you're like me or not, but I hate to see things go to waste. That's why I was pushing to take on more business even if we've got enough to cover the bills already. It's not as though I'm greedy, not at all, I just don't like throwing stuff away.

I hope I'm not going to regret this one. Jim seemed to be relaxed enough when I told him about the villa, but I could see it knocked him back a bit. Let's see what sort of mood he's in when he comes back from the chapel. He's a funny bloke sometimes. I mean Matisse was amazing and it's a nice building, but I don't really see why it's such a great place for thinking. I'd much rather sit and think in the garden or go for a walk up in the hills.

We've got it so good and easy here, it would be a shame to rock the boat by taking on more than we can handle. The thing is, in a business like ours, it's all about reputation. If you do a good job then people get to know about it. Individual owners know other owners and there are shedloads of small businesses down here who live off the second-home industry – estate agents, builders, swimming pool installers, gardeners, air conditioning repair people, you name it, there are plenty of us feeding off the wealth of property owners in a region like this.

It's mostly reasonably symbiotic – there is a need which gets filled – although most people would struggle to see estate agents that way. People who work in the industry tend to know, or know of, each other and if they reckon you won't make them look bad, they'll recommend you.

One trick, we've found, is to be picky about the clients you take on. Some punters, especially rich ones, have a professional approach to being dissatisfied. They don't feel right unless they've found something to complain about. I think that's why they invented seven star hotels. Find something wrong with this one, I dare you!

I suppose if you have that much money, it might eat away at you and make you feel as though everyone is always out to take something from you. I don't actually understand why, but anyway, if you're smart, you see that kind of client coming a mile away and avoid them like the clap.

When me and Jim first moved here almost fifteen years ago, it was still good but not so easy. We were skint and Jim was still a bit "fragile" for a while. We made do though. It doesn't take much.

We'd met a few months earlier. I was working as cabin crew on a huge yacht based out of Monaco. It was an amazing boat, but the work was tough and you were definitely a servant – or slave – when the owners, or their friends, were on board. The owner, Manos Patrides, had originally been a fisherman from a small village north of Athens, had worked his way up to captain and then, over a ten-year period, become a major ship-owner and one of the wealthiest Greeks since Onassis. There were a lot of stories about how he made the leap from poor, uneducated captain to uber-rich shipping magnate and none of them did anything to polish his halo.

Manos was getting on a bit now, which made the job of female cabin crew less hazardous and, fortunately, he didn't use the boat much apart from an annual four-week pilgrimage to the Sporades islands, which was where he'd originally come from.

M/V Oneira was a fifty-eight metre motor yacht with room for twelve guests in six huge state rooms and she had twelve crew on board. She was an amazing, beautiful thing but keeping her looking amazing and beautiful was a never-ending task.

It was quite a small crew for such a big yacht. By the time you took off the captain, first mate, chief engineer, chief stewardess, and chef, that left seven of us to do all of the grunt work. We always had to be smartly dressed and ready to serve guests, even when we were cleaning the loos or no guests were due for weeks. Those were the rules.

There were, of course, some days off and, once we were off the boat, the rules and formality were washed away by the first cold Amstel, leaving behind a group of young people out for a good time. People who work on boats have a well-earned reputation for letting their hair down when off duty and it's no different if you're working on a tramp steamer putting into Valparaiso or a thirty-five million euro super yacht mooring up in Skiathos harbour.

We always had a long weekend off in Skiathos while Manos and his family went to stay in his home village to see old friends and family, and six of us had rented a small apartment for a couple of nights just to be on dry land for a bit. Skiathos Marina was one of the few harbours which could take a yacht as big as Oneira – which is Greek for "Dreams" – and we were really pushing the depth limits even there. People talk about the wonderful freedom of boating, and that might be the case when you're in a smaller yacht, but moving around a mini-hotel like Oneira was a military operation and most places needed to be booked months, or even years, in advance.

Going ashore means drinking, and we were all very well oiled by the time we got to our favourite club, the Driftwood, soon after midnight. It was more of a bar than a club, but the music was pumping anyway and a few people were dancing in the middle of the room. For some reason, we had moved on to Mount Gay rum and soda and it was going down very smoothly. The barman looked familiar for some reason but I was too pissed to pay attention. As long as the drinks kept coming, I was happy enough.

It all started to go badly wrong when someone decided it was time to dance on the narrow bar. Before long we were all up there, swaying and stomping and singing along with the music; we were waving our glasses around like fifteen-year-olds. After a while, a couple of the regulars ran out of patience and asked us to get off. It was good-humoured enough and they reached up to help us get down. No harm done and there was plenty of laughter and backslapping. An average summer night in Skiathos.

There was one guy still up on the bar. He wasn't from our boat but had attached himself to us a couple of bars earlier. A fiery-headed Welsh boyo, he was either very pissed indeed or not quite right in the head; his eyes were all over the shop and he kept pulling his hands up and away from the guys who were trying to get him down, side-stepping along the bar, his falsetto giggling and rictus grin making him appear almost possessed.

The next bit happened in classic slo-mo. He pulled his hand free one last time and then started to go over backwards, arms slowly windmilling as he crashed into the bottle-filled glass shelves behind the bar. The destruction was impressive, he didn't leave a single bottle or shelf untouched, the noise was a teenage window-smashers wet-dream and, when it all stopped, he was lying stretched out, apparently unscathed, in a pile of glass and booze, still giggling like an idiot.

The good humour in the bar evaporated like water thrown onto molten pig iron, spitting red-hot gobbets in all directions, and everything kicked off. I must have fallen and cracked my head against something, because that was where it all faded to black for me ...

1995 - Fiona

They were just arriving at the pub as Alastair dropped his final bombshell about needing to disappear and be some sort of gap-year tramp for six months. Fiona could have killed him on the spot. His plan was to stroll off and peacefully pick grapes in the sunshine while she dealt with the shit-storm that he'd created. Well, there was no way that was ever happening. The selfish, selfish bastard.

Fiona couldn't take any more, she needed some quiet time to think things though and told Alastair she wanted to forget about lunch and take a taxi straight home. They could pick up on the unreal unravelling of their life once she'd had time to process everything. Alastair was smart enough to not argue.

In normal circumstances, it would have been very pleasant to sit over a bottle of wine and a couple of steaks, only the two of them, and on a quiet midweek lunchtime. Life wouldn't be too bad if it were a bit more like that, but this was a long way from normal circumstances.

Fiona couldn't stop her thoughts spinning around, and running through everything Alastair had just said. She couldn't stand back objectively, every thought stirred the crucible of her anger, and it was taking all of her self-control to avoid a huge public meltdown.

She wanted to be reasonable and understanding, but she only felt betrayed and let down. She could see how Alastair had made a genuine mistake and was doing the best he could to resolve it. He wasn't thinking of himself, but trying to make the best of an impossible situation, with his family's interests coming top of his priority list. Was that betrayal? Of course not. Her dalliance with Simon, however ...

The problem Fiona had was that, the more she thought about how angry and betrayed she felt, the more she was reminded that she was also a lying hypocrite, and that, of course, made her even more angry. The taxi journey home was a stiff, uncomfortable affair made up of formal, stilted conversation punctuated by long and painful silences.

By the time she'd picked up the kids and dealt with all of the normal bric-a-brac that families generate without thought – and usually thoughtlessly – the rest of the day had been swallowed up. It wasn't until she was getting ready for bed that she remembered she had promised to call Simon. Alastair was having a bath, so she had a five-minute window. She sneaked down to the kitchen feeling a bit like an intruder in her own home.

Simon picked up the phone on the second ring. 'Hello,' he said.

'It's me,' said Fiona in a stage whisper. 'Fiona.'

'Fiona. Thank God. I was worried something had happened to you. How did it go?'

'It went well, I suppose. As much as having the rug pulled out from under your life can go. I still haven't really got my mind around the whole shebang, and I think it's moved on since Alastair spoke to you.'

'Moved on better, or moved on worse?'

'Worse, I think. Yes, much worse. Look I can't actually talk now. Alastair's in the bath and I only have a couple of minutes.'

'I understand.' Simon was sounding very tense. 'Look Fiona. About yesterday. It was amazing. I can't stop thinking about you. About us. About the whole thing. I know we can't talk on the phone, but I have to see you. I must.'

Fiona felt a renewed tingle of excitement listening to the urgent passion in Simon's voice. She had never been unfaithful before, but it was clear now why people did it. Breaking the rules, naughty, mischievous, childish and dangerous, like a jamboree bag full of guilty pleasures.

She couldn't square those shallow, heartless feelings with the wrenching guilt she'd felt earlier when Alastair was telling her how much he loved her, but that was before he explained how he'd single-handedly destroyed their life. After all, Alastair was the real guilty party. Her sins were minor in comparison.

'OK, Simon. Alastair is going down to see his parents in the morning. I'll come into town again and we can meet for lunch. We should go somewhere different though, and just lunch. You decide and I'll phone in the morning to find out where. I'll call you around ten.' She heard the sound of the bathroom door closing upstairs. 'Look, I have to go. See you tomorrow.'

As she hung up the phone, a brief image of Simon flashed across her eyes, standing alone in his flat, speaking into a dead telephone. 'Goodnight Fiona. I'll see you tomorrow ... Goodnight darling.' She might be letting her imagination flatter her ego, but she did worry that Simon was taking the whole thing much more seriously than she was. He always took things too seriously. She should probably try and discuss that with him when she saw him.

'Who was that?' called Alastair from the top of the stairs. 'Are you coming to bed?'

'Nothing important,' Fiona replied. 'Only someone from the book club. I'm seeing her tomorrow for lunch while you're down at Jane and Mike's.' The lie slipped out slime-slick and effortless. 'I'll just grab a glass of water and I'll be up.'

1995 - Alastair

The kitchen where I grew up had always been a sanctuary; it was a big, light room with lead-paned windows and French doors on the garden-facing side. The full-size, black Aga cooker at the far end sat in a huge inglenook fireplace and grounded the whole space, providing a natural focal point and oozing warmth and comfort.

A large, rustic farmhouse table dominated the other half of the room – thick-boarded, rich-polished and solid, it looked as though it had been there forever. It was actually only about thirty years old, but had been made from the floorboards of a nineteenth century wool warehouse and the rich, luminous sheen came from years of fleeces polishing lanolin into the grain as they were dragged about. As an adolescent, I had always found this romantic, and redolent of those black and white BBC serialisations of Charles Dickens novels, where poor Victorian workhouse girls – probably young, bodiced and in need of rescue – slaved under the rod of a top-hatted, glowering mill owner.

My mother is fidgeting in her chair, looking, well, motherly, I suppose. I am certain the fidgeting results from resisting her instinct to leap up, wrap me in her arms, and rock me gently. 'Don't worry, darling, it will all be OK. Everything will be fine.' I also know what is stopping her. My father, who disapproves of such weak emotional displays and mollycoddling, is sitting stock still, the ramrod-straight military posture which has been a constant throughout my life still defining him completely. I can almost see the storm clouds building above his head – slate-black anvils preparing to unleash hell.

'Well, that's it.' I have finished my tale of woe. 'I've messed everything up. I didn't mean to, but I have. You know how much I hate to ask for help, but I don't know what else to do. Can you help us?'

My father stands and I brace myself for what is to come. This isn't the first time I've been on the firing end of one of his outbursts; the worst was when I was thirteen, and Simon and I were caught shoplifting in the local village post office. It was only a few sweets, and I think we did it because Jenny dared us, but we might as well have stolen the crown jewels and murdered three Beefeaters in the process. The strength and unbending righteousness of the tirade which followed was unparalleled. I think I actually wet myself.

It may have been the right way of dealing with misconduct in the army – although I somehow doubt it – but it wasn't the right way to manage a young teenager. I've tried to wipe the whole episode, together with a few others, from my mind, but they all flood straight back as I see my father looming over me. I even feel an urgent need to take a piss.

A few pregnant seconds pass before he turns, parade-ground sharp, and walks out through the French doors and into the garden. Not a sound, not a word, only a big empty space where he and his anger cloud had been. I don't know what to do. I've been so prepared for the inevitable onslaught – he never walks away from a fight – that I am left helpless and uncertain.

'He'll be back in a few minutes.' My mother breaks the silence. 'He's been trying to control his temper by taking time to walk around the garden and counting to one hundred. It won't work, I'm afraid. What the hell have you done, you bloody idiot? What about your family? You're supposed to look after them.'

I had obviously completely misinterpreted my mother's fidgeting. Wishful thinking, I suppose. I wasn't going to be on the receiving end of any mollycoddling today.

'I know, Mum. I didn't do any of this on purpose. I made a mistake and dropped the ball. I know it's all my fault and all my responsibility, but I'm doing the best I can to fix it.'

I want to curl up on her lap and sob like a six-year-old. Whenever I come home I always feel an overwhelming sense of safety and comfort. I grew up here and, throughout my life, this house and my parents have always just been there. I might not have visited or called very often, but the knowledge that they were there has given my life a basic underpinning, a rock-solid foundation to build on. The fact that I may now have compromised that foundation is both new and terrifying. I expected this point to come as my parents aged and needed support in return, but not yet. This is too soon and I'm not ready.

My mother remains unimpressed and definitely not happy. 'Don't behave like a child, Alastair. If your father sees you like this, I don't know what he'll do. This isn't a time for whimpering and excuses. You've let everybody down. I really didn't expect it from you. I really didn't.'

While she speaks, I am watching my father pacing up and down in the garden. His measured strides take him past the kitchen, off towards the orchard, and back again. I don't have a sense he is calming down.

My mother, meanwhile, hasn't finished. 'What about all the poor people who've lost their pensions?' she snaps, picking up her copy of the Daily Mail from the table and waving it at me. 'I suppose there'll be a scandal as well? Our family name will be dragged through the gutter like those Maxwell people? It's really too much.'

I don't know what to say. It seems I actually am alone and everyone is going to demonise me, even my own mother. Not for the first time, I start to feel sorry for myself. I don't want to hide from the facts: I didn't take enough care in my job and there have been serious consequences, but I wasn't acting in a deliberately fraudulent or negligent manner, and I didn't stand to gain personally. I was the victim of a deliberate pre-meditated fraud, which was carried out by others for their own interests. No one wants to accept this apart from maybe Fiona, and I'm afraid that, once she has time to think things through, she'll have changed her mind as well.

My father walks back into the room and sits down. I am surprised to see that the storm clouds have blown away. He just looks sad and old.

'No, Alastair. I'm sorry, but no,' he says, slowly and deliberately. 'It would be the wrong thing to do for a lot of reasons, not least as it potentially affects Jenny as well. But, in any case, we can't afford it. I've worked hard all of my life to build security for your mother and to make sure we can stay here as long as possible. There's also enough for some years in a retirement home if it comes down to it, but there isn't anything to spare and certainly not two hundred thousand pounds. We'd have to sell the Old Orchard, and I'm not prepared to consider that.'

'You can't extend the mortgage?' I reply. 'The house must be worth six hundred thousand.'

'Come on. You're the bloody finance guy.' His self-control is beginning to crack. 'Do you actually believe they'd give me a mortgage at my age? I'm sixty-four years old and living on a military pension. I might get one those equity release deals but you know as well as I do they're nothing more than legalised theft.' He slams his hand hard on the table. '... And that would mean the end of any chances Jenny has for inheritance. Or help over the next few years, for that matter. She and Danno don't have any real income and she's about to have a child. Do you really think that would be fair?'

'No, Dad, I don't.' The real problem is that I know he's right. 'I had to ask though. I don't see any other options. Whichever way I look at it, we're completely buggered.'

'Well, I suggest you get off your arse and find another solution pretty damn quick, then.' This is more like the father I know and, somewhat surprisingly, love.

My mother tries to get involved. 'Mike, can we at least look at ways to help? I don't want to think about moving out of the Old Orchard but there might be some other option. Surely it's worth speaking to your finance man?'

My father raises his hand like a policeman stopping traffic. 'I'm sorry Jane, my mind is made up. Alastair's got himself into this mess and he can get himself out of it.' He turns back to me. 'If you, Fiona and the kids get kicked out of your house, you can come and live with us until you get back on your feet, but that's it. This conversation is over.'

2017 - Fiona

'Could you do my zip please, darling.' Fiona reached back and pulled her hair up so Simon could see the zipper. Her immaculate wedding hairstyle had given up the ghost some hours previously, about the time when she had decided pogo-ing to a passable cover version of Billy Idol's White Wedding was a good idea.

'There you go.' Simon would normally at least go through the motions of stroking her shoulder or kissing the nape of her neck when he did her zip for her. Not tonight though. He usually hid it well, but Fiona knew Simon was in a terrible mood. He hadn't danced the whole evening, which was unusual for him. Instead, he'd adopted a couple of Maggie's single male friends and propped up the bar with them all night. Fiona had glanced over from time to time and had suspected a storm was brewing, but she was damned if she was going to let it ruin her daughter's wedding for her.

The taxi ride back had been no better. The rain had returned and the only noises were the rhythmic pumping of the wipers and the sizzle and swoosh of tyres on wet tarmac. The rain was fine and misty, turning each streetlight into an individual orange haze-bubble. She had known that nothing she could say would help, all she could do was wait until they got home and hope it somehow, miraculously, blew over.

After Simon had done the zipper, she allowed herself to believe the worst had passed and turned to him, smiling, 'What a glorious day,' she said. 'I don't think it could have been more perfect. I know it cost a huge amount but it was worth every penny. Thank you, darling.'

The slap came from nowhere. Knowing it might come did nothing to prepare her, and she fell sideways across the bed, instinctively curling up into a ball and rolling away, her right ear an explosion of pain. Surely her eardrum had been broken. She looked up and he was there, hunched over her, face thunderous, eyes popping and voice almost falsetto in its rage.

'Shut up. Will you just shut the fuck up,' he screamed.

'I'm sorry, Simon. I'm sorry. What did I do?'

She saw the next blow coming but it made no difference. A vicious, jabbing punch into the nerve bundles of her outer thigh took her breath away with a stab of pain worse than anything she had ever experienced.

'I said ... to ... shut ... the ... fuck ... up. Are you deaf?'

Fiona shook her head dumbly, numb with pain and fear, and watched as Simon paced up and down, his arms pressed to his sides. His fists were clenching and unclenching of their own volition, struggling to escape, to be wild and free. She'd never seen him so angry and knew she needed to be very careful. He might hurt her badly this time.

He was mumbling to himself as his inner fury boiled and bubbled. 'Typical ... so fucking typical ... always been the same ... happy to take my money ... happy to eat my food and drink ... just fucking ignored me ... always been the same, always ... second best ... good old Simon ... he'll be OK ... don't worry about him ... so fucking superior ... what makes them all so much fucking better, eh? ... posh, jumped-up twats, the lot of them ... he's been gone over twenty years and they still take his side ... but I've been here, I've been loyal ... I've always been loyal ...'

He stopped and loomed over her again. 'Did you have fun laughing at me when you were dancing with Piers?'

'Nnn ...' She cut off the word and shook her head instead as Simon lurched closer, face pushing towards her. She could smell the sharp stench of nervous sweat mixed with stale whisky, and braced herself for the next blow.

'I saw you looking over at me when you were dancing with him,' said Simon. 'You tried to hide it but I'm not fucking stupid. Little peeks and little giggles. I saw where Piers had his hands too. It's like I wasn't there. Poor old Simon sitting drinking in the corner on his own. He's paying for everything but no one wants him here. Not Jane, not Jenny, not Danno, not his wife, not even his fucking daughter. Everyone wishes goldenballs Alastair were here instead, even after he shat on the lot of you. How do you think that makes me feel? Have you any fucking idea how that makes me feel?' He was almost screaming now.

Fiona had her arms wrapped around her head, still curled into a ball, waiting and waiting for the rain of blows that would surely come. Knowing fighting back was not an option. She had learnt that the hard way a few years ago. Simon was much stronger than her and resistance only made it worse. She lay still, frozen in a flinch for what seemed like hours until she dared to open one eye and look out from under her arm. She couldn't see him. He must be behind her.

A second or two later, she heard the sound of his Mercedes starting outside followed by the screeching of tyres. He was gone. God knows where but, based on past experience, he wouldn't be back for a few days.

The breath left her in a rush and she lay sobbing gently into the duvet and quietly praying that the drunken bastard would manage to wrap himself and his precious car around a lamppost. As far as she could tell, her earlobe had torn where he had knocked out her earring and she would have a huge bruise on her thigh, but nothing was broken. She knew she had been very lucky. This couldn't continue. The next time, and there would be a next time, he could easily have something in his hand, a lamp, an ashtray, it wouldn't take much.

1995 - Jane

As Alastair drove off, Jane turned to Mike and screamed at him. 'Who the bloody hell do you think you are just shouting me down like that? I'm not one of your recruits. What makes you think you can decide everything for us, anyway?'

'I'm sorry darling,' Mike said. 'I shouldn't have done that. It was rude and uncalled for.' He managed a smile, but the vein in his temple was swollen and pulsing purple. 'But I am unbelievably disappointed and angry with Alastair. He was doing so well and now he's thrown it all away. He can't simply come crying for help from Mummy and Daddy. That's not how it works.'

'What are you talking about? That's not how it works. What a ridiculous thing to say.' Jane took a step towards him. 'He's our only son, for crying out loud. He's got a wife and two children. Our grandchildren. We can't simply abandon them on a point of principle.'

'We're not going to abandon them,' said Mike. 'We'll look after them, let them come and live here, help wherever we can but we're not going to tear down everything we have, everything we've built, to bloody drag Alastair out of the hole he's dug for himself. I won't allow it.'

'Why do you get to decide everything we do with "our" money?' Jane couldn't remember ever having felt this angry. 'It is "our" money isn't it?'

'Yes, it's "our" money,' said Mike, 'but you've always left me in charge of it and expected me to make the big decisions. I know what we can afford and what we can't. I read about mortgages and investments all of the time to make sure we manage things as well as we can. What I said to Alastair is the truth. It's not only a point of principle.'

Jane knew he was right about one thing at least; she didn't have a clue about their finances and relied on Mike to make sure everything worked out. She couldn't remember quite how things had become like they were. It was as much her fault as his, but there was no doubt that they had taken on very traditional roles. She had never expected it to be like that; she had been to university, which was quite unusual for her generation and, although she was well into her thirties when feminism really started to become mainstream, Jane had been a strong supporter of the movement.

It appeared that a good education and some strong principles weren't quite enough to resist the pressures of society, habit and, possibly, the natural, physical differences between genders. On top of that, Mike was about as far from being a "new man" as she could possibly imagine, so falling in love with the wrong person had probably been a major factor. He had occasionally shown his sensitive side, like the time when he'd told her about his experiences in Suez, but it was normally hidden so well that it might as well never have been there.

Jane seriously doubted Alastair had ever seen it. Unfortunately his relationship with his father was based as much on fear and respect as on love, although she had no doubt that Mike loved his children intensely. He had his own way of managing the relationship which had a lot more to do with cold showers and being a man than with sympathetic hugs and words of support.

Right now, however, Mike was standing between a mother wolf and her cub – a very dangerous place to be – and this situation wasn't going to be managed all his way.

'All right,' she said. 'I'm too upset at the moment to fight with you as well. Please promise me you'll talk to your finance man, find out what the options are and then you can explain everything to me. I'm not that useless. After that, we'll see.'

'I will,' said Mike. 'But you also need to promise to think a bit more about the reality of this situation. We do need to consider Jenny as well and we mustn't simply throw good money after bad. It doesn't sound to me like Alastair will be getting a job with a good salary anytime soon, so maybe they will need to accept a change in lifestyle in any case.'

Jane put her arm around Mike as they walked back inside, 'All right darling. I promise. There's no use in us fighting. We should just be concentrating on finding a way to help Alastair.'

2017 - Jim

The Mas d'Artagnon is the most stunning property on our books. It's in a small gated estate a couple of kilometres outside Saint-Paul-de-Vence and is an absolute gem. The building is modern, but designed by a well-known local architect using original beams and recycled stone so it looks like a traditional Provencal "mas" conversion, but without all of the problems which go with an old house. It's set back into the hillside, and the view from the poolside is huge. It stretches from Cap Ferrat in the East all the way across to the Esterel Mountains in the West, which is where the sun is now slowly setting, quite probably right above our favourite restaurant in Theoule.

The Mas d'Artagnon rents for ten thousand euros a week in the high season which means everything always has to be perfect. The current renters are a Russian family who have complained about too much chlorine in the pool. As a consequence, Sally and I have come up here with the pool engineer to check it while the Russians are out for dinner, probably at one of the many Michelin-starred restaurants which are within spitting distance.

There is, of course, nothing wrong with the pool water, which was only checked four days ago, but the customer is always right and Sally is persuading the pool man to dial the chlorine level down a bit for the rest of the week, even though it's actually against French health and safety regulations.

We've had a busy day and I'm taking a few moments on the terrace to relax; I'm enjoying the view and imagining what it would be like to live somewhere like this. My nagging feeling about that sort of wishful thinking is that it might actually be compulsory to be arrogant and spoilt if you can afford places this expensive. I'll carry on convincing myself that this is the reason why I don't have the option.

I needed a few days after the weekend to make up my mind, but I'm getting close to a decision and before I decide, I want to tell Sally what's been bothering me for the past few weeks.

She knows all about my wife – as far as I know, we were never divorced – and kids and all of the issues surrounding our separation. She also knows I'm a "wanted man", which is why I use my second name now, and I can't be formally registered on any of the paperwork for the business, house and car. Getting seriously ill wouldn't be a good plan either. We don't talk about it much, not because of any taboo, but the subject does make me feel uncomfortable and I tend to prefer to let sleeping dogs lie.

What Sally doesn't know is that my daughter got married last week. This is the thing that's been eating me up, and, to be totally honest, still is. The wedding has forced me to address a lot of questions about my children which won't go away. I am struggling with guilt about whether I should have been in touch with them over the past two decades. I can't change history obviously, but Maggie's wedding has brought everything into focus again. Should I contact her now? I could become a grandfather soon. Am I planning on never seeing my grandchildren, and never knowing my children as adults?

When I left, Hamish was nine and Maggie was only seven. They weren't responsible for any of the decisions made at the time, nor the consequences of my fall from grace, and my disappearance must have affected them badly. Being apart from them has certainly been painful for me. I was always taught to aim for win-win solutions to life's problems but that's not always possible and this has remained an open wound.

Thank God for social media. I've been following their lives on Facebook for the past seven or eight years, which has made it a lot easier for me, although in many ways it's the same as when I would look at them sleeping when I came home late from work; observing from a distance is a long way from physical contact and two-way interaction. My role as doting voyeur helps me a little but gives them nothing.

Jenny, my younger sister, is nothing if not predictable and I knew in advance what she would choose for her password when she eventually got round to setting up a Facebook account. It took her until 2009 to do it but, when she did, the password was Borrobil as expected. It was always her favourite book as a child. Hamish and Maggie were among her first Facebook friends so I've been able to log in as Jenny whenever I want and sneak into their lives unknown and unnoticed.

Before then, it was difficult to get any information about them without leaving a trace. I tried anonymously calling their schools once or twice, but the schools got suspicious very quickly and I ended up being extremely grateful that I'd used an untraceable pay phone.

To begin with I decided not to discuss my worries with Sally as I wanted to work through the dilemma myself, but the right answer has been stubbornly elusive. I was once taught a decision-making technique where you create a mental image of a big pointer like the Swingometer which the BBC always uses in its election coverage. If you think things through enough, and list the pros and cons, the pointer will eventually always tip to one side or the other.

That leads to the most important, and difficult part of the process – making a decision. One of the important lessons I learned from my father is that avoiding issues is weak and achieves nothing.

For instance, the choice I made about leaving home in the first place was actually absolutely clear and I'm still sure it was the right one. I don't think anyone else saw it the same way, and suspect they thought I was going mad, but, unlike me, they didn't have all of the information. For me, the swingometer was way over to the right and said, 'You have to go!'.

Whether, and when, to come back was a bit trickier in the early stages but the negatives started to build up as the weeks went past, while the positives stayed the same. The legal and financial consequences of coming out of hiding were always an issue but the factors that tipped it for me were my parents' reaction and the whole thing between Fiona and Simon. It still didn't mean I'd never go back, but I decided to wait.

The way Fiona and Simon had jumped into bed together had also pushed me off a bit of an emotional cliff. I really hadn't spotted anything was going on between them in the weeks before I left and their betrayal wasn't on my radar screen at all. Blind and naive as well as negligent, I suppose. By the time I'd dragged myself back out of the bottle a few years later, it had all seemed to be too late.

I can see Sally walking towards me along the gravel avenue of brutally-manicured lime trees, which leads from the house to the pool area. The strict lines of the *colonnade du tilleul* are more reminiscent of the Loire Valley than the Cote D'Azur and it looks out of place, contrasting starkly with the more natural Mediterranean softness of the rest of the garden. An ambitious idea which possibly didn't work out as expected? Who am I to say?

Sally is dressed in white shorts and crimson halter top, her long dark hair tied back and trademark Raybans pushed up. She is ethereal, filled with an inner grace and luminescence that never fails to give my stomach a little jolt. She has finished with the chlorine "disaster" and comes over to sit on the stone wall in front of me.

'All sorted?' I say.

'Da, komradski.' Sally has developed a good Russian accent working in this business. 'No lonka vil ze chemical veppons be blinding poor Georgi's beautiful blue eyes, or streeping hundred dollar peeses ov skeen from Natasha's fake tan. Eet is over.'

I laugh, but seriously doubt she's right. You can pick the villa owners to work with but not the tenants, and this lot will be back before the end of the week with something else to moan about.

I take her hands in mine. 'Sal, I know I've been a bit of a pain for the past few weeks. I do have reasons but I haven't wanted to talk about them. I'm sorry.'

'No worries,' she replies. 'You don't actually do such a great job of hiding things. At least not from me. Take your time. We can talk about it whenever you want.'

'I'm ready now,' I say. 'I've almost decided what to do but want to hear what you think first. The thing is ... the thing is ... my daughter, Maggie, got married last week.'

'Bloody hell.' She clearly wasn't expecting this. 'How long have you known?'

'I saw the engagement on Facebook ages ago but, for some reason, it didn't actually sink in until last month when she put up some pictures of her hen night.'

'... And you didn't say anything? Send a card or a present?'

I looked at the ground and shook my head slowly. 'No. I've been going back and forth, and round and round, about this, and haven't been able to make a decision. Deciding to stay away has been my default position for so long now that I can't seem to change it. I want them to know I think about them every day, but can't help feeling that, by throwing that grenade into their lives out of the blue, I would do more harm than good. I'm afraid it would only be selfish, trying to make me feel less guilty, whatever the cost.'

Sally waited until I'd lifted my head before replying. 'Or are you being selfish by not telling them? Taking the easy road?'

I turned and stood with my back to her, facing down the valley.

She carried on. 'All I know is that, if I were Maggie, I'd want to hear from you. Whatever the consequences, I'd want to know you were alive and hadn't forgotten me.' Sally walked over and put her arm around me. 'I'm not saying I'd forgive you, or even try to understand your reasons, but I'd still want to know.'

'I had a feeling you'd say that, and it's out of order to ask your opinion and then ignore it, but I realise I've made my decision anyway,' I said. 'Rightly or wrongly, I think it's too late to change things now. There's a huge risk anything I do will make everything worse and upset them too much. Maybe I am being selfish but, if so, that's the way it is. My life is here now, with you, and I'm terrified of doing anything which might risk that.'

Sally didn't speak. She just stood beside me and leant in closer, head resting on my shoulder, as we watched the last of the evening sun drift down through the valley and away.

1995 - Alastair

Jenny was early, and is waiting for me when I get there. We decided to meet at Kettners in Soho and she's managed to snaffle a window table. Even from a distance, I can see the luminous sheen lots of women have in the middle months of their pregnancy. She looks great. At least one of us does.

'Hiya,' she says as I walk over to the table. 'You're late.'

I look at my watch. 'No, I'm not. I'm dead on time.'

She laughs. 'Absolute rubbish, you're always late. It's a rule. And keeping a pregnant woman waiting as well. Disgusting behaviour.'

'Great to see you too. You're looking amazing,' I say, giving her a kiss and sitting down opposite her.

'Thanks. I'm feeling good too. I decided to give morning sickness a miss. You, however, look like shit, I'm afraid. Maybe even worse than last week at Mum and Dad's, and that was bad, even by your standards.'

I put my hands up in mock surrender. 'If it's any consolation, I feel as bad as I look. What's new with you? I'm so unbelievably bored with me.'

'Well, there is something,' says Jenny. 'I wanted to tell you at Easter but we never had a chance. It's all very exciting. Danno's got a song on the next Celine Deniau album, it might even be a single. We found out two weeks ago. He's been working so hard and everything is coming together at last. I haven't told anyone else yet. I guess I wanted you to know first. You're the only one in the family who understands that songwriting is a real career.'

I get up to give her a hug. 'That's brilliant news. He deserves it. And other stuff in the pipeline?'

'Yes, loads. And he's just signed a publishing deal with EMI. Good advance, above-average royalty split and they seem to be very engaged.'

'I'm so pleased for you,' I say, feeling something approaching happiness for the first time since I can remember. 'It's about time you both got a break. The last few years must have been a real grind.'

'Not like Mr Alastair "Highflyer" Johnson, that's for sure,' she says. 'The perfect son whose feet haven't touched the ground since he was a kid.'

'I'm afraid my feet are buried under a few feet of shit right now.' I am shocked by the wave of emotion sweeping over me, and my smile is half-baked. 'I feel a bit like Icarus, only in my version of the story I don't land in water.'

I'm sure Jen can see the tears building behind my eyes. She's seven years younger than me, but my little sis has always known me better than anyone.

'What's wrong? What is it? I've never seen you like this.'

And so, my voice cracking, and struggling to keep my emotions under control, I go through the whole sorry story one more time. Only ten days earlier, I was so desperate to share this with somebody, with anybody. Now, I am almost fed up with telling it. The difference with Jen is that I tell her everything, including my conversations with Fiona and the abortive trip to see Mum and Dad. Plus the minor detail that I'm likely to go to jail if I don't pay the penalty on time.

'Shit!' she says. 'What are you going to do? I'll have a word with Mum and Dad if you want. I don't give a damn about any inheritance. You know that.'

'Thanks. Much appreciated but, much as it pains me to say it, Dad's right. I can't get them into a mess over this and, in any case, it still leaves me broke, without a job and owing them two hundred grand. Not a great plan.'

'Put like that, you have a point,' she says. 'So what will you do? You can't go to jail.'

'Well, I do have a solution, but it's a bit, well ... unorthodox.

Promise me you'll hear me out with an open mind.'

'Of course. Tell me.'

'... And you won't ever tell anyone else about this? Including Mum and Dad.'

'OK, I promise.' Jen has torn her paper drinks mat into a hundred pieces and is trying to stack the shredded scraps neatly without much success.

'Well, I'll make it short. After my disastrous meeting, I had a drink with Piers and then ended up in the Palm Beach casino on Piccadilly – don't ask me how or why – and there was a girl working the roulette wheel. She had something incredible about her. She was glowing with this blue light, I don't know how to describe it any differently and I feel like a total prat just saying it, but it was there, she was ... well, she was radiant.' Jenny's mouth is beginning to drop open. 'Not yet, you promised to hear me out.'

The waiter arrives, cutting me off in mid-flow. We spend a few awkward moments placing an order while Jen stares at me with eyebrows raised to the heavens, clearly not sure whether I'm joking or not. The waiter leaves eventually and I continue.

'Well, as soon as I saw her, I had this incredible feeling, a warm, comforting glow deep in my gut telling me this was meant to be. I was destined to see her, it was a message, a sign of some sort. I know this sounds ridiculous, but you're the only person who might take me seriously. I know what I saw and I know what I felt.' As I spoke, I could tell it was coming out all wrong. I could hear my words from outside myself and it was obvious how ridiculous I sounded.

'Oh, for crying out loud, you must have just been pissed.' Jen still wasn't sure I was serious. 'You've been under a huge amount of stress recently. It's understandable.'

'That's what I thought the next morning, so I went back. I've now been back four times, stone cold sober. She was only working on two of those other visits, but it was the same both times I saw her. I've been researching it and there are loads of historical references about sightings like this. It's mentioned in the Mahabharata, there are quite a few legends in Greek history, and the Romans talk about the Goddess Fortuna, whose symbol was a wheel. There's one common thread to all of these stories. If you are lucky enough to see her, to be granted this vision, good fortune will follow.'

I wait expectantly for her response, but she just stares at me. 'I'm sorry, but I'm a tad confused,' she says, eventually. 'Leaving aside the fact that you're clearly losing the plot and imagining things, it doesn't look to me as though you've been granted a huge amount of good fortune recently. Or am I missing something?'

'No, but you don't get it. Seeing her is a sign of good fortune to come in the future. I know what I have to do. I need to go there and make a bet.' I can feel the truth and certainty embracing me and lighting my face as I speak. Surely Jenny will see that?

I take her hand and look into her eyes. 'I'll go to the casino when she's on the wheel. I'll bet on Red, and I'll win. I know it.'

'But how does that help you out of your mess?' she says, pulling her hand away. 'Even if you do win.'

'It's easy. I'm going to bet it all. Two hundred and fifty-thousand pounds. Everything on Red. Double or nothing.'

It's not very easy to shut my little sister up and I should remember this moment. She is a statue, she is freeze-frame motionless, her mouth forming a perfect Betty Boop 'O'.

'You really have lost it, haven't you?' Jen eventually finds her voice. 'Have you thought of seeing someone? ... I actually think you should see someone.'

'Actually, I've been seeing a counsellor for the past two months. It's been very tough, going through this whole process alone and it was great to have someone to talk to about it. That's over now, though. What's peculiar is that right now, I've never felt more together in my life. I feel calm and controlled, my anger outbursts have gone. I am sad at times but ...'

She interrupts me angrily. 'Look, even if you're right. Let's say, there is something special about this girl for you, I don't see how you make the great leap to assuming that means she's Lady Luck personified and you should throw your life savings into an all-or-nothing bet. What was that Monty Python quote about King Arthur and Excalibur? "... you can't expect to wield supreme executive power just because some watery tart threw a sword at you ...". Well, it's exactly the same, isn't it?' She is clearly lost for words.

'Not really,' I say, wondering which of us is making the least sense. 'Let's say I have flipped, and all of this is in my head, which is a definite possibility. What the fuck! It's still better than giving the money to the Serious Fraud Office, isn't it? If I lose, and the fine doesn't get paid, I'll stay disappeared. Fiona and the kids are in the same boat one way or the other. This way, at least there's a chance.'

'Oh, come on. That's a bunch of self-rationalising bullshit and you know it,' she says, frustrated now. 'I've said what I think. You should go back to your counsellor and talk it through with them before you do anything you'll regret. I know you though, and you're going to do what you want, whatever I say, so I might as well not bother.'

I smile at her and shrug my shoulders. I don't think for a second she actually believes me – she simply doesn't see the point in arguing and there's nothing more I can say.

'Look. You've always looked out for me and I've always trusted you,' Jenny says. 'I'm not going to change that now. You'll figure it out somehow, I know you will. Is there anything I can I do to help?'

'Yes, there is. One way or the other, I'm leaving next week on Monday. I won't tell anyone where I'm going and I won't be in touch with anyone. I think that's safer. Except you. If you're OK with it, I want to be able to contact you after a few days, to find out how everyone is getting on. The thing is, it has to be a secret. Like when we were kids, a "cross your heart and hope to die" secret. Can you do that? Even Danno can't know.'

'I guess I don't have a choice, but what about Mum and Dad? You're not going to avoid them for weeks and then leave with all that bad feeling unresolved. It'll kill Mum.'

'I can't face talking to them right now,' I say. 'It would remind me too much of how I've let everyone down. I know it's cowardly, but I just can't do it.'

'Can I talk to them?'

'Yes. That's what I was hoping you'd say. When I'm safely on my way, tell them why I've gone, and tell them I'm sorry to have let them down. Tell them I love them and don't blame them for not lending me the money. But they mustn't know I'm going to write to you. Can you do that?'

'Of course I can. Whatever you need.'

'Thanks. It means a lot. I'm going to take Simon to the casino tonight to see if he sees what I see. I know you don't believe me, but I'm not losing it. I'm really not.'

'Simon? Are you sure that's such a great idea? You must remember how weird he is about gambling. He wouldn't even play pontoon with us when we were kids. And the bets were only matches for Christ's sake.'

'Don't worry, we're not going to gamble. I only want to show him the girl.'

'Well, be careful. You know what he's like.'

1995 - Girl in Casino

I was wheel roller on the roulette as usual last night, showing that my school trip to Paris hadn't been a complete waste of time with my *faites vos jeux* and *rien ne va plus* rolling out like I was a native. My half-decent French may have actually been a bit more to do with this bloke Laurent I met a couple of years ago but that's a whole different *histoire*, if you know what I mean.

So this bloke turns up and starts walking around the tables looking at them all like he was trying to pick out a sofa in DFS or decide who to chat up at a school disco. It was the same guy I'd seen a couple of days earlier, Camel Eyes. I had a feeling he'd dropped in the night before as well, but he was sitting in the far corner, so I couldn't swear to it. He was still staring at me a lot and it was starting to creep me out.

He had a mate with him this time. His mate was very decent looking. It wasn't as though Camel Eyes was uninteresting as I said before, but his mate didn't have the same washed-out, stressed look and was in good shape. Dressed very sharply. A bit vain maybe, lots of brands on display; he probably did his part to keep the men's magazine industry in business.

Made me think of that bloke, Patrick Bateman, in American Psycho; half the book was about competitive brand name dropping and the other half about gruesome, pointless murders. Made for a strange read, but you really got the sense that the guy wasn't thinking like a normal person even when he was just rabbiting on about clothes. The obsession with detail – ties, suits, shirts, anything branded – was a neat way of getting you inside Bateman's head, which was definitely not a pleasant place to be.

Normally punters pick any old table and have a little flutter to get themselves started, but Camel Eyes only looked. Walked up and down with his mate and looked. Only at roulette though – I never saw him as much as glance at blackjack or craps or the slots – and he kept coming back to my table. We've been trained to keep an eye out for people who don't fit, in case they're trying to work some sort of system so, in my first break, I pointed him out to my pit boss.

He didn't seem too worried and typically made some random sexist comment about the punter probably liking my arse, but he did go and check with the girls on reception. We have a fairly stiff entrance fee and the drinks aren't cheap, so the casino makes a small profit even if people don't bet. That way, it's easier to turn a blind eye to time wasters which was what they decided he was; I was told to keep an eye on him and let them know if I saw anything specific.

Come to think of it, that's pretty much a standard policy for any casino; they'll turn a blind eye to almost anything as long as no one is trying to rip them off. Even then, the policy usually stays the same. I read somewhere that over twenty per cent of casino profits come from people who think they have a system to beat the odds. The truth is the odds are what they are – they're in our favour – and the only way to change them is to find a way to actually cheat, which can only happen if you've got someone on the inside.

Well, about half an hour after I got back to my table, it all got a bit more interesting. Camel Eyes was having this super-intense conversation with American Psycho and it looked for a moment like it was going to get physical; American Psycho was so angry. He stood up, looming over his friend, and started shouting and waving his arms like a crazy man before spinning on his heel – in a passable impression of a theatre luvvy having a hissy fit – and flouncing out.

I had to do some croupier stuff and, when I looked again, Camel Eyes was still sitting there on his own. The poor guy really looked like he could use a hug.

2017 - Sally

I like to think I'm easy-going. I was always told it's not my business to stick my nose in where it's not wanted, but Jim is wrong about his children. I don't know if he was right to stay away before; it sounds like it was all very complicated what with Simon taking on the role of stepfather and everything, but now it's different. Hamish and Maggie are both adults, they've got their own lives, and they need to know their Dad's alive and hasn't forgotten about them.

And, you know what? I'd like to meet them and try to build a relationship with them. I'm forty-nine now and it's too late for Jim and me to have children together. We've talked about it on and off over the years but it was never the right time and I think both of us were too afraid of taking on the responsibility until it was too late.

I like the idea of a continuity down through the generations though, and I'd be happy enough to be a stepgranny even if stepmum isn't realistic.

My family was pretty pathetic really. Mum and Dad moved down to Somerset from Nottingham when I was three and stayed in the same house, in the same tiny boring village, forever after. It was only the three of us and we completely lost touch with the rest of our family, which wasn't huge to start with. Mum died over ten years ago. She was only sixty-six but I reckon she finally decided death was preferable to living with Dad.

I suppose I was a bit of a handful for a few years but, for anyone who's grown up in a small village, it's more the norm than the exception. There's nothing, and I mean nothing, to do for teenagers which doesn't somehow come into the category of promiscuity or "causing trouble". We had two pubs in the village, The Plough and The Seven Stars and another handful in neighbouring villages. That was it for entertainment for the nearest twenty miles.

I had some mates who did stuff with their families like surfing or motocross, even golf and tennis, but that wasn't going to be happening in my family. Not ever. There were also a few bullshit things like the Young Farmers or the Guides, but they really weren't for me. Which left the pubs and, seeing as my dad used to drink in The Plough, it actually left me a choice of one.

I was working behind the bar in the Seven Stars from when I was fifteen. Totally illegal but the other barmaid was married to the local copper so no one was complaining. It was a nice enough pub, lots of oak beams, horse collars and farm implements from before the days when the beams were stuck on and the horse collars and farm implements came from a big pub supplies warehouse.

We'd have a lock-in most Fridays and Saturdays and I'd always get bought loads of drinks – just thinking about cider and black still makes me shiver. Unsurprisingly a pissed fifteen-year-old girl got her fair share of attention and I probably got a bit carried away on the odd occasion. It was cool to be treated as an adult. I could believe the day of my escape was getting closer.

The landlord looked out for me though and made sure the least savoury elements kept away from me. He was from East London and had quite a colourful past. Even the hardest of the good old boys knew better than to cross him. There were enough rumours about what had happened to those who had.

It had its points as a system, I suppose. Not politically correct and ignoring every licensing law you could imagine, but there was an element of control and care and the underage drinkers were better off in there than necking cheap vodka down at the rec or hiding out smoking dope in some farmer's straw barn.

Have you ever seen a straw barn burn? There's no stopping it once it's going, the heat is too intense. White hot and pulsing like the eye of a devil. All the fire brigade do is make everything around the barn wet and wait for it to stop burning. Much better if the kids are safely tucked away in the pub.

There was this one Saturday night, the 13th July 1985. I'll never forget it. It was a week after my sixteenth birthday and the night of the Live Aid concerts. They'd dragged the TV downstairs and set it up in the bar. Everyone was caught up in the whole spirit of the event. We felt for a moment like we were part of a world that was bigger than our poxy little shithole of a village. A blink of the eyes and the moment was over, but it changed me, and I think it changed everyone else who was lucky enough to see it.

Anyway, we'd had a great evening and a small group of us stayed on until after two, talking about the whole thing, arguing about which of the artists had been most amazing, saying how incredible Bob Geldof was and even trying to get our minds around what was going on in Africa.

I was still buzzing when I got home and slipped in as quietly as I could. Not quietly enough though. My dad was standing in the narrow hallway, face given a shadowy-yellow halloween mask by the bare bulb hanging just over his head. He was pissed and I could tell he wanted a fight, but I wasn't expecting what came next.

'What sort of time do you call this?' he slurred. 'Where the fuck have you been? You've been out shagging one of those blokes from the pub haven't you?'

'What the hell are you talking about, Dad? I've just come from work. There was this amazing concert, Live Aid, and we all stayed on after. You can ask anyone. What makes you think you can accuse me of ...'

He lurched forward, out of the light. '... You're no more than a little slag like your mother was, aren't you? I know what you get up to. D'you think I'm blind? I've heard them talking about you. Dressed like a fucking tart, and behaving like one too.'

'Dad. Leave it out. You're pissed and it's almost three in the morning. I don't know who's been saying what but it's not true. It's a bunch of lies.' To be fair, he wasn't so far off the mark, but I was buggered if I was going to let him accuse me of anything like that.

He moved closer to me, belching stale beer and cigarette fumes into my face like an insult. 'So what about your old Dad then?' he said, grabbing my arm and twisting me towards him. 'Have you got

175

something for him? Doesn't he deserve a little piece?'

I don't know where the strength came from but I pulled his hand away as though it belonged to a child and sent him flying backwards with a single push. His foot caught on the mat and he fell in a heap of drunken limbs.

I took a step forward and looked down on my pathetic, loveless excuse for a father. 'You keep away from me.' I felt the years of built-up resentment pouring out. 'You ever think of touching me again and I'll go straight to the police.' I turned, went up to my room and locked the door.

Later, I could hear him ranting on at my mother for hours. Someone always had to pay the price of his failures, and there were so many. I never really spoke to him afterwards, but I didn't tell anybody what happened as there didn't seem to be any point.

I got on OK with Mum, I suppose, but we weren't exactly close. I think I was always disappointed that she didn't stand up to my father more. Anyway, when I got a place at university, you couldn't see me for dust. I was out of there and not looking back.

The next time I went back was for Mum's funeral, which was predictably a dismal, grey affair. More people turned up than I'd expected though, and it reminded me that she probably did have a life and friends of her own, even though I'd never seen it. It was, of course, too late to find out by then, and Dad was still the same negative arsewipe he'd always been.

My dad's still alive but apparently he's now got bad Alzheimer's and, to tell you the truth, I'm mostly disappointed, because I think it means he gets off a bit lightly. I'd like him to be able to remember what a shitty husband and father he was, right to his last day.

It could've been worse, of course it could. I mean, there wasn't any actual abuse or anything. The odd slap, but nothing out of the ordinary and that one incident was the only time when he actually stepped over the line. The thing was that he was a small man, not physically small, just small and petty in all the ways that were important. He wasn't stupid, but it seemed as though all of his intelligence was used up on vicious sniping and put-downs. He actually thought he was witty as well, which made it worse.

I can't honestly think of one time when he ever said 'well done', or 'that's really good'. It wasn't in his nature. I'm struggling to think of better ways to describe him, because I'm now sounding ungrateful and petty myself and it's difficult to paint a picture of someone when you're only looking at negative characteristics.

That's him though, he is nothing more than a nasty, joyless, bitter man who has always diminished everyone and everything he touched. Like King Midas, only with shit instead of gold.

I suppose my father is one of the reasons why I want to be involved with Jim's children and future grandchildren. I'm not generally negative or cynical. I've met loads of brilliant, positive people over the years as well as a quite a few who were damaged goods. I'd just like to do my part in helping a few more people to make it through in one piece.

I also want Jim to be involved with his family. He is such a lovely man with a huge amount to give. Maybe he wasn't so great before, but I can only talk about what I know. He is the complete opposite of my father in every way – generous, kind, loving, thoughtful, always putting others before himself – and he has to find a way to overcome his demons and to be a father to his children. It's not too late. I'm sure of it.

The only slightly difficult side of our relationship is when we touch onto the past. Somehow we made an unspoken pact right at the beginning that we would avoid looking back. We both have history and experiences which we're not proud of, and would rather forget, so it seemed to be smart to start a fresh life together and to leave everything that happened before well alone.

It was the right thing for us at the time. I've been so happy with him and I think he feels the same, but there are a couple of nagging issues which won't go away. The first one is that the past is still with us and it will keep reminding us of that fact. Wishful thinking can't just make our memories disappear.

Does Jim's relationship – or lack of one – with Maggie and Hamish belong in the past or the present? I am pretty sure it belongs in the here-and-now and, whatever may have happened before, it is time for him to embrace that part of his life, however painful.

The other problem is that, however hard we try to repress it, our past remains an integral part of who we are. All of our experiences, good and bad, have played a role in building us into the people we are today. There was one evening when me and Jim shared a lot – the night we met again – but never since. I want to know the rest of Jim, warts and all, and I want him to know the same about me.

I've not mentioned this to Jim and don't know how he'll react when I do, but this whole business with Maggie's wedding is bringing a lot of things to a head and I think we're going to need to talk sooner rather than later.

1995 - Fiona

Simon was very geeky about his coffee machine but, it had to be said, the coffee was good. Fiona took a moment to savour the rich, slightly burnt smell and that bitter tang on the top of the mouth before the full taste sensation hit her. It looked so wonderful as well, a tiny, thick-shelled, porcelain espresso cup less than half full with biscuity crema floating on top. She closed her eyes, took another sip, and it was easy to imagine that she was sitting in a cafe in the centre of Rome.

It was the first time she'd stayed the night at Simon's place and he'd gone out to get croissants and a paper, leaving her to enjoy the coffee. The mid-morning city sunshine angled sharply through the sash windows and bathed "The Painting" in yellow gold. It may not have been the original but the reproduction was still hand-painted in oils and must have cost the earth. The natural light brought even more depth and contrast to the scene and the figures – which were barely defined shapes like the woman in Munch's "The Scream"– appeared to be moving imperceptibly, slowly writhing towards the king.

Alastair had gone away for the weekend with Maggie and Hamish. They hadn't spoken much since the day when he'd told her about the whole pension disaster. It was now only ten days or so before the money needed to be paid, but the most Fiona could get out of him was 'Just give me a few more days. I'm going to sort this out. I promise.'. He was in London most days, and quite a few nights, working on his solution.

Over the years, she'd realised that, when two people have been married for a long time, it's amazingly easy to live together "normally" without any real relationship – to go through the motions of a daily life but with no genuine connection as a couple. Fiona could think of quite a few friends of theirs who had been living like that for a long time. Some of them were probably open with each other about the situation, but she suspected others had simply forgotten what "normal" was supposed to look like.

She had never believed she and Alastair would fall into that trap; they had always kept the embers glowing and done whatever was necessary to keep romance alive. Many, many restaurant dinners had ended with discussions of those passionless relationships, and mutual vows to never let it happen to them. She didn't believe it was going to happen to them now either, they just needed to get through this nightmare.

And then there was this. Here. Now. Simon. She really didn't know what "this" was, didn't know what her feelings were or how she thought the future would pan out. In fact, she had made a subconscious decision not to think about "what next" with Simon. For the time being, it was great and exactly what she needed. He, or the situation itself, made her feel young and free, beautiful and sexy and, of course, terribly naughty. She was loving it.

Fiona couldn't help herself thinking of the affair as being "naughty", which she knew was an inappropriately shallow word to describe betraying your husband of eleven years. She had tried half-heartedly to look at the situation more seriously but some part of her refused to do it. Every attempt to tell herself off, to remind herself that she was a thirty-six-year-old, married mother-of-two, only resulted in a mischievous schoolgirl smile and sometimes even a giggle. None of it was real. A part of her realised she was subconsciously suppressing her guilt and that it couldn't last. There would need to be a reckoning soon enough but that would have to wait a little longer.

Simon was, of course, immaculately dressed when he came back in. Even when he was relaxing on a Saturday, everything was "just so". Smoothly shaven, crisp blue shirt, knife-edge creases in his tan chinos and perfectly polished brown brogues; he even had a different cologne for the weekend. A bit of a contrast to Alastair, thought Fiona and went on to wonder what, if anything, Alastair and Simon had in common. She couldn't think of a single thing.

Simon put the papers on the table. 'I got an FT and a Guardian Weekend for a bit of a balanced view on the world,' he said. 'The croissants are still warm. Juice? Another coffee?'

'Juice would be great,' Fiona replied. 'I'll wait on the coffee for now though. Otherwise, I'll be climbing the walls. It was amazing though. I thought I was sitting opposite the Trevi Fountain.'

Simon puffed up visibly; it was almost like he had feathers. 'It's all about the grind and the freshness of the beans. If you get that right, everything else follows ...'

Fiona didn't feel like listening to the coffee-making lecture again and picked up the Guardian magazine, which always brightened up her Saturdays. She was halfway through the cover article when Simon made an awkward little coughing sound.

'Fiona, you know I went out with Alastair a couple of nights ago?'

'Yes, you told me you were going.' Fiona sucked air sharply and stopped breathing. Had Alastair somehow found out about her and Simon? It had only been three times and she had been so careful. How could he know? 'He doesn't know about us, does he?'

'No, no, nothing like that.' Simon was definitely avoiding eye contact though.

'Well, what about it? You had me panicking there.'

'We went out for a drink, but then, afterwards, we went to a casino.'

'A casino, as in blackjack and roulette?' she said. 'But why? Alastair doesn't gamble. We've been to casinos a couple of times in places like Las Vegas, but only for a laugh and because we were there. Were you betting?'

'No, thank God. You know how I feel about gambling. Alastair promised me he wouldn't bet before we went in. He said he'd brought me there to show me something amazing.'

'Go on.' Fiona said, already jumping to conclusions. It had to be a girl. If Alastair was having a fling – and had lied about it – she was in the clear. Or at least not the only sinner.

'The casino is part of the Mayfair Hotel, where Alastair used to stay for work. We went in and they appeared to know him really well. "Good evening Mr Johnson", and all of that business. Once we'd got a drink, Alastair took me to the roulette tables and pointed out one table in particular. "*Can you see?*" he asked me, "*Can you see her?*" I didn't have a clue what he was talking about. The girl he was pointing at was the croupier. Nothing special, quite pretty but really nothing to write home about. I had no idea what he wanted me to look at.'

'So, he's having an affair?'

'No. Well, I don't think so, but it gets much weirder. We sat down at a table and, when I told him I had no idea what he was on about, he looked really sad and disappointed. I know it sounds crazy, but, as I understand his explanation, Alastair thinks there is something special about this girl, some sort of physical aura, which he can actually see. He was hoping I'd be able to see it as well.'

'Bloody hell,' said Fiona. 'I knew he was struggling, but it sounds like he's completely lost it.'

'I must admit I'm beginning to think the same,' said Simon. 'But there's more. To cut a long story short, he's apparently decided this girl and her aura represent some sort of message, a signal from fate. He believes he can't lose if he places a bet at her table, and he plans to take all of the cash he can get together and put it on Red.'

'He's going to do fucking what?'

'He's going to go double or nothing with two hundred and fifty grand of your money. He says he's got nothing to lose.' Simon put his hands on her shoulders and squeezed. 'I had to tell you.'

Fiona pushed him away. 'Damn right you had to tell me, Simon. Has he gone fucking doolally? What the fuck is he thinking? I have to stop him. Fuck, fuck, fuck!'

2017 - Jane

Her house had developed an echo, Jane decided. Unless she stayed completely still and silent, she was followed around everywhere by noises bouncing back at her. Closing a door, putting the kettle on the Aga, walking across the stone tiles or across the wooden floorboards, each creak and clack spoke back to her like a cheesy sound-effect from the cinema. The journey down the gloomy corridor from the living room to the kitchen was worse; her footsteps were like amplified, high-heeled shoe-taps on the tiles of a deserted hospital corridor. Maybe she should have her hearing tested again? Or her mind?

It wasn't only the echo. Jane had begun to see the house as a barren womb, a parched desert. It wanted more life, more energy, more oomph to restore its fertility and return to its earlier, fecund self. Her life was now lived between three rooms, the living room, the kitchen and her first floor bedroom. All of the other rooms had closed doors that were only breached from time to time if Jenny descended in one of her hyperactive, spring-cleaning moods. Jane was happy enough to avoid opening the doors and to conveniently forget how long it had been since the rooms had last been cleaned. It was only the odd spider's web after all.

One of the big selling points about The Old Orchard had been that it was half a mile out of the village. The perfect distance. It had allowed them to have their own space and privacy, but still to be a part of village life. Not so perfect any more. That had been fifty years ago. Fifty years this coming September.

It had been such a struggle keeping the place going without Mike. Apart from the fact she had less and less energy every day, there were so many things which needed to be done that he had previously just got on with. They had lived there together for forty-six years and had each settled into their tasks and responsibilities according to their preferences, skills and strengths. She hadn't realised how much she depended on him for all the little daily things that keep a house going. Despite everything, it appeared they had remained a good team right until the end.

She had been a little surprised to discover that he had continued to play such an integral part in their life, as she had never been able to forgive him for the fight with Alastair; she blamed Mike completely for driving him away. He had always been so one-dimensional. Right-wrong, good-evil, win-lose, love-hate, everything had been made up of absolutes for Mike. His solid, male certainty was a key part of what had made her fall for him in the first place and the same strength and certainty had kept her in love with him for most of their life together.

Strange how, for the last eighteen years of their marriage, it was that pig-stubborn intransigence which had stripped away her love, like a plaster being torn callously from a wound. She wasn't angry with him, at least not after a while. Not hating him, not even disliking him. It was merely an absence, an empty space where there was once something warm and permanent. If she looked back, it actually seemed to have happened from one day to the next. She went to bed one night comfortable in the love of her husband and woke up the next morning struggling to remember what, if anything, they had in common.

It hadn't, of course happened like that. For a while, there had been fights, recriminations and broken teapots until, after a few months, Mike refused to engage with any of it. As soon as anything looked remotely like an argument, he would just clam up and make himself scarce. Thinking about it, Jane realised that was probably the final straw; if you can't discuss things which are important to you with your partner in life, even in heated argument, what is the point?

Maybe that is what had happened to Alastair and Fiona? She didn't really believe it though. There was something more. She knew her boy and he wouldn't behave as he had without a good reason.

Jane sat at the kitchen table and realised she had begun to say goodbye to the house. She could now imagine having a small celebration party to toast the fifty years, and moving on. The house was built for a family with young children. It was time to give it what it wanted. Half a century was a decent innings by any standards.

She would ask Jenny to put in an offer on the cottage. It had been delightful after all, and it wasn't so far away from her few remaining friends. Not straight away. She'd tell Jenny when they came back from France.

The whole thing with France had been an incredible surprise. Amazing, and totally unexpected. Jenny had only told her about it a week earlier, as she'd wanted to wait for the final paperwork to come back from the notaire before saying anything.

Danno and Jenny had bought a villa in the south of France. Not just any villa though, they had bought the Villa Eugenie which she and Mike had owned for twenty years. The villa that had been the setting for many, happy family times while Jenny and Alastair were growing up.

Apparently, they'd been looking for somewhere down there for a while when Jenny had seen that the Villa Eugenie was on the market. She had recognised it immediately and persuaded Danno to go and have a look. He had fallen in love with it and, well, Bob's your uncle, they had bought it.

Jenny and Danno were going down for their first visit as owners the following Thursday and had invited Jane to go with them. It would be her first trip abroad for over ten years but she was ready — she had her shiny new passport and a little plastic folder containing Euros, travel insurance and health card — she had even packed her small suitcase.

It was a wonderful tonic for Jane to have a reminder of those days. The period when they had owned that house had spanned the best years of her life. She would certainly have some stories to tell next week, although some of them involving a sixteen-year-old Jenny and a certain young French man called Xavier might need to be censored. It would depend how well Jenny behaved herself, but a few little hints wouldn't do too much harm.

And then there was the "affair" with Alastair and that older girl, Isobel. She had been gorgeous and Jane had no idea why she had picked out Alastair. She had though, and Alastair hadn't known what had hit him. She could still remember him struggling not to cry as they left to go home after that summer. Heartbreak changes as people age. Much more contemplation and complication intrudes. In contrast, the end of a first love is naked and raw; fragile nerve endings left exposed to searing winds and scorching sun by innocent trust.

A shame we become old and cynical so readily.

1995 - Alastair

Even as I see Fiona open the door, I know something is wrong. She has that look on her face which means I'm in trouble. Big trouble.

'Hello you lot.' She is talking to Hamish and Maggie, not to me. 'You're late, and it's back to school tomorrow. Get your kit sorted out and ready. Supper will be on the table in twenty minutes and then it's an early night. Chop chop.'

We'd had a great weekend. I had discovered that both Hamish and Maggie had started to become people in their own right while my back was turned. We'd borrowed a Southerly 34 from an old schoolfriend; it was a smallish yacht and something I could handle on my own. As it had turned out, they made surprisingly good crew anyway. They'd obviously learnt something in the Caribbean.

I'd wanted to apologise to them both for being away so much, and for being mostly preoccupied even when I was around, but we never got around to it. We were having too much fun. I think they might still be young enough to not really notice what's going on, or at least I hope so. God, I'm going to miss them, but it will hopefully only be for a few months. I am seeing so many things more clearly than I have for ages. Better late than never I suppose.

Once they are out of earshot, Fiona turns to me dripping venom. 'You! You don't go anywhere. Let's get the kids fed and to bed and then we need to talk.'

I stand there speechless as she spins on her heels and returns to the kitchen to finish the food. I'm not quite sure what I've done. I've never seen her so angry. There is, of course, a long list of reasons for her to be extremely pissed off with me, but nothing really new, and nothing that should have got her this worked up right now. I

187

suppose she might have spoken with my mother. That wouldn't have been good. But even then ...

The bed-time routine runs its course – it's almost like normal family life – and I tell Fiona I need to take a shower to wash off the sea salt. I make it last, but can't avoid the inevitable. Fiona is in the kitchen.

'How long do you need to take a fucking shower?' It looks like there are marks on the tiles from where she has been pacing up and down. No sudden change of heart then.

'What's going on? You said you'd give me some time to fix things, and I will.'

'Fix things? Fucking fix things! So you think taking all of our savings and gambling them away is going to fix things. What planet are you on?'

Well, at least I now understand why she is so angry, but I have no idea how she found out. Has she been having me followed? Simon wouldn't have said anything. I made him promise before we went to the casino.

I am still calm. Something has actually changed in my head, like a switch. 'Look you're upset,' I say. 'I wanted to explain but I didn't think you'd understand. Where did this come from? Who have you been speaking to?'

'Simon told me of course. He's your best and oldest friend. Did you expect him to stand by and watch you destroy your life, and your family's life, even more than you already have? He came straight to me after your crazy display at the casino. Seriously, what did you expect him to do? His father's gambling destroyed his parents' marriage. Did you really think he would sit back and watch you do the same to us? Are you so far removed from reality you can't see anything any more?'

I feel the floor shift and slide and need to sit down. I had been certain Simon would keep his word. The foundations of my life are being pulled away one by one in a game of giant Jenga. Thank God this will all be over soon.

'Well?' Fiona is actually tapping her toes, like a caricature of an angry impatient harridan. 'Don't you have anything to say for yourself? I just don't know what I've done to deserve this sort of treatment.'

'Look, I can explain,' I begin. 'It's not as crazy as it seems. I'm trying to do the right thing and I know it will work. You need to trust me a little ...'

'... Trust you? Fucking trust you? I really, really don't need to trust you. Trusting you has got us into this mess. Sell the house, do whatever you need to do to get the money but this has to stop. I want you to promise me something. Promise me on our marriage and our children you'll put this crazy idea out of your head. Now and forever.'

We stand looking at each other as the big old kitchen clock ticks on. Everything else is still, two strangers in their own home, one furious, oozing hurt and righteous indignation, the other sad, resigned and disappointed. I know that nothing I say will achieve anything and understand I have to give up, to give in. It is over.

'All right. Whatever you want. I promise.' I turn and slowly leave the room. I feel nothing. Nothing at all.

2017 - Fiona

Simon didn't come home until the Tuesday after Maggie's wedding. He didn't say where he'd been and the incident wasn't mentioned. The only concession to what had happened was that he brought Fiona a beautiful pair of Louboutin shoes as a surprise present. Fiona played along with the airbrushing of history as she'd done in the past, but was finding it more and more difficult. She didn't need another pair of bloody shoes for Christ's sake, even if they did cost five hundred quid. At least if he'd given her the cash, she could have salted it away somewhere.

She'd calmed down since that evening and realised how difficult the wedding must have been for Simon. Jane and Jenny hadn't even tried to disguise the way they felt, and had completely avoided him. It was even more difficult with Maggie. She'd been so excited about the song Danno had written for her. Not only had it been performed in the church but it had also been recorded by the winner of X-Factor as her next single. Danno had given Maggie the writer's credit as part of the present and she was understandably over the moon.

Maggie had, of course, thanked Simon many times for the wedding and everything he'd done – she was properly brought up after all – but her gratitude was formal and perfunctory. Simon was a keen, sensitive observer and continuously compared the way people behaved with him with the way they behaved with others. Fiona knew he could see that there was no love or joy in his relationship with Maggie. She treated him with wary obligation. He knew it and resented it.

As far as Fiona knew, he had never hit either Maggie or Hamish, but they had certainly seen his anger. Fiona wondered if they had somehow become aware of the "incidents" between her and Simon over the years. God, she hoped not. If they had, what must they think of her?

It wasn't as simple as it appeared. She owed Simon so much. He'd had a difficult life and she knew he tried hard to manage his anger. There were times when it got the better of him, that was all. Overall, they'd had a good life together. Simon was interesting, good looking and usually good company. Fiona could tell he still loved her with a burning passion and, as the years had passed, she had come to love him as well.

Her problem was the same as it had always been – she still loved Alastair, and in a deeper, more visceral way than she'd ever loved Simon. She wished things had been different and couldn't understand how they had turned out like they did. It was all very well and good saying there was no point crying over spilt milk, but what if you desperately wanted some milk, and there wasn't any more?

She probably shouldn't have danced so much with Piers. Fiona knew perfectly well that he and Simon didn't get on and she should have seen how she was waving a red flag. It was such a special moment though, her little girl getting married, and she'd wanted to let her hair down and have some fun for once.

The past twenty-two years with Simon had been good years but, now the children had left, her life had steadily become limited and narrow without asking her permission. They had a beautiful house, she had amazing clothes and jewellery and a gorgeous car, they had smart friends and ate out in smart restaurants. Fiona was sure she'd never aspired to such superficial and shallow goals and, now Maggie had fully flown the nest, she was running out of excuses for accepting the status quo.

She had driven down a suburban cul-de-sac late at night and, try as she might, wasn't able to put the car into reverse. She could always get out and walk but was too afraid. She worried that her real fear was about managing financially without Simon – that she had become too comfortable and spoilt – but had she really become that weak and shallow?

A couple of nights after Simon reappeared, they were sitting after dinner watching TV, a perfect picture of the harmonious suburban couple. The film was Skyfall, which Fiona had seen a few times before and thought was one of the most ridiculous films ever made. On the other hand, action films were always great escapism and Daniel Craig was the sexiest man in the world.

There's one scene in a casino in Shanghai or Macau where James Bond gets into a fight with three or four classic baddie henchmen and, after feeding one of them to a giant Komodo Dragon, Bond ends up using an aluminium case stuffed with four million euros as a weapon. He finishes off the last villain, hands the case to Moneypenny and says, 'put it all on Red', before sauntering out.

It took Fiona straight back to that awful day when she'd found out Alastair had gone back to the casino after all. He'd gone back despite promising her on the lives of their children that he wouldn't and, in that moment, he'd changed all of their lives for ever.

Fiona tried to imagine what must have been going through Alastair's mind. What had possessed him to make him do it, even after giving her such a solemn oath? She still struggled to understand what could have made him break his word or, in fact, to believe it was true.

She'd made Simon go to the casino twice; he'd spoken to both the doorman and the barman and they had both confirmed that Alastair had gone back and had been involved in a major bet. It was in a private room where everyone was sworn to secrecy, but he had definitely been there.

Fiona had completely lost control when Simon came back the second time. She remembered him standing, almost cowering, in the corner of the kitchen while she took out plate after plate, glass after glass, and smashed them one-by-one onto the terracotta tiles. She was screaming and shouting hysterically and her head was threatening to explode.

After a cupboard-full of minutes, her screams of, 'Bastard. Stupid Lying Bastard.' became quieter and quieter, and she'd slowly sunk to the floor in the opposite corner from Simon, arms wrapped around her knees, her breath coming in short irregular snatches.

Simon had waited for a couple of minutes before walking over and sinking down beside her. He was sensitive and smart enough to say nothing and they sat together in a silent sea of broken glass and crockery as Fiona's fury slowly dissolved into emptiness and despair.

'Why would he do this to us?' she'd said to Simon, looking at him with pleading eyes. 'What did we do to deserve it? He's ruined everything.'

The days and weeks afterwards had been a blur. Alastair had gone, she had no means of getting in touch with him, and no idea what to do. The scandal hit the papers a day later and the media descended on their quiet road in Sevenoaks like locusts. They wanted Alastair, of course, but no-one knew where to find him and there was a growing sense of frustration in the press pack – perhaps wolves rather than locusts – which was making them even more aggressive than usual.

Simon took time off work and stayed with them – in the guest room – to help where he could. Fiona didn't know how she would have managed without him. Her world had been turned upside down overnight and she was struggling with confusion and self doubt. She tried to call Piers again and again but couldn't get a reply; her only hope was that he had a few answers.

On the second day, Maggie and Hamish came home in tears after one especially pushy hack had followed them all the way to the local shop and back, asking question after question and refusing to leave them alone. Simon had got up straight away and walked stiff-backed down to the end of the drive. Fiona had no idea what he said to the journalists, but it worked and they were much more careful afterwards. She knew she shouldn't have needed a man to do that for her, but she did.

They had a few thousand pounds in various bank accounts but, by the time the mortgage payment had been made, there was barely enough left to pay the bills for a few weeks. Another disturbing thing was that an additional fifty-thousand pounds had been taken out of the mortgage current account a few days earlier.

She'd eventually managed to speak to Piers, who'd been stuck at a conference in Barcelona. By that time she'd been through all of the paperwork and was becoming increasingly desperate. Piers had no good news for her at all. Apparently, three days before he left, Alastair had cashed in everything he could get his hands on.

All of the evidence pointed to the conclusion that he'd taken the lot and gambled it all away, leaving her nothing. There should be a law against it, some sort of "sound and disposing mind or memory" like with writing wills. There had clearly been nothing sound about Alastair's mind. Could she sue the casino? She doubted it.

Fiona and Simon had visited Jane and Mike to tell them what had happened. They'd decided it was right to let his parents know the facts of the situation, but things hadn't gone as expected. It didn't help that Jenny was there, as she was always suspicious of Simon but, in any case, the story they had to tell was the last thing Alastair's family wanted to hear. They'd all been sitting outside in the garden drinking coffee.

'So run that by me one more time,' Jenny said.

'Simon, tell them again what they told you at the casino,' said Fiona.

'Well, I went there twice,' said Simon. 'The first time, I couldn't get much out of the guy on the door, apart from to say he recognised Alastair from the photo I showed him and he'd seen him go in there a few times.'

'So, you went back?' said Jenny. 'What happened then?'

'Yes, I went back. Fiona insisted,' said Simon. 'She needed to know what actually happened, so I went back and offered the guy a hundred quid if he could tell me a bit more. He told me that, if I had another hundred for the barman, they'd both meet me in the cafe around the corner and tell me everything they knew.'

'This is all sounding ridiculously cloak and dagger isn't it,' said Jane.

'Yes, it is,' said Simon. 'But I didn't see any other option, so I went there and met them. They told me Alastair had been at the casino that night and he'd gone into a private room for something called a Midas bet. A huge and unusual bet which only happens every few years.'

'And what did they say happened? How much was the bet?' said Jenny.

'That's the thing,' said Simon, shrugging his shoulders. 'They had no idea and couldn't find out. I offered them more money, but they insisted they didn't know.'

'So, we don't actually know that Alastair bet all of the money, or whether he won or lost?' said Jane.

'No, we don't,' said Fiona. 'But what we do know is that he cashed in all of our shares and savings and borrowed as much as he could on top. We also know he was obsessed with this girl at the casino and believed he couldn't lose if she was the one to spin the roulette wheel. I made him promise he wouldn't do it, but it appears that he broke his word. If he'd won, I can't believe he would have just taken all of the money and disappeared. That doesn't bear thinking about.'

'The bit about the girl fits,' Jenny had nodded her agreement. 'He told me about her when we had lunch. He was definitely sounding crazy, but I didn't believe for a second he would actually do it.'

Mike had been sitting back in his chair and listening quietly until then, but after Jenny's revelation he leant forward. 'Jenny, what do you mean you knew about this girl and Alastair's mad plan?' he said. 'Why didn't you bloody well tell us? Maybe we could have done something.'

'I promised him, Dad,' said Jenny. 'I gave him my word that I wouldn't tell you.'

Before Mike was able to respond, Jane had jumped to her feet, screeching her chair across the tiles. 'I'm sorry, but I've had enough of this,' she'd said. 'The pair of you waltz in here telling us our son's disappeared and, completely out of character, he has abandoned his family with nothing because he has lost his mind. It doesn't make sense. There's something more to all of this than meets the eye and I think the best thing would be for you to leave now and allow us to fully understand what's going on. I'm sorry if that appears rude but that's how it is.' She'd stood facing them, hand stretched out for a formal handshake. 'Fiona, Simon, thank you for coming and Fiona, please send our love to Maggie and Hamish.'

And at that, they'd been ushered out of the gate and away. Both Simon and Fiona had been dumbfounded until they were a few miles up the road at which point they'd burst into hysterical, embarrassed laughter.

'Did you see the look on Mike's face?' Simon had spluttered.

'Yes, I think that went quite well really,' Fiona had replied. 'When all's said and done.'

Simon had been there for her throughout that crazy time. When the press were camping outside, he'd been there to hold her hand. When the money ran out, he'd stepped up. When the Serious Fraud Office applied to the courts to force her to sell the house, Simon was there to buy out Alastair's share so they could keep it. He'd even sold his beautiful flat to raise the money. Fiona couldn't imagine what would have happened to her and the kids without Simon's help over that period.

When the press realised there wasn't much to the Polaris story without Alastair, they dug around to find something else and, a couple of months after the initial scandal, they seized on the relationship between Simon and Fiona, looking for anything to add a juicy human element to their increasingly thin articles.

Fiona had insisted that she and Simon take care to keep their relationship a secret after Alastair left. At the time the press got involved, she'd begun to believe they had pulled it off, and she and Simon had started to talk about how they might tell people that they had become a couple.

It was sod's law that a journalist from the bloody Daily Mail had smelled a rat and then extended his sniffing around to the weeks prior to Alastair leaving. It was nothing but rumour mongering until an unhappy ex-waiter from Julie's recognised a picture of Fiona and Simon in the paper and called the journalist. The resultant exposé covered three pages, gave a detailed timeline of their torrid affair, and even listed – with surprising accuracy – what they had eaten and drunk at lunch that day.

Simon wanted to sue them for libel but Fiona pointed out that, for something to be libellous, it needed to be untrue and, although the paper had filled in a lot of gaps with guesswork, the main story was true. They couldn't avoid the kids finding out about it and that article had sounded the death knell for their already-strained relationship with the rest of Alastair's family.

Fiona had added the stigma of adultery to that of being married to a white-collar criminal, and it hadn't gone down well in Sevenoaks. Her group of close friends dwindled away and she was even snubbed completely on a few occasions. Now, as a publicly-outed scarlet woman, she was also a predator and likely to seduce any, and all, of their husbands if she were given the slightest opportunity. It was ridiculous behaviour but there had been nothing she could do. Even Elaine had kept her distance, which was the ultimate hypocrisy.

Fiona had no close family and, without Simon by her side through those dark days, life would have been unbearable. He was kind, loving and supportive as well as providing a necessary father figure for Maggie and Hamish. She occasionally doubted whether she should really describe her feelings towards him as love, but they had a good time together more often than not, and she could never forget how much she owed him.

Besides, without Simon, where would she go? What would she do?

1995 - Jane

Jane and Mike weren't talking.

Mike was almost sixty-six and Jane was sixty-two. She believed they should probably have reached a level of maturity where they didn't behave like ten year-olds, but apparently not.

They hadn't been talking since shortly after the last time they had seen Alastair. He had looked so lost and lonely and had clearly hoped for more motherly love from her. Jane remembered watching his face collapse when she had given him a piece of her mind instead. Well, what had he expected? Alastair had always been her golden boy, he could normally never do anything wrong in her eyes, but to present them with such a catastrophic failure was really too much. And just like that, out of the blue, without so much as a by-your-leave. Really, what had he expected?

Jane regretted it now. The poor boy was obviously struggling and, although she liked Fiona, she wasn't convinced she would be giving him much support in the circumstances. Who else did he have?

Fiona, like Jane herself, had made the decision to forgo her own career in order to focus on bringing up her children. It was very difficult to manage both, despite what they told you in the women's magazines, and Jane had always supported their choice. Obviously, most people couldn't afford that luxury but they had been able to and there was no reason not to take advantage of their good fortune.

The quid pro quo was, however, that the working partner brought home the bacon and Jane imagined Fiona was feeling sidelined and betrayed by Alastair's fiasco even though it actually did appear as though Alastair had simply been foolish and hadn't deliberately done anything wrong. Jane now believed the authorities were behaving like bullies and treating her son very unfairly, but she suspected that Fiona — somewhat understandably — wouldn't care and would be mostly worrying about herself and the children.

She had tried to telephone Alastair several times over the past weeks but could only get replies from that awful answering machine. She refused to speak into a tape recorder. It was just so rude.

As if by magic, her telephone rang. Maybe it was Alastair?

It was Jenny. 'Hi Mum, how are you guys doing?'

'Well, I'm fine, thank you darling,' replied Jane. 'But, as for your father, you'll have to ask him yourself as we aren't talking.'

'Oh Mum, how totally ridiculous. You're behaving like babies. How long has this been going on?'

'It's been two weeks now,' said Jane. 'He was so angry after Alastair came down and started by refusing to discuss the subject and then moved on to refusing to discuss anything at all. He's behaving as though he's cut Alastair off completely. I really don't know what to do.'

'Much as I love him, Dad can be a total plonker sometimes,' said Jenny. 'Anyway, I saw Alastair last week. We went for lunch.'

'Why didn't you call? How is he? I'm very worried about him and he seems to be avoiding my calls.'

'Sorry, I meant to, but we've had a lot on,' said Jenny. 'I had a scan yesterday. Everything is fine, but we've decided we don't want to know if it's a boy or a girl, so you'll have to wait before you choose between pink and blue.'

'That's wonderful. It's all so exciting. And you're feeling well?'

'I'm fine thanks. Danno and I are both over the moon about it.' Jenny paused for a moment. 'I'm not so sure about Alastair though. This has all been a huge strain for him, and I'm afraid he's not coping well.'

Jane sat down and gathered herself. She had known that, but hadn't been there for him. Hadn't been there for her only son when he needed her, and still wasn't. If only Mike weren't so obstinate and aggressive.

'Mum,' Jenny shouted. 'Mum. Are you still there?'

'Yes, darling, I'm here. I was just catching my breath. The poor boy. Is he going to be all right?'

'I hope so Mum. He's pretty tough and once he's gone, I think he'll get himself back into shape.'

'Gone. What do you mean gone? Where's he going?'

'I don't know,' said Jenny. 'He's decided that the media are going to have a field day with this. Probably led by the awful rag which you insist on reading. He believes the best thing would be for him to make himself scarce for a few months. I think he's planning on hiding out in southern Europe somewhere. He wanted me to tell you, and to tell you that everything will be OK. He's leaving on Monday.'

Jane felt a metal band tighten around her chest. This mess got worse and worse. 'Thank you Jenny. Thank you for letting me know. Can I call you back later? I need to take a loaf of bread out of the oven.' She hung up the phone and walked over to the French windows, breathing slowly and deeply, in and out. There was no bread.

She could see Mike sitting under the rose pergola, reading his Daily Telegraph. Cover-to-cover, every day. Jane had always found Mike's structured personality and regular habits to be comforting and something to rely on. Now they just made her angry.

2017 - Jim

... The orchard is beautiful, although the trees are strangely blurry like smudged charcoal and the table is brightly lit as though we are sitting in the middle of a theatre set. I feel great. Fiona is next to me, hand resting on mine, both of us a little merry, but only a little. We're staying over anyway so it doesn't matter.

I've actually taken a couple of extra days off work and we have loads of fun plans with Hamish and Maggie, including a trip to Thorpe Park on Tuesday. It's great to have some relaxed family time, I'm really looking forward to it.

Simon is sitting across from us with his latest girlfriend. Six months this time, it must be a record. Simon's girlfriends all look the same – blonde, stick-thin, stylish and very posh. Still, whatever makes him happy ...

My mother has been up to her usual mischief and has been ploughing through lots of sugary toasts and speechettes. She's actually quite good at speaking and it wouldn't be Easter in the Orchard without them.

'I've saved the best for last,' she says, a huge grin spreading over her face. 'Next year, there'll be one more of us at this table.' She pauses for several seconds for dramatic effect, and we all lean forward obediently. 'Jenny is expecting a baby. It's due on the tenth of October.' The announcement gets the open-mouthed surprise it deserves. Mum's glass is raised really high this time. 'To Jenny, to Daniel and, most of all ... to family.'

The sheets are soaking wet and I sit up, breathing heavily. Daniel! Daniel! I knew that name meant something to me. I get up on shaky legs and creep through into my small office. It's still the middle of the night. The ancient PC takes forever to boot up and I find myself tapping my fidgety fingers on the table as the pointless blue Microsoft graphic swirls in inane patterns, doing everything it can to irritate me.

Eventually the damn thing finishes, and I type "Daniel Miller Musician" into Google. There are 156,456 positive matches. I go straight to the Wikipedia entry:

Daniel Antony Miller[1] (born in Croydon, London)[2] is an English songwriter, musician and record producer, best known for his work with Sam Williams, although he has written songs with other artists including Sally Wainwright, Marlon B, John Johnson, Miles Routedge, Marky P, Celine Deniau, Ayshe, The Found, James Green, Katie Mars, Tina Thomson and many others. He has been a part of 32 Gold/Platinum certified albums (UK and US) including 11 (UK) number 1 albums, and 17 (UK) Top 10 singles including 12 (UK) number 1 singles.

I knew there was something about him. How could I have been so thick? Daniel Miller is Danno, my sister's partner of twenty-seven years. My brother-in-law, Danno, is the new owner of Villa Eugenie.

1995 - Fiona

Fiona sat in the kitchen alone, sipping a camomile tea. It was almost ten o'clock, but still quite light outside; summer wasn't far away. She stared blankly at the wall, which was crying out for a new coat of paint. In fact the whole kitchen was looking tired, but there wasn't much chance of anything happening about that. She slumped in the chair, suddenly overcome with exhaustion. The journey of the previous three weeks had drained her, a twisting mountain road winding down into a sunless valley, throwing her around like a doll with each hairpin turn.

She could remember how, as a small girl, she would sit in the back seat of her parents' car with her best friend, intentionally exaggerating every curve in the road and both making wild tyre-screeching noises as they threw themselves back and forth across the seat in time with the swing of the car. That had been fun.

Alastair had told her his plans a few hours earlier. John, his lawyer, had been tipped off that the authorities planned to issue a press release in two days, on Friday morning, which was three days before he had expected.

'I need to leave earlier than I thought,' he'd said. 'I have to be on a ferry tomorrow.'

'But ... but ...' Fiona had been completely thrown, and suddenly realised she hadn't actually expected him to go. '... but what about telling Hamish and Maggie, your parents, Jenny? You can't just go.'

'I have to. It's the only way. I know it sounds melodramatic, but I need to be gone before the press get hold of this. I've posted Piers a power of attorney and detailed instructions so, anything you need, you can speak to him.'

'Where will you be? How can I get in touch with you?' So much was unresolved. They had been avoiding this conversation for days and now it was suddenly upon them, unasked for, and very unwelcome. 'What will we do about money?'

'That will all be sorted out. You'll see. I'm seeing someone this evening in London to organise everything. You shouldn't worry about that.' Alastair had been confident and strong, back to his old self and she found herself believing him, not that she had any choice. 'You won't be able to able to contact me though, at least not for the first month or so. I'll try and get messages to you from time to time. Six months is not so long, and it might be less. I'll get back as soon as I can.'

Fiona had felt bitterness and resentment well up inside her, acid bile pooling in the back of her throat. 'So, you're basically going to run away and leave me to deal with all of the shit? I have to tell the kids what you've done, explain everything to your family and to our friends? I have to deal with a pack of parasitic journalists and distraught employees? I have to do all of this on my own, while you bugger off to pick bloody grapes or something in the sunshine?'

'I can only say I'm sorry so many times Fiona,' he'd said, hands laid open on the table. 'I'm doing the best I can to get us through this. I know it's not your fault in any way. I know you don't deserve any of it. I'm sorry. What more can I say?'

'Don't say anything. Nothing more. I don't want to hear any more of your words. They don't mean anything, anyway. If you're going to go, just fucking go.'

'Fiona, let's not leave it like this,' Alastair had pleaded. 'Please don't ...'

'Just go!' She'd turned her back on him and stomped upstairs to the bedroom.

When she'd come back down to the kitchen half an hour later, Alastair hadn't been there.

Fiona sat at the table, replaying those last words in her head, regretting them and wishing for another chance. Simon was only a dalliance, he wasn't going to replace Alastair. What if Alastair never came back? What if something happened to him? She didn't want their last conversation to be like that. They had too much invested in each other to just throw it all away.

She began to sob. Quietly to begin with and then building into deep, racking, snot-filled snorts of anguish, face pressed into the tablecloth, hands clasped behind her head. Whatever had happened, she knew she only wanted to be with Alastair. There wouldn't ever be anyone else. Why hadn't she told him? Why had she been so cold?

1995 - Girl in Casino

Have you ever had one of those days that seem to go on forever? Not because it's a boring day, but more because there's too much going on. The kind of day when you're afraid there isn't enough room to fit every emotion, every action, every bit of excitement, every fear, into twenty-four short hours.

Yesterday was one of those days.

I wasn't supposed to be working as I'd just pulled three straight long shifts – that's from eight in the evening until four in the morning – and I was due a bit of sleep. Imagine my surprise then, when my shift manager, Janet, turned up in person at my crumby little flat and told me the casino manager wanted to see me. She wouldn't, or couldn't, say why and I assumed I was for the chop. Why it couldn't have waited until the next day when I would be in anyway, I didn't have a clue.

So I'm sitting in Jeremy Kaizer's office together with Janet, the head of security and a couple of the bookkeepers who I don't really know. Jeremy is the General Manager of the casino and he's got a nasty reputation among the female members of staff. I'm glad I'm not on my own.

Mr Kaizer passes me a photo taken from one of the security cameras. 'Do you know this man?' he asks.

It's a picture of Camel Eyes. 'Yeah, I've seen him around,' I say. 'He's been in a lot over the past couple of weeks. I already told our shift manager he was acting a bit strange.'

The head of security turns to Mr Kaizer and nods. 'We received a report on Wednesday 22nd April from the floor and checked him out. His name is Alastair Johnson. Nothing appeared out of the ordinary, so we took no further action.'

'Have you ever spoken with Mr Johnson? In the casino, or outside?'

It takes me a moment to realise Mr Kaizer is speaking to me. 'No. Never,' I reply. 'He kept looking at me strange as I said, but I never spoke with him.'

'OK. Thank you, Miss Richards.' Mr Kaizer pushes a gold-coloured gambling chip across to me. 'Have you ever seen one of these before? Pick it up. Have a look.'

So I pick up the chip. It's really heavy, feels like it's actually made of solid gold but the outside is just plain; there are no markings apart from the number "250" stamped into the metal on each side.

'No, I've never seen anything like this,' I reply, handing it back. 'What is it?'

Mr Kaizer licks his pink lips. 'It's called a Midas chip. Specially made out of twenty-four carat gold for one bet, and one bet only.' He really is a very creepy man. 'Every now and then, a casino will get a special request from someone who wants to make an unusually large bet. If the casino is able to cover the bet, it's traditional to make one of these Midas chips for the gambler. The gold in the chip alone is worth several thousand pounds and the gambler will keep it, win or lose. It's not common knowledge and Midas chips are extremely rare. I believe the last time this casino made one was in 1989.'

'So what's this got to do with me?' It's starting to look less and less like I've been called here to be fired.

'Your Mr Johnson wishes to make an unusually large bet and has made an additional special request; he insists you be the one to spin the wheel. He will make the bet on Red or Black. No other combinations or individual numbers will be permitted.'

'So how big's the bet?' I have to ask. 'What's that chip worth in real money?'

I can now see that Mr Kaizer's smile is mostly creepy because he's shitting himself. This is obviously a big deal for the casino.

'Mr Johnson will be making a bet of two hundred and fifty thousand pounds.'

We're all sitting around the table. Camel Eyes is calm and relaxed, but Jeremy Kaizer is sweating buckets as he takes out a small, polished wooden box and pushes it, almost grudgingly, across the table to Camel Eyes.

'Your personal Midas chip, as discussed, Mr Johnson,' he says. 'It is yours to keep. I wish you the best of luck.'

Camel Eyes takes the chip out of its purple velvet cocoon and turns it over briefly between fingers and thumb before placing it onto the table. 'Thank you,' he replies, and looks over at me. 'Whatever happens, I would like the croupier to have the Midas chip afterwards, please. As a personal gift from me.'

I can't quite believe it and nod my head in thanks, head spinning with thoughts of the things I could do with a few thousand quid, all of which involve getting out of this dump. What just happened? Incredible.

The special gold chip sits on the green baize, placed perfectly symmetrically inside the red diamond. I spin the wheel with a flick of my wrist and the numbers blur. I hear a sharp intake of breath from Mr Kaizer as the ball goes in.

Time is a funny thing. I flash back to that first moment in Bangkok airport and remember standing frozen just inside the airport entrance, imagining two possible futures. Each future was real, playing out in slow motion cinema quality. In one I walk through customs as normal and board the plane, a deep sense of relief flowing through me, and a glass of champagne helping me to celebrate how I'd got away with it; in the other, I'm almost through immigration when I hear that voice behind me, 'Excuse me, Miss. Could you come with us please'. I had known though. Known for sure which future would be the real one. I have no idea how I knew. I just did. I knew exactly what would happen if I didn't get rid of the washbag.

This time is different. The futures are playing out and again there are only two options. Either he'll win, or he'll lose. I have no idea, or sense, of which will be the actual future, but Camel Eyes does. He knows he'll win. I have no idea how, but I'm certain he has no doubts whatsoever.

The wheel slows, throwing the ball up and out, slipping into a number, flicking out again with a disjointed click-clack, once, twice, three times, flick, flick, flick until it settles and finds its final home. The wheel is still turning a bit too fast to be sure where it has landed, but it is looking like ...

I can't believe Camel Eyes gave me that gold chip. I took it to a jewellers first thing this morning to get it valued and they said they'd give me four thousand eight hundred for it, so near as dammit five grand. I don't want to sell it though – not unless I have to.

Last night must have been one of the craziest nights of my life. The casino had wanted to get all sorts of press and publicity around the bet, but Camel Eyes wouldn't budge. He'd drafted some kind of confidentiality letter which everyone had to sign. It was like the bloody Official Secrets Act or something. I wanted to tell my mates about it, to stop it feeling like a dream, but all I could do was to write it in my diary which really wasn't the same.

The funny thing is that I don't think he ever said one word directly to me. Even when he was giving me the chip he was looking at Mr Kaizer. He'd been stalking me for weeks, had asked for me especially, gave me a gold coin worth five grand and then didn't even say 'Hello', 'Thank you', or ask what my name was. What was that all about?

I'd known he was weird when I first saw him, but I don't think he's weird in a bad way; it's just that there's something else going on, something else which is behind the whole thing – the bet, the way he looked at me, everything. It's unfinished business and I feel empty and washed out. I thought about trying to contact him but the "Official Secrets Act" says I can't. I don't actually know why I care. I'm up five grand which is more than I clear in half a year, I should be doing my share of punching the air.

I do care though. I want to know the rest of the story, but I guess I never will.

My crazy twenty-four hours isn't done with me yet – not by a long shot. After four shifts in two days, I've got a day off and I don't know what to do with myself. I can't calm down or concentrate on anything. It's like trying to go to sleep on Christmas Eve when you're a kid. You know you should sleep so you can get up early and enjoy all of your presents but, however hard you try and concentrate on counting sheep jumping over gates in a field, your mind can't help focusing on the scratching sounds coming from downstairs.

There isn't a real Santa Claus of course. You know that, you're not a baby. And even if he did exist, he wouldn't actually come down the dirty chimney, that's plain silly. So what are those scratching sounds then?

I go down to the caff on the corner to treat myself to a fry up and to chill and read the newspaper. It pretends to be a proper caff, but this is nineties London and they also do great cappuccinos, which wasn't an option in the caffs I remember when I was growing up. An Italian bloke called Paulo runs it with his wife and son, and it's a great place to sit and people watch.

There isn't much interesting in the paper, except for Elizabeth Montgomery dying. She played Samantha in Bewitched. The one who wiggled her nose and made things happen. Either something funny or fixing some sort of mess her husband had got into. She had a little daughter, Tabatha, who was about my age at the time, and I wanted to be her and wished my mum was Samantha. Tabatha was a witch too, but wasn't so good at wiggling her nose and, either nothing happened, or she messed something up. I spent so much time wandering round wiggling my nose that my mum wanted to send me to the doctor to check that I wasn't retarded.

I am humming the Bewitched theme tune to myself as I wander back to my flat, *dah dah dah, dee dee dee dee dee dee ...* , when I see a man coming out of the main door to my block. I stop dead and shrink into the wall, my stomach is churning and I need to fight the urge to turn and run. It's fucking Anders, I know it is. He may be a hundred yards away and, thank God, walking in the other direction, but I'd know that Swedish hunk anywhere.

It's been two years since I dumped those drugs at Bangkok airport. I can't believe he's still looking for me. I'll bet they were worth shedloads and got him into a bunch of trouble with his Thai dealer. He must know I haven't got two beans to rub together, so the only reason he can have tracked me down is for some sort of revenge or to make a point of some sort. Do people really do that? After two years? I thought it was only in the movies, but I guess I was wrong.

Well, he's gone for now, but he knows where I live and I'll bet he knows where I work. He'll most definitely be back, so I need to get the fuck out of Dodge, and I need to do it now.

When I get up to my flat – more of a room really – the door is hanging half open and the poxy Yale lock is completely trashed. It looks as though a tornado has hit the place and I begin to wonder if Anders thinks I kept the drugs rather than dumping them at Bangkok Airport. That would make more sense than some crazy vengeance kick, but it doesn't make me any keener to cross paths with him.

Luckily, I always carry my passport and cash, all of twenty-three quid, on me and I don't have anything else worth taking, so everything is just scattered around. He's been thorough though. The carpet has been pulled up, the lid pulled off the cistern and the mattress slashed open. My landlord is going to love this.

It takes me five minutes to throw everything I need into a small bag. A few clothes, my pathetic jewellery collection which Anders completely ignored, and I'm done. I also take my Gambling Commission Certificate of Approval from the broken frame it was in and tuck it in the bag. I'll need that if I'm going to get work in another casino wherever I end up. It's quite pathetic that I framed it though. How sad is that? I make sure no-one is waiting for me outside and set off down the street to the tube.

My short term plan is simplicity itself. Get away from here, go somewhere crowded and completely random, and then figure out what to do next.

My work is in Mayfair and my flat's in Shepherds Bush, so I figure the Hand and Shears pub next to Smithfield market is about as

211

random as I can get. I used to meet a bloke I knew there a while back, but it's got nothing to do with anyone I know these days, or a place I normally hang out.

It's a proper London pub hidden in one of the backstreets next to the meat market and is a favourite haunt of some of the city boys who work around the Barbican. They also do the best rare beef sandwiches of any place I've ever been: juicy, tender beef; soft, brown granary bread; too much butter and a smudge of horseradish to give it a kick.

It's almost one o'clock by the time I get there and the pub is filling up. I grab a pint and a sandwich and find a stool at the end of the bar up against the wall. I'm beginning to calm down, but can't help imagining what might have happened if I'd come back earlier or, even worse, still been in the flat when Anders got there.

What am I going to do now? If he's found me in London, he must have some serious contacts, probably people who know people in the police. I suppose he could have traced me through Nicki, who I abandoned in Koh Samui, but I've hardly seen her since and I don't think she knows where I live. She probably knows I work in a big London casino so that might have been it. There aren't that many of them and Anders could have gone through them one-by-one. Surely they wouldn't have given him my home address though? I suddenly realise this isn't only Anders; his Thai friend must be involved as well.

Well, anyway, I'm not going to find out. I'm never going back to my flat or the casino and I don't think I'll feel safe unless I get out of the UK. It might be an idea to move my cruise ship idea forward a bit. Most of the jobs I've looked at before ask for two year's experience as well as needing you to be certified, but I've got eighteen months under my belt now and I'll find a way to get them to make an exception. I can't believe they'll find me on a cruise boat; I'll be safe there.

2017 - Sally

I'm happy Jim has changed his mind and decided to face up to his past. I don't know whether I'll need to start calling him Alastair now. I'd rather stick with Jim.

When he realised the Villa Eugenie had been bought by his brother-in-law, I think he felt overwhelmed by the coincidence and that he was being swept away by a wave of inevitability. He couldn't hold on any longer.

It's a bit of a worry, turning over this family stone. Neither of us knows what he'll find underneath. After twenty-two years, there will be lots of dark, damp possibilities, some of which probably won't look so good in the light of day.

Circles tend to want to close eventually and it's time for this one to be complete. So much of life is defined by luck – a throw of the dice or a turn of the wheel. You can't just 'do the math' as the Yanks would say. Probabilities are what they are but, if there wasn't something else, lines of fate or whatever, I can't believe any of the big things in my life would have turned out as they did. The odds are much too long.

That night in Skiathos was the biggest one, of course. That must have been more than a chance encounter, it really must have.

When I recovered consciousness and opened my eyes, I was in a strange room, in a strange bed, apparently naked under the sheet and with a wet towel draped over my forehead. It must have been late morning and my head was a war zone. It wasn't only a hangover, although the acid spasms in my stomach told me I certainly had one of those. I reached up to my temple and could feel the soft, swelling bump and the dried blood of a serious knock.

I closed my eyes again, it didn't help much, but anything was worth trying. In fact, it didn't help at all and, seconds later, the pain behind my eyes dragged me puppet-like into a sitting position, head between knees, fighting to control the waves of nausea which were threatening to burst out through the top of my skull.

'Here.' The disembodied voice was accompanied by a washing up bowl which I grabbed just in time ...

... There was nothing left but I kept retching, unable to stop despite the agony of each choking, spitting spasm.

'Some water?' I took the glass and managed a couple of careful sips as my breathing began to return to normal. I risked opening my eyes again and looked up at my nurse. It was the barman from Driftwood. I couldn't see him properly with the sun behind him, and my eyes full of tears, but I knew it was him.

'Take these. They'll help.' I don't know whether the pain had overwhelmed my reason or whether I just trusted the guy, but I took the offered pills without question and choked them down.

'Thank you,' I said, as he took the bowl away and gently helped me to lie back onto the pillow.

'You're welcome. Rest now. You'll feel better when you wake up.'

The pain stayed behind while I drifted away into the white mist.

When I woke again, it was dark outside. Gentle, yellow streetlight slipped through the shutters onto the wall facing me. We must have been on the second or third floor and you could hear the noises of another Skiathos party evening getting under way down below. God, even thinking about it made me feel ill.

I could see the shape of a man sitting opposite me. He saw I was awake, got up from the chair and came over. 'I'm Jim,' he said. 'How are you feeling?'

'A lot better, thanks. I thought I was going to die before. What happened to me? How did I get here? I'm Sally, by the way.'

'Pleased to meet you, Sally,' said Jim. 'There was a big fight after that idiot fell off the bar and the police were called to break it up. You'd been knocked over and cracked your head on the edge of a table. Your friends were arrested, but I told the police you worked with me in the bar and I'd look after you.'

My self-preservation instincts were back and it all sounded a bit iffy to me. 'I don't want to be ungrateful,' I replied, trying to get a better look at him in the half darkness, 'and I don't even want to think about how I got out of my clothes, but why did you do that? Why did you help me?'

'Sorry about the clothes,' Jim said, laughing. 'I tried to look the other way, I promise. But, seriously, you were covered in blood, glass and every imaginable type of alcohol so I didn't actually have a choice. As for why, I was moving you into the recovery position when I saw this around your neck.'

He was holding out my gold medallion. My lucky charm. I hoped he wasn't smart enough to figure out it was solid gold.

'That's mine ... it's mine.' I sounded like bloody Frodo Baggins. 'Could I have it back please.'

'Of course you can,' he said, handing it to me. 'I only wanted you to tell me where you got it.'

'It was given to me. It was a present.' I actually had turned into a hobbit.

He switched on the bedside light and looked at me. 'Do you remember who gave it to you?'

I would have known those dark eyes anywhere. It was Camel Eyes, the bloke from the casino.

I can still remember the dizzy mix of emotions which were churning inside me as I tried to understand the situation, and the impossible odds against me meeting him again like that. The strongest emotion by far was fear. Not fear he was dangerous or anything, but more of a panic that life was taking control of me rather than the other way around. I had always wanted to see him again and to understand what actually happened, but that didn't mean that I wanted my life to be part of someone else's grand master plan.

Being in charge was the only thing in my life I really had to be proud of. I'd certainly made my fair share of bad decisions and, to be fair, it could be said that my life had mostly involved me lurching from disaster to disaster. But they'd been my disasters, my bad decisions and, who knows, maybe I would eventually figure out how to make better ones. The idea of being a pawn on destiny's chessboard didn't appeal to me at all.

Eventually one of us had to say something and, as I've never been short of a word or two, it was no surprise that it was me. 'Bloody hell. Jesus H Christ,' I said, barely managing a falsetto squeak. 'I don't believe it's you. What the hell are you doing here?'

'Well. As I live here, and it was you who came into my bar,' replied Jim with a smile, 'you may want to ask yourself that question. I was quietly minding my own business until you and your wrecking crew piled in.'

'Good point, well made,' I said. 'We'll park that for now. But your name's Alastair, isn't it?'

'Yup. That's my first name, but after everything that happened, I decided to use my second name, James. I've been Jim for five years now. I think I actually prefer it to Alastair.'

What with the shock, the sleep and whatever drugs he'd given me, I was feeling surprisingly normal, but the situation was still surreal enough to make me dizzy. 'I read all about you in the papers after the bet,' I said. 'I saw your photo, and even cut out a few of the articles. I felt like I was an important part of your story, but nobody knew who I was.'

'I didn't actually know who you were either,' said Jim. 'To be fair, I didn't even know your name until a few minutes ago. But you were definitely an important part of the story. I would never have made the bet if it hadn't been for you. How did you manage to keep away from all those journalists?'

'It wasn't so difficult. After they found out about your crazy bet idea, I think they spent a few weeks looking for the mysterious girl in the casino, but they couldn't find me; I'd already left England and I've never been back.'

'Why, what happened?' Jim looked worried. 'There was no reason why you needed to leave.'

'There was actually. The morning after your bet, something from my past caught up with me. It was just bad timing, but I had to get away quickly.'

'As long as it wasn't my fault,' he said, dropping his shoulders. 'I caused enough trouble for enough people in one way or another. I wouldn't want to add one more to the list.'

'No. Really nothing to do with you,' I said, closing my eyes and shivering as I thought about Anders and his Thai friend. I looked at Jim sitting calmly by the side of the bed. 'There's one thing about the whole saga that still bugs me though.'

'Go on,' he said. 'You seem to know more about it than I do anyway.'

'Well. You've got to remember that, unlike everyone else, I know you actually won the bet. You don't seem like a total shit, so why did you bugger off and leave your wife and kids with nothing? And, for that matter, what did you do with half a million quid in cash? If I had that sort of money, I wouldn't be working as a barman in Skiathos and living in a one-room flat.'

'You need to be very careful what you believe just because it's written in the newspapers,' said Jim, running the fingers of his right hand up and down from his cheek to his temple, pressing hard as though he was in pain. 'I left all of the money for my wife and family. I took ten thousand pounds for me, and gave her the rest.'

'Bloody hell,' I said. 'But it doesn't make any sense. Why would she hide that?'

'I have no idea,' said Jim. 'I don't know what she had to gain, apart from hurting me and turning my children and family against me, which she certainly did. I still don't understand it. I'd been a pain in the arse for quite a while but we had a good marriage. I'm sure of it.'

'There must have been something,' I said. 'That's plain nasty. Perhaps it was because of that other bloke? Your friend?'

'Maybe. I don't know and, to tell you the truth, I've stopped caring. One thing I do know, is that I'll never, ever, forgive her for it. I might have been able to forgive her for jumping into bed with my shit of an ex-friend, but lying about the money was so malicious and vindictive that I can't forgive her. It's cost me too much.'

Although it was a bit of a convenient explanation, he appeared to be genuine enough; he certainly wasn't living like someone who had money and, for some strange reason, I was certain he was telling the truth.

'What a bitch,' I said. 'And you've never tried to tell anyone else what happened? Surely you could have explained it to your family. Wouldn't you want them to know? And your children?'

'Maybe,' said Jim. 'Maybe they'd have believed me, but my sister ignored my letters and my parents publicly disowned me in the press. I was on the run by then, a convicted criminal with a drinking problem, and it seemed less and less like a great idea. For the last couple of years, I've been trying to concentrate on moving forward step-by-step.' He smiled and looked down at the floor. 'Unfortunately, I don't seem to have got very far yet.'

He then sat quietly for a few seconds, still looking down at the floor, before continuing. 'When I realised it was you on the floor of the bar, it took me straight back to the night in the casino and reminded me that, whatever happened afterwards, my luck held that night. It made me believe I still have time to get my act together and find something a bit more than ...' he said, waving his hand at the small, sad room, '... this.'

Even five years on, he was a looking a lot better than he had in the casino; he was tanned, lean and, the dark depths of his eyes had an added sparkle. I needed to be back on the boat by eight the following morning, but we sat and talked all night, not only about the casino and the negative consequences of what happened afterwards, but about everything – our hopes, our dreams, how much he missed his children and his family, the things we both still wanted to see and to do.

I have never learned so much about someone, about who they actually are, so quickly. It seemed our shared experience in the casino gave us the permission to be open and honest about everything, to each dip our hands into the well of the other's soul. I can't really explain it. Maybe it was love at first sight. Of course, I'd seen him before, but that didn't count; this was starting afresh, writing the first pages of our common future on crisp and creamy sheets of thick parchment.

My mind was on fire as I walked down through the sleeping streets of Skiathos Town and back to the Marina. Even at seven in the morning the temperature had started to build; the morning sun already making its contribution to the previous day's heat which still glowed from every stone and rock.

Jim and I had swapped contact details and, while a part of me was certain something wonderful was beginning, the battle-scarred realist inside me was telling me it was nothing more than a crazy coincidence and the only thing that had happened was that I'd just spent a surreal, hungover night with an older guy. I mean we hadn't even kissed. It was only a conversation, after all.

My reception back on the boat was very predictable and full of shouts, whoops, applause and innuendo. Most of the others had managed to escape from the bar, although the skipper was at the police station trying to get the engineer and the chef released from jail where they'd spent their Sunday. I had no doubt that a mention of our boss's name would have the cell doors open quickly enough.

The others were relieved to see I was OK, but no-one had actually bothered to look for me when I didn't make it back to the flat. Shit often happened on a shore run and it was every man for himself.

There were always a few good stories to tell after our nights out, but that weekend was a classic even by our standards. And that was ignoring the whole Camel Eyes coincidence, which I had no intention of sharing with any of the others. I let them believe whatever they wanted about how I'd spent the previous day. They would anyway. I had a big cut on the side of my head, but my hair covered it and things could have been much worse.

True to form, our captain had the prisoners freed by ten and we managed to get everything shipshape before the Patrides family rocked up in the afternoon. We all knew how exhausted the others were, but no-one let it show and we only needed to make it through until after dinner when the old man went to bed. A good night's sleep for all of us and everything would be back to normal.

As I lay in my bed and started to drift off, that was the one thought floating around my head. Not a thought, a wish. A young girl's eyes-squeezed-shut wish that everything wouldn't actually go back to normal this time.

The two week's sail back from Skiathos to our base in Monaco was largely uneventful. The sun shone all day every day, chrome railings needed polishing, decks were scrubbed, bathrooms cleaned, beds made, drinks poured, food served and cleared. Task after task, hour after hour, no time for anything more than work or sleep. It wasn't so bad, but it felt even more pointless than it had before. Was this it? Was this life?

When the dolphins came, it was like a cool, refreshing breeze. They were there when the sun rose, about twenty of them, skipping and flashing around us, and they stayed with us all day. Everyone – crew, owners and guests – was transformed by their company. The childish, playful joy which they displayed as they showed off their acrobatic skills was contagious, and normal life was suspended for a while.

Kirios Petrides even insisted on opening champagne for all of us, so we could toast our good fortune. The old shipowner knew the importance of Poseidon's favourite companions and, for a moment, it was possible to imagine him as an intrepid young boy, starting out on his first voyage, stuffed to the gills with passion and ambition.

When we arrived back at base, it took over four hours to get everything cleaned up and organised and it was after six o'clock by the time I finally set foot on solid ground again. I had friends in Antibes and we were going to meet at the Blue Lady pub which was always a good laugh, although the thought of another big party night wasn't massively appealing. I was getting old.

Although Monaco is a dump, the row of big yachts at the Hercules Marina is enough to take anyone's breath away and I was totally engrossed with voyeuristic boat watching as I walked along the concrete pontoon. The disembodied voice coming from behind jolted me out of my dreams.

'Hello, Sally.'

I turned and there he was, sitting on a bench, looking up at me and smiling.

'I didn't want to waste any more time,' said Jim. 'I can't believe this is all coincidence and I'd never forgive myself if I didn't do something about it.'

He stood up, and I ran over to him, filled with instant dolphin joy. I took his face in my hands and kissed him, not trusting myself to speak. Things like this only happened in films or to other people. Not to me.

When I eventually released him, his smile was like a cheshire cat who'd discovered a cream factory. 'So I take it you might feel the same way?' he said. 'It wasn't a wasted trip?'

'No. I mean yes,' I said, stroking his cheek. 'I am so happy to see you. I never hoped for this. I'd decided it was just a crazy dream.'

The fifteenth of July. That was when we began our real story. That's our anniversary and I can't imagine anything could ever be half as romantic as that moment.

1995 - Fiona

'Simon, is that you?'

'Fiona? What's wrong? You sound upset.'

'I'll tell you later. Can you come to the house this morning? I need to see you. I'm going swimming now, but I'll be back by eleven-thirty. Please come.'

'Don't worry, I'll be there. See you later.'

Fiona had woken early with a headache and wandered around the house. She had cried out her grief the night before and was moving back to the mood of self-righteous anger which had been her default state for several weeks. As she paced from room to room, her somnambulant stroll gradually morphed into a stroppy stomp, each step jarring her throbbing head and reminding her of how Alastair had let her down.

These thoughts and the headache had been washed away by the maelstrom of preparing the children for school. Forgotten bags, lunches, books and notes had swirled by, only to be grabbed and re-organised as usual. It was only once she had waved them off that she had allowed her thoughts to move back to Alastair. *Bastard. Selfish, selfish bastard.*

She imagined him setting off, strolling down a sunny country road swollen with relief, carefree freedom humming and whistling its merry tune to him as he ambled along. Was she supposed to feel sorry for him? And what about the money? She had seen nothing but a few weak promises.

Getting engaged and married hadn't worked out exactly as she'd hoped it might when she was a little girl. There was a proper sequence of steps for every romance, which were followed to the letter first in Disney films and by her Barbie doll, and subsequently in all of the trashy bodice-rippers she'd read as a teenager.

Her own life had not followed the proper sequence at all; the discovery that she was pregnant with Arabella was certainly not supposed to predate Alastair's marriage proposal and the romance of proposal and engagement was somehow lost in the discussions about how they were going to manage, and what she should do about her job.

It wasn't really Alastair's fault she'd decided to give up her career. She had been doing well, but it might have taken a while before she was earning decent money and even longer before she actually got paid. There was also the awkward problem that a man simply can't carry a child for nine months and give birth. It did interfere with so many elements of the equality discussion.

They had made the decision together and agreed to review it in three years. She'd even managed to get an informal agreement from her chambers that she would be welcome back if it was no longer than three years.

Worrying about the proper sequence of things went out of the window when Arabella died. Fiona's life was on hold for a long time and, once she got pregnant with Hamish, work was something which never crossed her mind. She was going to do everything in her power to look after him. Nothing else was important.

She had looked at the possibility of going back to work when Maggie had started primary school, but the options for a thirty-four year-old former barrister were somewhat thin on the ground. Alastair had started to earn good money by then and she found herself looking for excuses to keep putting off any decision about looking for a job.

Yes, it wasn't entirely Alastair's fault that she had no real prospect of finding a job now, but the condition of her giving up her potential career was that he provided for them. The terms of the deal were absolutely clear and now where was he, and what was she supposed to do?

She would call Piers later to find out what her options were, but before then she had no intention of missing her swim which was the one thing that had kept her sane for the past few months. When she got back, Simon would be there. It might be pathetic and childish but the only thing Fiona could come up with to get back at Alastair was to take Simon into their marital bed. She would need to be reasonable and mature later, but for now she would stick to being childish and spiteful.

When she got back from swimming at quarter past eleven, Fiona wasn't surprised to see that Simon was already there. He was so keen. Like a puppy.

'Fiona.' Simon rushed over and hugged her. 'What's wrong? You sounded really upset on the phone.'

'Alastair's gone,' she said. 'He's gone.' She held Simon tightly, burying her face into his neck and scrunching up her eyes to hold back the tears. Sadness-loss-anger-frustration, they had blended into a shapeless emotional mush, which had survived eighty lengths of the swimming pool with ease.

Simon took her by the shoulders and held her away from him, looking deep into her eyes. 'Fiona, he doesn't deserve you. He really doesn't. Don't worry, I'll look after you.'

Fiona knew that wasn't what she actually wanted but, on the other hand, just then it appeared to be a very solid second-best alternative. 'Come on Simon,' she said. 'Let's go inside. People will see us.'

2017 - Jane

'Almost there, Mrs J,' said Danno, turning back to her with a big grin. Jenny was driving the hire car, which was a huge black monster, and Danno was giving her directions, from his phone of all things. He was fidgeting around in his seat like a little boy who needs to have a wee wee, and was obviously very excited about the new house.

'I can see that, Daniel,' said Jane. 'I might be ancient, and a lot of things have changed, but I haven't forgotten what the *rue des Singes* looks like. And, rather surprisingly, neither the mountains nor the sea have moved much since I was last here.'

'Now, now, Mum,' said Jenny. 'You know that sarcasm isn't attractive in a lady.'

She was doing it again, the cheeky, little minx. Using all of Jane's old aphorisms against her. She could see she needed to acquire some new ones. It really was too much.

They pulled up in front of the gates of Villa Eugenie and Jane was transported back in time. Many things might have changed but the gates hadn't. They were classic, silver-painted, wrought iron, with vertical metal bars leading up to a row of circular motifs and topped off by elegant scrolls which rose to a joined heart in the middle. She had always loved them.

Danno was fumbling in his pocket. 'Hang on a sec,' he said. 'The estate agent sent me the remote control for the gate. I've got it here somewhere ... here we go.'

As the gates swung smoothly inwards of their own accord, Jane had to admit that even they had actually changed a little.

'How are you doing, Mum,' said Jenny. 'You must be exhausted? Do you need a nap?'

It had been a long day for Jane already what with all of the waiting around that flying inevitably entails, but she didn't feel tired and doubted she would be able to sleep anyway. She was struggling to control the avalanche of memories which was sweeping her along and threatening to bury her. A lot had changed, of course, but the main features of the villa were the same and the view down over the sea was exactly as she remembered it. How many hours had she spent looking out over this view? It was wonderful to be able to do it again.

'Thank you darling,' she replied. 'I'm fine for now. I'm simply trying to take it all in. It's so wonderful to be back. I had no idea how much I missed this place. I'll take a stroll around, if you don't mind.'

'Knock yourself out, Mrs J,' said Danno. 'We'll get the stuff out of the car and get everything switched on. You have a little wander and reacquaint yourself with the old place, eh?'

Jane took the gravel path beside the fat-stemmed climber which ran up along the south-west facing wall. It had to be the original wisteria she'd planted so long ago. She could remember taking such care to keep it watered on one of their drives down. Jane had grown it from a cutting at the Old Orchard as she had been determined to have a piece of England at the Villa Eugenie. The wisteria had finished flowering now, but looked happy enough and she ran her hands over the bark noting that they were both equally wrinkled, and showing their years.

The main garden had changed quite a lot. One of the previous owners had added another, lower terrace to make the swimming pool into one of those infinity pools which seemed to be all of the rage. Jane couldn't quite see the point but imagined that it might be nice to stand in the pool, resting on the edge with an uninterrupted view out over the sea. She would have to give it a try, but not today.

The new, lower terrace was made into a gravel piste for petanque, which was rather charming. There was even a little, round table with a Ricard sun umbrella. Perfect for a glass of pastis as the sun was setting. Nothing was, in any way, offensive and she and Mike might have made similar changes to things if they had kept the place for longer.

There was a big rattan chair on the terrace padded with fat, enticing, white cushions. The furniture was different, but the comfiest chair was in the same spot as it always used to be and Jane sat down to enjoy her favourite view for a little longer and to give Jenny and Danno time to explore their new house.

She must have fallen asleep in the chair – she was obviously more tired than she thought – and it was dark when she woke up.

'In the nick of time, Jane,' said Danno as he laid plates out on the table. 'Supper's almost ready. Jen got one of those spit-roast chickens from Carrefour and she's just making the salad dressing. Can I interest you in a glass of rose?'

'That would be wonderful. Thank you Daniel. Could I also have some water please? I'm parched.'

'On their way.' Danno gave a little waiter's bow and flourish, and disappeared into the kitchen.

As Jane got up and took a seat at the table, Jenny came back in carrying a bowl of dismembered chicken, flesh steaming and sticky, grill-black skin begging to burn impatient fingers. She held up a small jug. 'I remembered the sauce, Mum. I haven't had this since I was a kid. I don't think there's anything like it anywhere else in the world.'

Jenny and Jane had always been the biggest fans of the spit-roasted chicken with its rich, meaty gravy, sticky and salty with herbs. It smelt like a walk in the hills, and was as delicious as Jane had remembered.

Jane lifted her glass. 'To your beautiful new home,' she said. 'To Villa Eugenie. I know you'll spend happy times here. Thank you for letting me share in this.'

'Thanks, Mum,' said Jenny as she and Danno joined in the toast. 'To Villa Eugenie!'

Jane looked down at her plate, overcome with a surge of emotion, which prickled behind her eyes. She took a few deep, sighing breaths. 'I've got one more toast,' she said. 'It's been very difficult, but I've finally made up my mind.' She lifted her glass one last time. 'To The Old Orchard. Thank you for fifty wonderful years. Up and down maybe, certainly happy and sad, but wonderful all the same. It's time for me to move on. I've decided to sell up and buy the cottage.'

'Oh, Mum, that's great news,' said Jenny. 'I have been worrying about you rattling around in that big house on your own, and it'll be super to have you just down the road.'

The rest of the meal passed in a blur with Jenny moving into practical mode and starting to plan all of the logistics, estate agents, solicitors, removals, and dealing with an accumulated lifetime of "stuff". She was in her element. After a while, Jane wasn't able to keep pace with the busy stream of words and she pushed herself up from her chair.

'Thank you for a lovely meal, darling,' she said. 'I think this old lady is ready for her bed. We'll have plenty of time to talk about this in the morning.'

They had argued over who should have the master bedroom. Danno was insisting Jane should have it as it was a trip down memory lane for her, but Jane wasn't having any of that. It was their house now and she was only one small woman. The guest room would be perfect. She won, of course. Danno was a lightweight when it came to marathon arguments.

Jane preferred the guest bedroom anyway. It was smaller but had the same open view from the window, as well as its own private terrace with a couple of café chairs and a small round table. It was still almost too hot, even at eleven o'clock at night, but Jane had always loved the heat. Now she was older, she found there was an added benefit. It made her ache a little less.

She could hear Danno and Jenny talking as they cleared up the last few dishes. Jane loved the fact they were still happy together and hoped it would stay like that for them. They made one another laugh and seemed to be in tune with each other all of the time. She had learned from her own experience that finding happiness with a single partner and holding onto it for a lifetime is a much rarer thing than one would once have imagined.

Their quiet voices talking about ordinary day-to-day things was comforting and familiar as she lay there looking up at the ugly glass ceiling light hanging above her. That would have to go.

'Will you blow the candles out, please.'

'Already done.'

'Leave the chicken dish. We can sort it out tomorrow.'

'OK. Don't forget the agent's coming round in the morning at ten thirty.'

'I'll be up way before then. I have to ...'

As Jane fell asleep, the soft sea breeze floated the curtains in and out as though the room was breathing with her. For the first time in a very long time, her dreams were full of light and warmth.

The moon was a sharp sliver cut into a clear, star-bruised sky. Tomorrow would be another sunny day.

1995 - Alastair

I have one last thing to do before I go. I don't need to be on the ferry to Calais until late afternoon which gives me plenty of time to go back to the house while Fiona is out swimming. I know she won't miss her pool session even with everything else that's going on.

I feel buoyant, energised, and ready to take on the world again. I've been struggling to cope with the body blows which have been pounding me one by one over the past few months and which have seemed to materialise from nowhere. Now the luckometer has swung firmly back in my favour, however, everything makes sense and the earth is back on its proper axis.

Clearly, it is not ideal that I need to leave my family for a few months, but they are now well provided for and it will soon all be forgotten. I will come home a new man and find work I can believe in and which allows me to be a better person, to spend time with friends and family, to get my priorities right. Yes, a few months of separation is a small price to pay for that.

As expected, Fiona's car isn't there when I arrive. I should have at least forty-five minutes before she's back. We've been living in the house for almost five years now and, as I walk into the hall and move from room to room, everything is superficially normal, just as it always is. My perspective has changed though and I'm seeing everything with new eyes. When did it move from being my home to "the house"? It is all beautiful, of course. The house is lovely and Fiona has very good taste, but I can now see how it's missing a bit of soul or something. I can't quite put my finger on what.

Neither Fiona nor I are big "keeping up with the Joneses" people but, in a place like Sevenoaks, it does creep up on you. It seeps into your skin while you sleep. Maybe we should move when I get back? Look for a simpler life which isn't so dominated by the acquisition and display of objects. There'll be plenty of time to think about such things.

I leave the envelope on the kitchen table, leaning up against the pepper grinder. It took me an age to write the letter. I wanted to say so much more, but it was important to get across the practical details without writing an essay. Fiona will understand.

2017 - Jim

My teaspoon chatters nervously on the saucer of my coffee cup as I walk back to the table. I've always had a steady hand, but not today. Sally left home before me and is already sitting under a sun umbrella, nursing her *infusion de tilleul* with both hands. 'You know you look like shit, don't you?' she says.

I put the cup down and sit next to her. 'Yup. I looked in the mirror before I came out. I remind myself of Tom Hanks in Philadelphia, but more gaunt, and without the lesions.'

I'm usually quite comfortable with how I look for my age. I'm slim, physically fit and tanned, not too many wrinkles considering how much time I've spent in the sun, and I've still got all my hair. That man wasn't looking out at me from the mirror this morning. Someone had stolen my body during the night.

'You need to find a way to relax. Take slow, deep breaths and lay off the coffee.'

Easy for Sally to say. It's been three days since I realised our new client, Daniel, is actually Danno, my brother-in-law, and I've not slept properly since. Sally and I talked about what I should do for ages, but I suppose I knew deep inside that these ridiculous coincidences were more than just happenstance. One way or another, it was time to stop running.

And so I gave in and agreed I would come to today's meeting and face up to my past. Apart from anything else, I wanted to understand why Jenny never replied to my letters. That had always been the final straw for me and probably the biggest "if only" of all.

Running, hiding and keeping under the radar has been my life for so long that it's become an integral part of my world. I've built so

232

many walls based on foundations of self-justification and rationalisation that I haven't known what to think or feel as the clock has inched forwards over the past three days. My guilt has always been balanced by self-pity and righteous indignation. I tried to do the right thing in an impossible situation and it wasn't all my fault. I managed to provide for my family despite everything. Why hadn't Jenny replied to my letters? How could Fiona and Simon have got together so quickly? Why had no one ever tried to find me?

A flash of my looping mental slideshow was enough to jolt me out of my attempts to find comfort in excuses. I was slapped with visions of Maggie walking down the aisle with Simon by her side, the wedding's top table without me, the father-daughter dance with no father. I had let her down, let both my children down. What had they done to deserve that?

I didn't actually believe my own publicity. I had created this mess and, whatever happened after I left, I should have done more to try to rectify the situation. Instead I went on a pathetic quest for justification and stayed in hiding, moaning about my bad luck and dulling the edge of my pain with cheap whisky in the dingy corner of some poorly-lit dive or other.

Once, when I was younger, I was ordering a beer in a Singapore bar when the middle-aged man sitting at the bar turned to face me. He looked up, raised his glass, and composed his soft, sagging features into a smile of sorts. 'Cheers,' he said. 'Welcome to paradise. I'm just travelling the world. Me and my friend, Johnny Walker.' It was as though he was playing a looped tape recording and I remember wondering how many times he'd said the same words and in how many places. He then turned away and looked down at the bar, watching the ice cubes in his whisky glass spin slowly to a standstill.

I had often told that story – half joke, half salutary tale – and always wondered what could happen to turn someone into such a sad excuse for a man. I realise now that, after leaving, I had been that very man for many years. Probably worse.

Even once the Polaris CEO had been extradited and the threat of a jail sentence had gone away, I was still too cowardly to slink home.

Afraid of bankruptcy, loneliness and shame, I convinced myself the window of opportunity had closed and I would do more harm than good.

As the years went by, the walls got stronger and I didn't have to try so hard to buttress them. It really was too late and everyone was better as they were. My father's death shook things a bit but not for too long. It was only when I heard about Maggie's wedding that my defences began to crumble.

This morning, the situation got worse. Sally called to confirm the meeting at Villa Eugenie and Danno mentioned in passing that his mother-in-law was staying with them. I had been starting to regain my balance and to prepare myself to see Jenny again after all this time, but this took things to a whole different level.

My mother. My mother for Christ's sake. We haven't spoken for more than two decades and I've been angry with both her and my father for all of this time. They cut me off, abandoned me when I needed their help most. Told the world how much I'd shamed them and let them down. Again, my pathetic attempts to stoke the fires of righteous indignation are too feeble and fail miserably.

I should have at least tried to be in touch, to explain myself one more time. Maybe she would have forgiven me, even if my father couldn't. Maybe she'd never actually given up on me anyway. I add one more slide to the show. My mother is standing under a black umbrella at my father's graveside, framed by the hard, merciless rain. As the coffin is lowered, she lifts her gaze from the single anemone clutched in her hand and looks up, searching the gathered faces hopefully, desperately wishing for the prodigal's return.

It is no wonder I look terrible. I feel even worse, standing alone in an empty field, surrounded by piles of rubble. All of my walls have collapsed and I have nowhere left to hide.

'Jim ... Jim ... Snap out of it. We need to go or we'll be late. You know what traffic on the A8 can be like.' Sally's voice is an instant tonic and reminds me that I don't have to do this alone. 'Don't worry darling. I'm here. I'll be with you.'

As we drive over to Eze, I have another flashback to that moment, almost half a century ago, when I sat in my parents' car as we drove home. The feeling of not trusting myself to speak is the same but there is something else, something dangerous, sitting beside me and my self-centred sadness.

My dangerous companion is hope. A part of me can't help being excited and imagining glass-half-full champagne moments of reconciliation and redemption. Dangerous indeed. I need to manage my expectations. The best I can hope for is to have a chance to explain myself and to try to understand why the other players in our small Greek tragedy acted as they did. I doubt reconciliation is on the table. That ship will have sailed long ago.

As our little jeep bounces and rattles along, Sally is more chatty than usual. I think she understands that I need to avoid sinking too deeply into my thoughts. 'You know you've never really told me why you cut yourself off so completely from everyone,' she says. 'I understand why you thought it would be good to be away for a while, and the Fiona-Simon thing must have been very hard, but it doesn't seem like enough.'

'Well, there isn't anything you don't already know,' I reply. 'But you're right, and that's what goes round and round in my head the whole time. When I look back with 20:20 hindsight, what happened didn't justify me staying away. In retrospect I think I was wrong, but the only thing I can say is that it seemed right at the time. I wasn't in my right mind, and everything that happened – the penalty not being paid, Fiona and Simon, my parents disowning me, and my sister not replying to my letters – piled up one by one until something finally broke inside of me, and that was it. I gave up.'

'That sounds so sad,' she says. 'Look, we don't have to talk about this now, if it's too painful.'

'No. It's all right. I'm going to have to dredge these memories back up again when we get there, so a bit of a rehearsal is probably not such a bad idea. My final lifeline was always Jenny. I told her everything and I knew she wouldn't judge me, or listen to what the media had to say. I had agreed she would be my link to home. We would write to each other and no-one else would know.'

'... And?'

'... And it turns out I was wrong. She obviously did judge me, and sided with my mum and dad and everyone else. I wrote to her three times but she didn't reply. I've never understood why.'

'Well, you're going to find out soon enough,' says Sally, as we pull up outside those beautiful wrought-iron gates. 'Don't worry. It'll all be OK. I'm here.'

There isn't a good way to soften the shock of my arrival, so we walk up to the front door together and ring the bell. Danno answers. He's changed, of course – he must be almost fifty now – but he still looks like Danno, a successful, manicured Danno.

The double take is almost classic slapstick as he sees me. He flinches backwards. 'Alastair? Alastair? Is it you?'

'Who is it?' Jenny's voice echoes from inside.

I stand still, arms by my sides, and nod. 'Yes, it's me.'

'It's only the people from the management agency,' shouts Danno back into the house. 'We'll be through in a sec. Put the kettle on will you?'

'Alastair. Fucking hell.' Danno steps forward and throws his arms around me. 'It's so good to see you, man. Jesus. Jenny's going to wet herself.'

I can't help myself and burst into tears. I had no idea what to expect but it wasn't this. We stand hugging while I get my act together. 'You too,' I struggle out eventually. 'It's great to see you too.' I take a step backwards. 'This is Sally, we're business partners and, well, everything partners really.'

'Pleased to meet you Sally,' says Danno and then turns back to me. 'This is fucking insane. It must be over twenty years. I never thought I'd see you again. Where have you been? What have you been doing?' He pauses for breath. 'Shit, we can't stand around here all day. It's not me you need to see. Better face the music.' He moves back towards the house.

I put a hand on his shoulder to stop him. 'Before we go in, how's my mother? Is she well? Will she want to see me?'

'She's in pretty good shape for an old girl,' says Danno, 'and, yes, of course she'll want to see you. She might have a coronary, but she'll die happy.'

We walk into the living room...

Danno leads the way and goes over to Jenny, who is standing by the window. My mother is sitting in an armchair concentrating on some sort of newspaper puzzle. He clears his throat. 'Ladies, you won't believe this, I've got some really quite amazing news ...'

Jenny screams, runs over, and throws her arms around me.

'... Alastair's here,' says Danno.

My mother's head snaps up, birdlike, but she can't see me behind Jenny. 'Alastair? What do you mean, Daniel? What are you talking about?'

I half extricate myself from Jenny's hug and face my mother. 'It's me, Mum,' I say gently. 'It's me.'

She lifts one hand to her mouth. 'Oh ... ' She half rises, but drops back into the chair. 'Oh, Alastair. Alastair. It can't be you. I don't ...'

I walk over to her, kneel in front of her and take her face in my hands. 'It really is me, Mum. I'm sorry it's been so long.'

The vacant look of shock disappears from her eyes and she's herself again. I can see at least some of the golden-boy-who-can-do-no-wrong is still there as she gently pulls my hands from her face and envelopes me in her arms. 'Oh, my boy. My poor boy. Why did you stay away from us for such a long time? We missed you so much, and I've worried about you every day. Why didn't you get in touch?'

'I did try, Mum,' I reply, 'but it didn't work out. I'm sorry about Dad. Did you get my flowers?'

'Yes, dear. And I knew they must be from you. No one apart from you and Jenny would have known what to send.' She pulled away and looked at me, her eyes sharp and glittering. 'In what way didn't it work out? It must have been possible to let us know you were all right.'

'I wrote three letters to Jenny, but she didn't reply to any of them and, on top of your article in The Telegraph, I assumed you must have all decided it was better for me to stay away.'

'That bloody newspaper article.' My mother spits out the words. 'I never forgave your father for that. But that doesn't explain twenty-two years. Why didn't you get in touch afterwards?'

I stand up, helping my mother stand, 'It's complicated, Mum. I was in a dark place for a long time. It was as though something had snapped inside of me and I wasn't much use for anything, or to anybody, for years. I think I had some sort of breakdown and, by the time I surfaced, with the help of Sally, it all seemed to be too late.' I turn to Sally. 'This is Sally, by the way. Sally, my mother, Jane.'

'Very pleased to meet you, Sally,' says my mother, 'I'm sure we'll have a chance to meet properly shortly, but you'll understand this is all a bit overwhelming.'

My mother and I stand in the middle of the room, hugging for long, wonderful moments and I can feel her tears soaking into my shirt. I've waited so long for this moment. 'I missed Maggie's wedding,' I say, eventually. 'How can I have missed my daughter's wedding? Is there any way she'll forgive me? And Hamish? They're all grown up now, and they don't know me at all.'

My mother looks up at me. 'Yes, you should have been there,' she says. 'It was a wonderful day, but it wasn't right without you. You should have been there, and I doubt Maggie will ever forget that you weren't, but she's a lovely, sweet girl and she might forgive you one day. They both might, but it won't be easy.'

Despite her age and all of the shock and emotion, my mother is still the sharpest tack in the room. She turns to Jenny. 'Jenny, what's this about three letters? You never told me about any letters.'

Jenny is looking down at the floor. 'Well, I was so pissed off with everybody at that stage,' she says. 'You and Dad for not being there for Alastair and giving that horrible newspaper interview, my useless brother for running away and leaving his family penniless, and Fiona for jumping straight into bed with that creep, Simon. I was four months pregnant with my first child, hormonal and irrational. I threw the letters in the fire without reading them. I've relived my decision a million times since, but it was too late and I didn't know how to get in touch with him.'

'You stupid girl,' says my mother. 'Do you have any idea what ...'

'Hang on,' I interrupt. 'I didn't leave my family penniless. That's not true.'

Now, everyone is confused, and the three lead actors – my mother, Jenny and me – are locked in a Mexican standoff of blank stares.

'But Fiona told us you did,' Jenny says. 'She and Simon came around to see me, Mum and Dad a few days after you left. She told us you'd lost all the money at a casino and left her, Maggie and Hamish with nothing.'

'We were all so disappointed, darling,' says my mother. 'We understood you were under huge amounts of strain but nobody expected you to behave like that. Not you.'

'But it's not true.' I am almost lost for words. 'It's complete rubbish. I didn't lose the bet. I won two hundred and fifty thousand pounds. Sally can tell you. She was there.'

'It's true, Mrs Johnson,' says Sally. 'I was the croupier, and this was the biggest win ever in a British casino. Alastair bet a quarter of a million pounds on Red and won.'

I don't know who is the most confused and shocked. My mother takes two steps backwards and slumps down into the sofa, one hand pressed to her chest. Jenny's face is a picture of anguish, loss and pain and I am a complete mess; thoughts and emotions buzz around inside of me with no direction or control. My head is a beehive which has just been knocked over, and the bees haven't yet figured out what has happened and who is to blame.

'Oh my God,' says Jenny, eyes red and hands clenched in front of her. 'I am so sorry. I should have known. I should have trusted you. How can you ever forgive me?'

For a few long seconds, as I think of everything I have missed out on over those long years, I consider the possibility of never forgiving my sister, but this is surely a time for reconciliation and rebuilding and I must remember that. I look at Jenny. 'It won't be easy,' I say. 'There's so much to take in and understand, but you weren't to blame for what happened. We'll get there.'

'So what happened to the money?' says my mother in a quiet voice.

'I left four hundred and ninety thousand pounds in cash for Fiona before I set off. I put it in a safety deposit box in her name.'

'But she didn't say anything about that,' says my mother. 'And in fact, quite the opposite, she appeared to be furious with you for leaving her with nothing.'

'Thinking about it,' says Jenny. 'Fiona and Simon have always lived unusually well considering what he probably earns. Nice cars, designer clothes and posh restaurants. It makes more sense now.'

'Oh, my dear boy,' says my mother. 'You poor angel. Why would Fiona do such a terrible, selfish and spiteful thing. I always knew you wouldn't just leave your family with nothing and disappear.'

'Oh God,' I blurt out. 'All this time, you thought that about me. No wonder you didn't reply, Jen. Twenty-two years, twenty-two stupid, bloody years and all this time ...' I walk towards the terrace doors. 'We've got so much to talk about, so much catching up to do, but this is too much. Give me five minutes. I need to get my head around everything. I won't be long.'

I stand alone on the terrace, looking over the pool which hasn't yet been opened for the season. Swimming pools always look so sad when they haven't changed out of their winter clothes. The cover is sagging, a bubble of rainwater floats on top, rotting leaves and pine needles cover everything with a black, gritty scum.

It's a magical process, opening up all of our villas for the season. It takes so little to transform this dismal image of death, despair and decay into a clean, sun-glinting blue oasis, a picture of invitation and hope, filled with memories of years of laughter and joy. A true metamorphosis.

I am still lost for words. A part of me knows what I want to say. I want to scream out that Fiona is a fucking bitch and has ruined my life with her lies, but it's not true. At least not the bit about my life being ruined. I'm reserving judgement about the fucking bitch part.

If I'm honest with myself, my life is better than it ever was and better than it ever could have been if I'd stayed. There have been unecessary and tragic misunderstandings, but that can't be changed and Sally makes up for those and more. Even now, she is here for me, I can see her through the window, laughing and joking with my mother.

Now my family knows the truth about me, and I know why they behaved as they did, maybe we can start to repair some of consequences of those lies. Most importantly, I might be able to see my kids if they haven't been too poisoned against me. It won't be easy, but I'm going to try. You can't turn back the clock and revisit the past, but you can always hope to compensate in some way in the future.

Simon turned out to be even more of a devious, fucking Judas than I could ever have imagined, and I suppose he may have influenced Fiona's decision, but that's no excuse; she was a grown-up with a mind of her own. She made her choices and it had never crossed my mind that she might decide to keep all of the money and then lie about it. Perhaps she was always that selfish and materialistic and I just hadn't noticed. If so, they were made for each other and good luck to them.

I have been thinking a lot recently about the whole episode with Sally and the casino. I still can't explain the visions which I saw and am now convinced I'll never be able to. The thing I have come to realise, however, is that — whatever it was I saw — it probably didn't mean what I thought it did at the time. I now believe some part of me was telling me to be with Sally, that she was special for me. I suspect the whole business about the bet and Lady Luck was nothing more than me rationalising the taking of a delusional, insane risk when I was desperate and saw no other alternative.

As far as the bet goes, I now think I just got lucky. No magic. No fate. As far as my relationship with Sally is concerned, I thank fate every day.

Sally and I don't need much to be happy and I am thankful to be living the simple life that we do. One day at a time. There is a great quote from Edward Norton, which hangs on the wall above my desk:

We buy things we don't need, with money we don't have, to impress people we don't like.

That was me, once upon a time. But no more.

1995 - Simon

Fiona went straight upstairs and Simon wandered into the kitchen. It was strangely exciting being in Alastair's house, not as Alastair's friend or a friend of the family, but as Fiona's lover. He didn't feel guilty. It was his turn, his moment. Alastair had always been the golden boy. It was about time the tables were turned.

On the kitchen table, propped up against the pepper grinder was a blue envelope, 'My Dearest Fiona' scrawled across the front. That was strange. It was unopened, so Alastair must have come back to leave it, and not long ago. Simon shivered. Whatever was inside, he knew that it wouldn't be good.

He needed to know what Alastair had to say, but took great care not to tear the envelope as he slipped out the single sheet of paper. There was something else inside – it was a small brass key. He examined the key for a few moments before putting it carefully on the table and starting to read.

Darling Fiona,

By the time you read this, I'll be gone. I'm certain it's for the best and, hopefully, it won't need to be for too long.

I've let you and the kids down so badly over the past few months and I can only say again how sorry I am. I am so lucky to have someone who's prepared to stand by me despite my behaviour.

I knew that you thought I'd finally lost it when I told you about my casino plan. I realised I was never going to be able to explain why I was so certain I would win. So, I lied to you one last time.

I went to the casino last night with two hundred and fifty thousand pounds in cash. All of our savings. I placed it on Red and the girl spun the wheel, but I

242

wasn't nervous because I knew I couldn't lose.

The winnings are now in a safety deposit box in your name at Coutts on Piccadilly. The key is in the envelope.

I hope you will use four hundred thousand pounds to pay off the penalty and my lawyer's fees, but it's up to you. If you've had enough of me and you want to move on, just use it to make a new start for you, Hamish and Maggie.

If the penalty isn't paid, I'll know from the tabloids. I'm sure I'll be convicted, but they probably won't look too hard for me and I'll stay hidden.

I am so sorry for all of the pain and heartache I've caused.

With all my love,

Alastair

Simon stood for two long minutes, staring at the sheets of paper, struggling to focus. His lips were twitching as though he were half speaking. The writing blurred as he read the letter one more time. It was typical of Alastair to be so gracious. And so bloody lucky. He could see exactly how this would pan out.

Fiona called from upstairs. 'Hurry up, Simon. Oh, and be a dear and grab a bottle of white.'

'OK. I'm on my way.' Simon resealed the letter with the key inside and placed it carefully back in position. He opened the fridge and picked out a bottle of wine – Chablis. Domaine Louis Michel Grand Cru 1993. Not bad. Fiona was obviously learning.

His legs were heavy and he could feel his shoulders sagging as he walked out to the hall. Looking up, the stairs seemed to rise forever. As he gathered his breath and forced his right foot up onto the first tread, he felt the anger and frustration building inside him and his head started to shake, small staccato movements from side to side.

He sucked in air and spat it out between clenched teeth before turning around, putting the wine and glasses on the hall table and making his way back to the kitchen.

He then picked up the letter and carefully, methodically tore it into small pieces, which he scattered one-by-one into the bin. He took the safety deposit box key and slipped it into his trouser pocket.

Simon smiled as he left the room. It was his time, after all.

Epilogue

There's something about ferries. They're not luxurious – you could hardly describe a Dover-Calais trip as a cruise – nor are they purely functional. I somehow doubt the truck drivers making their twice-weekly crossings are contemplating the romance of the voyage but, even in the depths of winter, there are always a few people taking the ferry who are filled with a sense of adventure, passengers for whom the rumble and roar of the smoke-belching marine diesels means a beginning, the first step in a journey.

Especially emotive for islanders like us, the ferry is an umbilical connection to different worlds and cultures. It only takes an hour and a half to cover the twenty-six miles from Dover to Calais but, from the moment you feel the soft nudge of the jetty on the other side, you know you're in a different country and all of the rules have changed.

I've taken this ferry many, many times, but I still feel the same childish excitement as when I was a six-year-old holding my mother's hand and watching the dirty, grey Channel waters seethe in the growing rift between hull and quayside. It looks the same today as it always has but I am, if anything, even more excited than before.

For the past four months, I have been rudderless, left adrift and, let's face it, weakened by my powerlessness and the uncertainty of my position. Since I learned the size of the penalty which I'd been given, it's been even worse. I've worked hard all of my life and been successful, but I still found myself in the position of not being able to provide for my family, which was something my privileged silver-spooned past left me poorly equipped to handle.

Last night, I made my offering to the Fates. Are you still on my side when the chips are – in my case literally – down? The answer was a resounding 'yes' and I can now leave with my head held high, knowing that, at the very least, I have made sure my family has what it needs while I'm away. When I come back, I will figure out a way to earn a living. I feel confident now that my skills and experience will find a home one way or another. We don't need so much, and I'll make sure I spend much more time with my children as they grow up. It's not too late.

As always, I stand at the back rail, the sea breeze filling my lungs and whipping my hair, until the White Cliffs are chalky smudges. Only then do I make my way to the bow where I wait, not for long, for the first signs of the French coast. There are no cliffs on the French side, only scrubby dunes, and we are well over half way before the line of the horizon begins to thicken. Gradually the flat, grey ribbon becomes more than a mirage and solidifies into something real and tangible. We are almost there.

After I left the letter for Fiona, I had a busy few hours in London, buying everything on my list. I might be overdoing the cloak and dagger business, but I am keen to do everything I can to make it impossible to trace me. I am hoping I will only be hiding from the press but, if Fiona decides to not pay my fine, the police will also be looking for me. I can't believe she won't pay it, but I wouldn't have given her the option if there weren't some part of me that wonders whether I've broken things irreversibly between us.

There's nothing I can do about the ferry journey as it's booked in my name and I have to go through passport control on both sides of the Channel. They'll find out I went to Calais easily enough but, once I am in France, I will try to disappear and I think I should be able to stay "off the grid" after that, unless I am unlucky enough to get arrested for some reason.

France is part of the new Schengen area, which means I can move around between five or six countries without showing my passport, and the number of countries included is set to expand to cover most of the European Union by the end of next year.

My main shopping trip was to Evans Cycles in Waterloo Cut,

where I collected my bike, a steel-framed Dawes Galaxy with a narrow leather Brooks saddle, agony for the first few hundred miles but super-comfortable afterwards. I had asked them to fit racks and waterproof panniers front and back and a full set of tools and spares. I had already picked up my tent and sleeping bag and was set for the first few weeks at least. My plan was to get south as soon as possible and follow the weather.

I'm not too worried about changing my appearance; it's not as though I'm a mass murderer and, in any case, I have a suspicion that a couple of weeks of cycling in the open air and sunshine will make me unrecognisable anyway.

I received my ID card from the Camping Club International last week. It's a private association but the ID looks quite official and it should work as proof of identity in most campsites across Europe. I intend to travel under my second name, James, and have used a fictional address for the CCI card. I don't see why I should raise any flags with Interpol.

Hotels are out of the question as they always require a passport and registration in France. The same goes for credit cards, I need to avoid leaving any paper trail in my name. My one exception is the small hotel I have booked in Calais for tonight; it's now almost eight in the evening and I want to start fresh in the morning. They won't be looking for me yet and they will find out I came to Calais anyway.

I converted the ten thousand pounds I took from the winnings into smaller bills, as using fifty pound notes might be difficult and make me stand out. I've kept two thousand pounds worth with me, half in francs, half in deutschmarks, spread out in different pockets and with five hundred pounds sterling hidden inside the seat pillar of my bike.

The rest of the money is winging its way in equal shares to five campsites in France where I've made reservations for later in the summer. Using the normal post is a bit risky but it's not traceable and I don't really expect problems. Even if I don't find any work, I am pretty sure I could live for at least two years on what I have, and I will hopefully only need to be away for six months at the most.

And so, on a gloomy May evening, I wheel my bike over the sharp ridges of the metal ramp and onto the quayside. I throw my leg over the crossbar, slip into the toeclips and, filled with nervous excitement, wobble my way into France.

The place I am staying, the Hôtel Pacific, is a sad dump, set in a dreary, run-down block right in the middle of town. The guy behind the desk is equally dreary; his droopy moustache and laconic monosyllables clearly masking a lively personality full of warmth and joie de vivre, and masking it well. Although it appears to inconvenience him enormously, he takes my passport, hands me a registration form and points me in the direction of the garage where I can put my bike. The garage is damp, unlit and smells of stale urine; there is also nowhere to lock the bike, but I have to assume it will be OK. I am tired and ready for a quick meal and my bed.

When I come back to the reception, he raises his head and gives me an "oh you again, what do you want now, can't you see I'm busy" look before handing me a key attached to a huge lump of metal and flicking a nonchalant hand in the direction of the stairs. The lights in the hallways are another challenge. They're the type which automatically switch off on a timer to save power, and these ones have been set to five seconds or less, only giving me time to get half way to the next switch before darkness rules again.

There's a technique to it though and, as I'm a quick learner, it doesn't take me too long to get to my room. I almost wish I hadn't bothered. Room 312 is dark, musty and cramped; the grey, washed-out sheets hang limply over the saggy bed and the draughty window is no barrier to the noise and fumes of the busy Rue Royale. It's as far from the shared bathroom as you can get, and of course the five-second light switch is all of the way down the corridor. Welcome to France.

I can't remember the last time I stayed somewhere that wasn't reasonably luxurious, but it's been a while. When I was younger, I had strong views about wasting money on expensive hotels. Apart from the fact I couldn't afford them, I believed it was unnecessary and, after all, it was only a bed for the night. On top of that, it had seemed to me that the more people spend on hotels – the more they search for luxury and perfection – then the more they find to complain about and they eventually end up in a permanent state of righteous dissatisfaction.

Well, years of business travel and a demanding wife seem to have corrupted me a little. I can still hear myself spouting the same trite opinion at some dinner or other, but my minimum standards have increased a lot and my reaction to the lovely Hôtel Pacific reminds me of how quietly hypocrisy can sneak up on you.

Let's face it, I wasn't going to get a great night's sleep anyway. Once the initial euphoria of setting off has faded, I realise I am looking at a bleak and lonely future, at least in the short-term. If I want to stay hidden, I can't contact anyone I know. The only way I'll be able to find out what is going on with my family will be via the newspapers and they're unlikely to tell me much apart from the basic facts, which I already know, and a lot of spurious speculation. Hopefully, I'll be able to get some updates from my sister Jenny but, even then, I'll need to wait a few weeks and will have to be very careful.

A dank morning mist from the Channel fills the streets of Calais as I set off on my first day's ride. I am still unfamiliar with having panniers on the bike which, combined with cobbles, potholes and French road signs, makes for a shaky start. I haven't been cycling for over five years and am under no delusions about how much it is going to hurt. I used to do quite a bit of mountain biking, so the muscles are probably still there somewhere, but the first few days are going to be a challenge.

My target for the first day is fifty miles to Etaples-sur-mer which should be an easy ride south along the coast road. I've planned the first week's riding more or less which will get me as far as Dijon. Once I'm there, I'll look at the weather forecasts, see how much my bum and legs are hurting, and take a view.

I'm expecting the first articles to appear in tomorrow's papers but it will be a day or two before I find out whether Fiona has decided to pay the fine or not. I'm still confident she will, but it is a lot of money and I can't actually be sure of anything anymore. She has been behaving strangely for the past few weeks and I don't know why. She is certainly pissed off enough to do anything. I'm hoping she'll talk to my parents or Jenny before deciding. They'll help. I wrote to Jenny last night, telling her I am safely on my way and giving her a poste restante address in Avignon to write to.

If Fiona does't pay the fine, I don't know what will happen but, assuming my lawyer and that awful woman from the Serious Fraud Office are to be believed, they will start criminal proceedings and I will probably go onto all sorts of Interpol databases fairly quickly. One way or another, I will need to stay hidden.

I've brought a copy of The Lonely Planet book for France with me, and I intend to read up on everywhere I go and to keep a diary. If everything goes to plan, I'll be able to read tales of my adventures to Maggie and Hamish.

Etaples, where I'm headed, used to be a famous destination for artists in the nineteenth century, especially the impressionists. They came here for the special light and named this part of the coast the Opal Coast. I can see why, as there's a unique and silky smoothness to the landscape.

The sun is a ball of softened crimson, hanging low over the dunes and the last stubborn patches of mist seem to cling to the edges of each shape they touch, smoothing out sharp angles and allowing colours and objects to melt into one another, actually more like a painting than the real world.

There is nothing, no one, not even a sheep or a cow. Only scrubby dunes and flat fields. The damp air swallows every sound apart from the distant, desolate cry of gulls. An icy pebble drops into my gut sending out sudden ripples of sadness and despair which threaten to spill into tears, but don't quite manage. What's the point? There's nobody to share my sorrow, to wipe away my tears. I shiver reflexively.

For the first time since I can remember, I am alone. Really alone.

BEST EATEN COLD by Tony Salter

The Bestselling Psychological Thriller you can't put down.

Imagine that someone wants to do you harm. Someone you once knew, but have almost forgotten. Now, imagine that they are clever, patient and will not stop. They'll get inside your head and make you doubt yourself. They'll make you question who you are, and ensure that everyone you care for starts to doubt you too.

Each perfectly-orchestrated doubt will slowly, steadily, build to a crescendo and destroy you.

This is real and it could be happening to you.

Fabiola lives an idyllic life in Oxford — beautiful house, adoring husband, happy healthy baby. She thinks she's left her past behind her, but in a world of smartphones and social media, it's not so easy to wipe the slate clean.

Best Eaten Cold is a chilling reminder of how quickly — and how blindly — we have learnt to trust in the online world, although none of us really understand it at all.

***** "Fast-paced, terrifyingly believable, chilling at times... the kind of book that's hard to put down"

***** "I admire any author who can hold my attention so thrillingly from beginning to end"

***** "Much superior to Girl on the Train."

AVAILABLE NOW in paperback or eBook format from Amazon and most booksellers.

Thank you

Thank you for reading The Old Orchard. I hope you enjoyed it.

Writing gets more and more satisfying when people enjoy reading your work. There are a huge number of books released every year and it is increasingly difficult for each of us to pick out the good ones – those which grip and hold you all the way through to the end ... and maybe leave you feeling a little differently about the world.

I think that The Old Orchard is one of those books. If you agree, please tell your friends or local book club about it. It would also be very helpful if you could let me know what you thought by leaving a review on Amazon or Goodreads

To read my (occasional) blog, learn more about my writing or stay informed about future novels, please visit my website at www.tonysalter.com

Acknowledgements

Writing novels is a solitary task but I don't think I could enjoy it without some company along the way. Feedback, encouragement and patient support are essential emotional props, but so are the sweeping blows of honest criticism which help to remind me that I am writing for readers and not only for myself.

I need to thank all of my readers for their patient support and, in particular, Sue Brown, Annie Eccles, Fiona Aris, Emma Newman, Aliki Radley, Gro Salter, John and Di Cronly, Siobhan Neiland, Raffaella de Angelis and Michael Salter. The detailed feedback from all of you was invaluable. Sue, Annie and Fiona deserve special thanks for reading The Old Orchard three times at different stages (and apparently enjoying it every time!). I am also very grateful to Jamie Groves at Story Terrace.

Huge thanks are also due to the people who have helped with my marketing, as there's no point in writing novels if no-one knows they exist. So, thank you Hugo C, Sue B, Cath N, Julian G, Anita M, Jenny C, Phil E, Anthony S, Janette S, Sandra T, Sara C, Ben O, Bridie G, David S, Carlene H, Peter N, Claire B, Shuna M, Claudine G, Jason E, Teresa C, Chris S, Emma P, Rem N, Sue T, Tamsin T-J, Muir P, Mark P, Lynne S, Richard R, Kipper, Dana O, Rose G, Rory H, Liz G, David L, Mark G, Mike G, Dave C, Sue H, Julia E, Angela R, Richard P, Janet Poppe and Charlotte S.

Finally, I must again thank my wife of twenty-nine years, Gro. Without her love, support, patience and tolerance, none of this would have been possible.